Acknowledgements

No man is an island and no writer can do it all by themselves.

I'd like to take the time to thank Scott Hoover and Ellie of Lovenbooks for providing me with the gorgeous cover photo of model Hollis Chambers. He is the perfect Rhett in my eyes. Thanks to Louisa Maggio of LM Creations for designing the wonderful cover. It makes my heart soar and my smile expand. Thanks to Emma Mack and Lorelei Logsdon for the editing and proofreading jobs. Especially to Emma Mack for taking me on at such short notice and working her heart out to get the book up to scratch.

Thanks to Katrina Jaekley and Tanya Kay Skaggs for reading Rhett chapters at a time and providing me with love and feedback. I appreciate the time you take out to bring me up from the lows and self-worry of the writing process. Thanks to all the members of the J. S. Cooper Indie Agents for all of their support and love and daily interactions.

Thanks to all the readers that have helped to promote me and spread the word about my books. I love the emails and messages I get and I wouldn't be writing and making a living if you didn't enjoy my books.

Last, but certainly not least. Thanks to God for all his blessings, for without him nothing would be possible.

Rhett

Prologue

It all started with a note and a piece of candy when we were seven years old. She sat next to me in class and as the best student in the class, she was always winning pieces of candy from the teacher. One day, I'd had enough of watching her eating candy. I wanted to share in the candy with her, so I sent her a note:

Do you want to be my best friend?

Yes

No

She responded with a "Maybe" and that was the beginning of our friendship.

Chapter One

There are a few things you should know about me. I'm a fine young Southern gentleman. I open doors for women, most of the time. I know how to ballroom dance. I know how to woo. And I know how to drink with the best of them. Many women think I'm hot, or sexy, or whatever you want to call it. I'm not sure if I'm really that hot or if there's a drought of hot men in South Carolina. Yes, I'm a good ol' boy. Though, in reality, I'm not a good ol' boy in anyway. Though, that's no secret. I like to have a good time, I like women, and I'm not afraid to speak my mind. The only other thing you should know about me is that I have one friendship that I cherish above all others.

That's my friendship with Clementine O'Hara. She was my best friend and the only person in the world I didn't try and screw around with.

Clementine O'Hara had been blessed with one of the worst names I'd ever heard. It was hard to say her full name with a straight face. It was even harder to say her nickname without bursting out laughing. "Clemmie, what are you doing tonight?" I stared into her serious brown eyes as she scribbled something in her notepad.

"Why?" She looked up at me and frowned. Her lips were stained navy blue from the pen she'd been nibbling on every few minutes.

"I was hoping that…"

"No." She shook her head and went back to scribbling furiously.

"You don't even know what you're saying no to."

"I know you, Rhett and the answer is no."

"Come on, Clemmie."

"Does it involve a girl?" She cocked her head and looked at me with narrowed eyes.

"No," I shook my head and gave her my lazy smile. She rolled her eyes at me and I laughed. Clemmie was not one to fall for my sweet smile and big blue eyes.

"So what does it involve?"

"It involves girls, plural." I grinned. "I kinda double-booked tonight."

"So cancel on one."

"I don't want to cancel on either of them." I sat down on the edge of her bed. "That wouldn't be fair to either of them."

"Why not?"

"I'm sure they've been planning what they're going to wear since I asked them out."

"Rhett Madison, you're an asshole." She shook her head at me. "Now leave, I'm trying to write."

"Some friend you are." I tried again. "I thought I could count on my best friend to help me out in a jam."

"Then I suggest you get a new best friend, preferably a guy." She laughed as I made a face at her.

"Because you are never going to convince me to act as your wingwoman again. No way, Jose. Not after last time."

"You weren't my wingwoman, Clemmie." I pulled her ponytail and laughed. "You were just helping me out in a jam."

"Well, Brittany sure didn't seem to think I was helping out." She shook her head and shuddered. "What a mess that night was."

"Did I blame you?" I grinned at her.

"Blame me?" Her jaw dropped open. "I know you're not going there. I was stuck listening to her going on about how great you were for two hours. I've never met a more boring, insipid woman in all my life."

"Is that why you told her I was on a date with someone else? After I told you that I absolutely didn't want her to know?"

"Rhett, you should be thanking me. What did you see in her?" She gave me a look. "Oh, wait, I know, her big boobs and blonde hair."

"Hey, she was hot and she was willing." I shrugged. "I'm 21, in the prime sexual peak of my life. I wasn't about to say no."

"Trust me, I know." She rolled her eyes.

"Come on, Clem. Please?" I gave her my best puppy-dog face and she laughed.

"Unlike you, Rhett Madison. I can say no quite easily."

"Clementine O'Hara, please do not make me beg."

"I'm not going to make you do anything."

"I'll take you out to a nice dinner next weekend."

"Hmm, steakhouse?" She grinned and rubbed her stomach. I knew the way to Clementine's heart and goodwill was through her stomach. It was ironic in a way seeing as I was the man, but I knew she was always down for a good steak dinner.

"Any steakhouse you want, baby."

"Let me think…" She stared at me and then grinned. "That's still a no."

"What if I add a couple of bottles of wine?"

"Do you want me to run my mouth again?" She raised an eyebrow at me and started laughing. Her brown eyes flashed at mine in humor and I groaned. "You know I'm likely to slip up and say something I shouldn't."

"You suck." I lay back on the bed. "What am I going to do?"

"Just cancel on one of them. It's not going to kill you."

"You don't know that." I grabbed her fluffy white pillow and placed it under my head. "Why does this smell so good?" I buried my nose into her pillow and sniffed. It smelled sweet and flowery and totally girly.

"Because I did laundry yesterday." She shrugged. "You would know the smell if you did laundry as well."

"That's not going to happen."

"I can't believe you still take your laundry home." She shook her head. "That's crazy."

"Do you want to do it for me, then?" I smiled at her sweetly. "I'm sure Dolores would be happy to have one less chore to do."

"Dolores gets paid. I don't." She shook her head.

"I can pay you if you want." I gave her one of my signature looks. "I can pay you in any way that you want."

"Are you offering me the job of your maid?" Her eyes were full of light and mischief and I laughed.

"I'm not sure I could afford you."

"I'm glad you realize that." She grinned at me. "And for the last time, no way. I'm not going."

"Come on, Clementine. I really want you to be a part of this with me."

"Be a part of what? Fooling two girls into thinking you're interested?" She laughed and looked at me with incredulous eyes. "You think I want to be a part of that, why?"

"Because you want to experience everything with me." I grinned and winked at her and she burst out laughing.

"Rhett Madison, I'm not sure what dream world you're living in, but I surely don't want to be a part of your cruel and unusual punishment against women."

"How is dating me a punishment?" I pursed my lips and gave her my sad face.

"You tell me how it's not?" She jumped up and put her arms on my shoulder. "Now scoot, boy, I've got homework to do."

"Come on, Clem." I sighed, ignoring the feel of her hands on my shoulders. Clementine had always been a touchy-feely girl, but it had never bothered me until recently. And it wasn't that it bothered me, but made me more aware of her as a woman. I didn't want to think of her as a woman.

"I need to finish this tonight, Rhett. I've got to work tomorrow morning before class."

"You've always got to work." I sighed, annoyed that she was kicking me out.

"That's what poor people do to make money. We work." She grinned at me and winked. "Now go try and convince two bimbos that you didn't make a date with both of them tonight."

"They're not bimbos." I grinned. "At least not that I know of."

Rhett | 9

"Uh-huh." She raised an eyebrow at me and wiggled it for a second. It was a trick I had taught her in fourth grade and she never stopped using it now.

"Who knows, maybe they'll be cool with it and offer to have a threesome."

"Yeah. Maybe." She shook her head at me and mumbled under her breath. "Pervert."

"I'm not a pervert, every guy wants a threesome."

"No, they don't." She shook her head. "Some guys respect women. Some guys actually want a relationship with just one woman."

"Uh, who?" I looked around the room. "Show me a guy who will turn down a threesome with two hot women and I'll show you a guy who used to be a woman."

"Whatever," she said and laughed while shaking her head.

"It's true. Statistically speaking, more men want sex than want relationships."

"What's the statistic and where is it from?"

"99% of men want sex." I paused. "The statistic is from me."

"I'm guessing you're not part of the 1%."

"You know it." I laughed. "You ought to try it some time."

"I'm saving myself for marriage." She played with the cross around her neck. "You know that."

"Yeah, good luck with that." I laughed at her, but secretly I was pleased. For some reason it made me feel better to know that Clementine wasn't dating much or sleeping around. I never thought about it much to understand why, but I knew that it made me happy to know that she was saving herself.

"Who knows what will happen when I get a boyfriend, though." She shrugged and I tensed.

"What boyfriend?"

"Any boyfriend." She made a face and screwed her cute little nose up. "I'm not a nun, you know."

"Yeah, just be careful. You deserve a Prince, not a loser," I muttered, thinking about all the guys that had approached me and asked about trying to hook up with her. I'd told all of them that she wasn't interested and to back off. Not that I'd actually asked her, but I knew what was best. I knew guys like me: they only wanted sex and there was no way in hell that I was going to hook her up with a guy like me.

"So..." She started hesitantly and paused. "So..." She started again.

"What?" I looked at her curiously.

"Penelope thinks that I hang out with you too much and that's why a lot of guys aren't asking me out."

"What?" I frowned. Penelope was Clementine's best girlfriend, a girl she'd met in freshman English. She was cute and funny, but we'd never really hit it off as friends.

"She thinks that guys see you with me all the time and get the wrong impression."

"What are you talking about? We hang out a lot because we are best friends." I rolled my eyes. "Do girls assume you're a lesbian because you hang out with her a lot?" My voice rose. "Maybe she's the problem!"

"Rhett." She rolled her eyes at me. "I'm just letting you know what Penelope said." She bit her lower lip. "I mean I see her point."

"So what are you saying? You don't want to be seen with me?"

"No." She sighed and shrugged.

"Do you want me to hook you up with one of my friends?" I suggested lightly, though my stomach was in knots.

"Have any of them ever mentioned me?" She asked lightly. "Like do any of them think I'm cute or anything?"

"What?" My heart thudded. Was she joking? All of my friends thought she was hot as hell, though they knew better than to make suggestive comments around me. Clementine was gorgeous with her light brown hair and big brown eyes. Her skin had a natural olive tan that made it seem like she was constantly glowing and her body was curvy in all the right places. It didn't hurt that she had a nice size chest and a cute pert ass. I frowned as I stared at her nibbling on her pen. She was too beautiful for her own good and the fact that she didn't know it made her even more attractive to guys.

"I was just wondering." She shrugged and gave me a small smile. "Maybe you can see if any of the guys that have mentioned me want to take me out."

"Are you joking?" I frowned, my heart beating fast. "I thought you were concentrating on your studies and waiting until marriage."

"Rhett, I'm not going to wait to date until marriage." She giggled. "Don't be silly." She looked up at me with a wide smile and a carefree expression on her face. She reminded me of sunshine on a cloudy day. I felt my stomach relaxing as I smiled back at her. She was my Clementine, my best friend, and as much as I wanted to keep her under a rock, I knew I had to let her fly.

"I'll see if I can think of any good guys." I said finally.

"Or guys at your truck club." She grinned.

"Hell no. They just wanna get laid in the back of their pickups." I shook my head.

"Is that what you want as well?" She raised an eyebrow at me.

"Been there, done that, wasn't all that. The space is too tight."

"TMI," she groaned.

"I'm telling you, it sounds hotter than it is. Shit, the girl can barely move and it gets so cramped. And I can't even adjust and..."

"Rhett." She gave me a look. "I do not want to know about your sex life."

"I was just saying." I grinned. "You don't want to be with a guy from the truck club."

"What about the country club?" She smiled. "Chad is pretty hot."

"Chad?" I made a face. "He's a douche."

"He's hot."

"You think he's hot?" I made a face at her and thought about Chad. He was tall, blond, with blue eyes, richer than everyone but my family. But he was totally a dickhead. He'd fucked half the girls at the club and didn't keep it to himself.

"He's totally hot." She collapsed on her bed and smiled. "I'd totally make out with him."

"Clemmie." I groaned and stared at her on the bed. "You'd catch something if you made out with him."

"Whatever." She smiled and rolled around on the bed.

"Clemmie, stop that." I muttered as I watched her, images of her doing naughty things suddenly entering my mind.

"Stop what?" She sat up and brushed her hair over her shoulder.

"Nothing." I shook my head. "I gotta go."

"Okay." She nodded and stood up. "I should get back to my homework."

"You sure you don't want to come tonight?" I asked hopefully.

"I'm sure," she nodded. "Very, very sure."

"Fine." I walked towards the door and looked back at her. "Thanks for nothing."

"You're welcome." She beamed and walked over to me, giving me a small kiss on the cheek and a quick hug. "Have fun tonight and good luck."

"Bye, trouble," I rubbed her hair and walked out of the apartment. It had freaked me out when Clementine had hugged and kissed me every time she saw me or departed from me. I wasn't used to a family that was so loving and tactile, but she blamed it on her Nanna's Cajun roots. Though her grandma was from the North and I'm not sure where the Cajun roots came from. At first, I'd been uncomfortable getting hugged all the time, however I had grown to appreciate how loving her family was. I truly felt that I was a member of the O'Hara clan.

"Yo Tomas, what you doing tonight?" I called to one of my friends from college as I walked into my house.

"Fighting the good fight. What's good, bro?"

"Wanna go on a double date?"

"Que?"

"Your girl is a hottie. Trust me." I held my breath waiting for his response. Tomas was the only guy I knew that liked the game as much as I did. Plus, he was a man that women loved. I think it was his Latin roots, but Tomas had a suaveness that made me look like a little boy. With his jet-black hair, brown eyes and dark tanned skin, he was the picture of tall, dark and handsome. It didn't hurt that he had an accent and flung out Spanish poems as if it was his job. I knew if anyone could help me tonight, it would be Tomas.

"You know I find my own chicas, Rhett." He laughed. "Unless there's a reason you called me?"

I laughed at his question. Tomas really did know the game well.

"Dude, I double booked. I don't want to cancel on either and was going to play it like I thought they knew it was a double date."

"Risky move."

"Yeah, but once they see you, they'll be happy."

"You know which one I'm getting?" He paused. "What does she look like?"

"She's hot. Tall, blonde, big tits." I paused. "Do I need to go on?"

"Nah." He laughed. "What time we going out?"

"I told them both I'd meet them at Q bar at 8. That good for you?"

"I'll be there at 7:45 with flowers." He laughed.

"You're going to make them both ditch me." I laughed as well.

"Hey, don't hate the player, hate the game."

"I taught you the game."

"You wish."

"Perhaps." I grinned into the phone. "So I'll see you there at 7:45. Just go along with whatever I say, okay?"

"That's fine. I don't suppose Clementine will be there, will she?" Tomas continued talking and I could feel the smile leaving my face.

"No, why?"

"Dude, she's hot. I can't believe you haven't smacked that ass."

"She's like my sister, dude."

"The operative word in that sentence is 'like', bro. She's not your sister."

I rolled my eyes at the phone and waited to calm down before I continued. "Anyway, she's not coming."

"She seeing anyone?" He asked, not realizing how pissed I was getting.

"Clementine isn't dating right now. She's trying to concentrate on school first."

"Nerd alert." He groaned.

"Tomas." My voice was short.

"No diss, man. Nerds are hot. I'd fuck a nerd. She could mutter the periodic table while I went down on her."

"Dude, that's not cool."

"I'm having a laugh." Tomas laughed. "Chill."

"I'm chilled." My voice was anything but chilled.

"I was just wondering. I know she's your friend, but I was just curious. She's cute. I'm sure you'd rather her date me than some schmuck you don't even know."

"Hmm." I didn't want Tomas to back out of the date, so I ignored his comment.

"You know Brody thinks she's hot too."

"No, I didn't."

"Yeah, when we saw her with you at the library, he said something, but you know he won't do a thing. He's too much of a pussy. Though, Clementine might enjoy that."

"I wouldn't say that." My tone was definitely annoyed.

"We should all hang out some time. Invite her to the party I'm holding next week."

"We'll see." I sighed. "Anyway, I gotta go, Tomas. I gotta make reservations. I'll see you tonight, okay?"

"Okay, see you bro." Tomas sounded a bit put-off, but I hung up before he could say anything else. I walked into the kitchen and grabbed a beer before walking to my living room and relaxing on the couch. Clementine had helped me pick out the dark brown leather recliner, though it wasn't really her taste. She'd wanted me to buy a blue and white pinstriped linen couch and I'd vetoed her choice quickly. I'd been deciding between a black, dark brown and red leather couch and I let her choose between the three. I settled into the couch, trying to get comfortable, but I felt uneasy. I wasn't happy that Tomas had been talking about Clementine. As if she would ever go out with anyone like him. It annoyed me that he was talking about her like that, like she was some sort of object. I shuddered just thinking about them dating. There was no way in hell that I would ever let anything like that happen. Clementine and Tomas would date over my dead body. And I didn't think Brody was a step up, either. Though, he was nothing like Tomas and I. He seemed like a quiet guy. I didn't really know him well, but he was in some of Tomas's classes and hung out with us at the bar a couple of times. He definitely didn't seem like a player. In fact, I'd never seen him with a girl, but that didn't mean I was going to let him go out with Clementine. None of those guys were good enough for her. I smiled to myself, as I remembered that I didn't have to see her dating either of those guys any time soon.

Clementine was a romantic and lived with her head in the clouds when it came to relationships. I didn't anticipate her dating anyone serious for a long time and that suited me just fine. I grabbed my phone and called Q bar and made a dinner reservation for four. I knew that the two girls would be slightly put out that it was a double date, but I also knew that once Tomas and I turned on the charm, they'd be like putty in our heads. Shit, I wouldn't be surprised if one of them decided to go down on me at the bar. I grinned to myself as I pictured Sally or Jackie blowing me under the table. That would be hot as hell.

Chapter Two

I woke up with a smile on my face, grinning as I remembered the events of the previous night. Sally and Jackie had both been pretty upset as they realized that they were on a double date, but when they'd seen Tomas they had both turned into blubbering messes. I shook my head as I remembered Tomas saying line after line in Spanish. None of us had any idea what he was saying, but even I had to admit it sounded pretty in Spanish. The funniest part was that Tomas had basically been speaking gibberish. He didn't even speak Spanish and only knew a couple phrases. I'd nearly burst into tears of laughter as he'd said, "Voulez-vous coucher avec moi?" I'd had to whisper in his ear that I was pretty sure that was French. He'd laughed and winked at me as the two girls played with their hair and licked their lips. It had been a pretty good night overall. While neither of them had blown me, Sally had grabbed a hold of me a couple of times and rubbed her pretty little derriere on top of me as she'd given me a pretty lame lap dance.

I stretched and jumped out of bed and walked to the window and looked outside. The sun was shining and I knew that it was going to be a pretty day. My mind immediately turned to Clementine and I wondered if she wanted to go to the park and play some Frisbee or something. I sighed as I remembered it was Sunday. Sundays were always reserved for family time. Clementine always went home for Sunday lunch with her parents, Nanna and her brother Jake. I knew that I was always welcome to go, but I didn't like to impose and go too often. I walked back to my bed and sighed as I plopped back down, the smile gone from my face. I was bored living in this big house by myself. I grabbed my phone and called Clementine and waited impatiently for her to answer.

"What's up, Rhett?" She answered breathlessly and I wondered what she was doing.

"Nothing much. Just woke up."

"Must be nice." She laughed.

"What are you doing?" I asked curiously. "You sound like you're out of breath."

"Playing Frisbee with Jake."

"Oh, cool." I smiled as her brother's face entered my mind. "Tell him I said hi. Tell him to call me. I got tickets to see the Gamecocks."

"Okay." She paused. "Rhett says hi, Jake."

"Hi." I heard Jake mumble in the background. "Tell him to come over."

"Jake says you should come over."

"Tell him next time." I muttered, even though part of me really wanted to go.

"Rhett says he'll come next week." She shouted at Jake and I rolled my eyes at how loud she was being. I was pretty sure that Jake wasn't that far away from her.

"What are you doing tonight?" I changed the subject.

"I'm watching Devious Maids."

"You don't have a maid." I stared at my bed as I spoke into the phone.

"It's a TV show." She laughed and I smiled at the sound of her girlish giggles.

"I was about to say."

"No Rhett, I didn't win the lottery and I didn't marry a Madison or a Vanderbilt."

"You already know I'm not getting married and I think all the Vanderbilts are gay."

"Rhett!" Her voice rose in disapproval.

"I'm joking. Well, not about the 'me not getting married' part."

"No one wants to marry you, Rhett Madison."

"There are a hundred girls that would disagree with that statement."

"Only a hundred?"

"Clemmie," I sighed and sat down on the bed. "Do you want to hang out or not?"

"Not. I told you I have TV shows to watch."

I rolled my eyes as she spoke. "I thought you had a DVR?"

"I do."

"So then you can hang out."

"I don't want to hang out."

"Come on." I frowned annoyed. If it was any other girl I would have forgotten them by now. I wasn't a guy who bothered with girls who played games. Fortunately for Clementine, she was my best friend and I knew she wasn't playing games.

"Don't you have a little black book? Call one of those girls up."

"I don't want to go on a date. I just want to chill."

"Ask Tomas."

"Tomas went out." I was starting to get upset at the fact that she didn't want to hang out. "And anyway we hung out last night."

"Are you getting angry at me?" She laughed. "Oh Rhett, you think every girl should drop all their plans just to hang out with you, don't you?"

"No."

"If you want to hang out, you can come over and watch TV with me."

"Crazy Linda's not going to be there is she?"

"She'll be in her room. We'll watch TV in my room."

"I don't want a repeat of last time." I groaned and closed my eyes as I remembered Linda trying to corner me in the bathroom to kiss me.

"When did you get so picky? I thought you would have been happy that Linda tried to kiss you."

"She had a mustache."

"So?"

"And she has crossed eyes."

"She's having surgery."

"On her brain? Because she didn't seem too smart."

"Rhett, you're horrible."

"That's why you love me." I laughed. "I'll be over at 7, is that okay?"

"That's fine."

"What do you want me to bring over? Actually don't tell me, let me guess. Salt and vinegar chips, chocolate chip cookies, a bottle of wine and some gummy bears."

"You know me too well." Clementine laughed and I could picture her eager smile in my head and it made me grin.

"You're going to get so fat, you know that, right?"

"Don't tell me. I can't be your best friend once I'm fat?"

"You wish you could drop me that easily. I'm not going anywhere."

"Well you never know. I might be."

"You might be what?" I frowned and sat down on the edge of the bed.

"Nothing, I gotta go. See you at 7."

"Okay."

"Oh, and Rhett?"

"Yes?"

"Bring a t-shirt if you plan on staying over tonight. You stretched out my last one."

"Well if you insist on buying girly-sized t-shirts, that's going to happen. I'm a man, you know."

"No need to worry too much. You'll be able to fit into my fat t-shirts quite soon."

"Clementine you're silly." I laughed and jumped up feeling excited. "I'll start training you at the gym if you want!"

"I don't want." She made a noise that made me think of sex.

"Don't make that noise." I groaned.

"What noise?"

"That grunting moaning noise."

"Are you going crazy? What grunting moaning noise?" She groaned again.

"You just did it again." I frowned, not wanting to think of her in that way. Clementine was the only girl that I had as a friend. She was the only girl I hadn't tried to sleep with and I wanted it to remain that way.

"Rhett, you have sex on the brain. I'm surprised you want to hang out with me tonight."

"I got cancelled on." I said lightly and waited for her to say something.

"Wow, don't I feel special! I'm back-up girl number two."

"Number five." I laughed. "The four other girls I wanted to take out were busy."

"Rhett, did you really have to tell me that?"

"No, but I value honesty." I laughed easily even though it was a lie. I hadn't asked any other girls out for the night.

"If we hadn't met as kids there is no way that we'd be friends right now." Clementine's voice sounded a bit annoyed.

"I can't help being hot."

"I know. Just like you can't help being rich or smart or cocky."

"Hey, hey now." I frowned. "You okay?"

"I'm fine." She sighed. "Be at my place at 6:30. I don't want you chatting away once my shows start."

"We wouldn't want those maids to feel like they're being ignored now, would we?" I joked and she groaned.

"I gotta go, Jake's giving me a look 'cause I keep throwing the Frisbee to the side." She huffed out and then hung up the phone. I threw the phone onto the bed and then I checked my appearance in the mirror before leaving my room. I stared at my handsome face and frowned. Sometimes I wondered what life would be like if I wasn't so handsome. Would girls react differently if my eyes weren't so blue and sparkly? Would they still want to tousle my silky hair if it was ginger and coarse? Would they still longingly stare at me if I was average-looking? I took a deep breath and walked out of the room and wondered how much I took for granted in my life. My grandma had always told me that I was lucky I had such beautiful baby blue eyes. I had learned from a young age that all I needed to do to get out of trouble was to give a wide smile and a quick look of sorrow. I'd gotten away with almost everything with my mom and grandma. Until everything changed, of course.

It had been different with my dad and Clementine. Clementine seemed to be immune to my looks. She'd never flirted with me or expressed any sort of interest. We'd been friends since we were little kids and we'd stayed friends all the way through college. There'd never been one time that she'd ever expressed a romantic interest in me. Not even in high school, when all the girls had started flirting with me hardcore. We'd even been assigned as lab partners in chemistry and she'd spent more time staring at labels than she had staring at me. It had been disconcerting at first. I'd assumed that she'd eventually be like every other girl once I'd hit puberty. I had even daydreamed of her begging me to kiss her and be her boyfriend once we became teens, but she'd never treated me as more than her best friend. Of course I'd blamed her lack of interest on her being a lesbian for a couple of months, but then she'd started gushing about some junior called Tony and I'd realized that she was as into men as most of the other girls in school. She just wasn't into me. It had stung at first, but then I'd liked the idea. She would be my first real female friend that was really only interested in being friends. I wouldn't have to worry about her falling in love with me and I didn't worry about falling in love with her. It was high school that cemented our forever friendship. She was the one stable person in my life. The one constant. She cared for me above my looks and my money. She wanted nothing more than to be my best friend. She didn't demand emotions and promises from me that I couldn't give. She understood that I didn't do love and never would.

"Move over." I pushed Clementine over on the bed. "Bed hog."

"Sit on the chair." She stuck her tongue out at me.

"Your chair's not comfortable. I want to sit on the bed."

"You're annoying." She shook her head and her long brown hair went flying as she moved over. "Come on, then." She patted the mattress next to her.

I promptly plopped down on the bed next to her and lifted my feet up.

"Rhett, take your shoes off." She hit me in the arm and I laughed.

"Okay, okay." I leaned down and undid my laces and dropped my shoes on the floor and lay back. "So is Catty Maids about to come on?"

"It's called Devious Maids, and yes." She looked over at me. "You better not fall asleep."

"I'm not promising anything." I laughed and pushed my head back in her pillow. "Your bed is so comfortable."

"So, why no date tonight?" She peered at me with a curious expression on her face. I didn't want her to know that I hadn't asked anyone out.

"I guess they're all busy because of finals."

"Finals are not until next week." She made a face. "I don't think the girls you date are studying this early."

"You've been studying."

"You don't date girls like me." She laughed and I reached out and grabbed her.

"What do you mean by that?"

"I mean that you don't date smart girls." She shrugged and her brown eyes flashed at me.

"Some of the girls I date are smart." My hand rested on her arm for a few more seconds. "Maybe not as smart as you, but they're smart."

"Uh-huh." She rolled her eyes. "You don't do smart girls."

"I do all girls." I grinned and she groaned. "What?" I laughed. "It's true."

"You need to fall in love."

"Ugh, don't mention love to me." I shuddered.

"Come on, Rhett."

"I'm not interested." I sighed and thought back to my parents' abusive marriage that had lasted way too long because they loved each other. "I'm not made for love. I'm made for lovemaking."

"You really think you're some sort of pimp, don't you?" She sighed.

"Not a pimp." My fingers ran to her cheek. "I remember when I kissed you, you didn't object."

"We were playing spin the bottle." She rolled her eyes, but I could see a red hue rising in her face. "And we were thirteen."

"You didn't have to use tongue." I grinned at her and licked my lips and she groaned and pulled away from me.

"Let's just watch TV." She grabbed the remote and turned the volume up. "Now be quiet."

"You're so bossy."

"Shhh." She put her finger to her lips and I laughed and watched the TV screen. The screen flashed with a bunch of hot girls and I wondered what it would be like to sleep with a maid. I was busy staring at one of the actress's chests when Clementine screamed and jumped up in the bed, making me almost fall off.

"Dude, what's going on?" I looked at her in concern and she glared at me.

"Shh." She put her finger to her lips and looked back at the screen. "He has a gun."

"Who has a gun?" I whispered and looked back at the screen.

"Shhh." She groaned and elbowed me.

"Ow, that hurt." I looked over at her face as she stared intently at the TV screen. Her eyes were alert and I could see that she was concentrating hard. I grinned to myself as I thought about tickling her and distracting her. She'd be so pissed if I did that. I was debating risking her wrath when the TV went to commercial break.

"Rhett, you're not even watching the show." She looked at me with pursed lips.

"It's boring." I shrugged. "Let's go out and do something."

"I already told you I don't want to go out tonight." She shook her head.

"Fine." I lay back and yawned. "Boring."

"I don't know why you came over if you wanted to go out."

"I wanted to hang out!" I turned on my side and spoke to her. "You haven't even asked me how my date went last night."

"Because I don't want to know." She shook her head with a small smile.

"What do you mean you don't want to know?" I raised an eyebrow. "You always want to know."

"Rhett, I don't want to encourage you in your shady dating habits." She shook her head.

"So you don't want to know what drama went on last night?" I cocked my head and looked at her. I watched as her eyes widened in excitement. I knew that she totally wanted to know what had happened the night before. Clementine was as into gossip and drama as any girl I knew. I wasn't even sure why she was pretending that she didn't care.

"What happened?" she gasped finally, unable to stop herself.

"I thought you needed to concentrate on your show."

"These are the moments DVRs are made for. Pause." She grinned and pointed the remote at the TV. "Now spill."

"You sure you want to know?" I raised an eyebrow and almost laughed at the eager expression on her face.

"Yes, yes." She nodded and leaned towards me. "Spill all the details. Did they scream at you? Did you get slapped?" Her voice rose eagerly. "Oh my god, did they fight?"

"Clementine." I shook my head and laughed. "You're watching way too much of that TV show."

"Tell me." She groaned and grabbed my arms. "I need to know." I tried to ignore the warmth of her fingers on my skin. Her fingers felt smooth and pressed into my flesh tightly. I shifted on the bed at the slight buzz of electricity I felt at her touch.

"Let's just say that Jackie didn't mind at all." I raised an eyebrow. "At least, I don't think her breasts minded as they rubbed up and down on my chest."

"What?" Clementine's jaw dropped and her eyes narrowed. I saw a flash of disappointment in her eyes, but it faded quickly. "They still slept with you?"

"No," I defended myself, even though I wasn't sure why I wanted her to know I hadn't slept with them. "We didn't have sex. She gave me a lap dance." I shrugged.

"What? You booked a date with two girls on one night and one of them gave you a lap dance?" She shook her head.

"Well, I took Tomas with me for Sally."

"How nice of you." She rolled her eyes.

"You think I'm a pig?" I grinned.

"Let's just say I wouldn't want to date you." She lay back and her brown eyes looked at me in disgust. "You just don't care, do you?"

"I care about you." I reached over and pinched her cheek. "But only because you're a brat and I've known you for years."

"I mean about the girls you date."

"I care." I shrugged. "I ask them on dates, I pay, I give them what they want."

"No you don't." She moved away from me and frowned.

"Yes, I do."

"You've never given one girl what they really wanted." She shook her head. "Not one. You've never made one of them your girlfriend."

"Ugh, don't say that word." I shivered.

"I don't understand why you won't get a real girlfriend." She sighed. "We don't all have cooties, you know."

"Trust me, I know." I licked my lips suggestively and she groaned.

"All you care about is sex."

"At least I don't lie and tell them I want a relationship." I sighed, not wanting to get into a conversation over me being a commit-ophobe. "I'm not interested in having a relationship."

"Yeah, yeah. I know." She grabbed the remote. "Now, shh."

"Wait, what?" I grabbed her hand. "You're turning the TV back on already?"

"Yeah." She smiled at me and winked. "You know how I need my drama. And it looks like tonight I have to get it from the maids and not your pitiful love life."

"Whatever." I stared at her. "I should leave if you're going to be mean to me."

"Uh-huh." She stared back at me with a challenging gaze. "We both know that's not going to happen."

"Bully." I made a face and she grinned.

"You're a mess, Rhett Madison."

"You're a bigger mess, Clementine O'Hara." I grinned at her and showed her my perfect white teeth and dimple.

"You can't charm your way with me, Mr. Madison." She batted her eyelashes at me and I bowed my head.

"But I sure can try." I pretended to lift off a pretend top hat and she laughed.

"Shh." She pressed play on the remote and the maids came back on screen. I leaned back and tried to understand what she saw in the show, but my mind started drifting within a few minutes. I pulled my phone out of my pocket and checked my text messages. There was a message from Jackie asking if I was busy and if I wanted to watch a movie. I knew exactly what that meant. She wanted to move on from lap dances to the real thing. I tried to picture her face, but all I could remember was her rubbing her smaller-than-I-normally-liked breasts across my face. I deleted the text and put the phone back in my pocket. I had a rule that I never let a girl interrupt one-on-one time with Clemmie. I'd created the rule in high school when I'd nearly destroyed our relationship by flaking on her one too many Friday nights to take random girls out to the movies at the last moment. I could still remember the flash of anger in Clementine's eyes as she'd accused me of taking her for granted.

"I don't know about you, Rhett, but I would never put a date in front of my best friend." She'd fumed, her eyes sparking darts at me.

"It wasn't on purpose," I'd muttered, annoyed that she was getting angry.

"This is the fourth time you've ditched me at the last moment to go on a date." She'd counted her fingers. "And it's the last time. You will not do this to me again. I'm not some second-class girl, just because I'm your friend."

"I never said you were second-class." I rolled my eyes at her dramatics. Girls!

"You didn't have to say it. That's how you've been treating me." Her finger had poked me in the chest as she pushed her shoulders back. *"This is the last time. The next time you ditch me at the last minute will be the last time you call me your best friend."* Her words had been melodramatic and slightly over-the-top, but they'd scared me. I couldn't imagine a life without Clementine being there for me. I'd rolled my eyes at her and pretended that I thought she was being over-the-top, but I had never ditched her at the last moment again.

"Oh my god, that was crazy." Clementine's squeals distracted me from my thoughts. "I totally didn't see that coming. Do you think he's going to kill her?"

"Um, I guess?" I mumbled and gave her a smile.

"You weren't watching, were you?"

"Truth or Lie?" I grinned and watched her jump off of the bed. "Where are you going?"

"Getting some water. Want some?"

"I'd rather have a beer."

"Fine. Hold on." I watched her walk out of the bedroom and looked around the room. It was small, but it was totally Clementine. It was decorated in blues and greens and there were at least fifteen framed photographs on the walls. I grinned as I saw one of us at Disney from the previous summer. I jumped up off of the bed and looked at the different photos that chronicled our friendship. They brought back so many happy memories. I walked around the room and looked at all the photos and then frowned. There was a photo of Clementine and I at my eighth birthday party. It was a picture of us cutting my cake together and my mom and dad were standing behind us grinning. I stared at the photo for a few seconds and then turned around. What a farce that had been. We'd looked like such a happy family. Only we were anything but that. My dad's smile had hidden his affair with his secretary. It was so clichéd it wasn't even funny. And my mom, well, my mom was the biggest liar of all. Her smile hid her alcohol problem. And it hid the fact that she didn't give two shits about me. She'd walked away from me and my dad just a few years later and never looked back. She didn't care about me and she didn't care about our family.

"Okay, I'm back. I decided to have a beer as well." Clemmie walked into the room grinning. "I know, I know, you're shocked. We have class tomorrow and I'm drinking, but after the week I've had, I deserve a drink." She paused and handed me the bottle and then looked in my face. "Hey, what's wrong?" She frowned and studied my face.

"Nothing." I grabbed the beer and took a long swig. The bitter cold taste felt welcome in my mouth and throat.

"Nothing like 'nothing', or nothing like 'I'm not going to talk about it'?" She took a step closer and peered into my eyes. I looked away from her. I wasn't in the mood for her to do her body intuition tests. Clemmie figured she could tell my mood just from staring into my eyes or studying my body language. It annoyed the shit out of me. Sometimes a man just needed to be a man. That was the problem with having a girl for a best friend. They wanted to talk through everything. She wouldn't let things go and she always needed to know what my real feelings were. Sometimes I just wanted to tell her to leave me the fuck alone, but I knew how sensitive she was to just about everything, so I'd resisted so far.

"I'm fine." I plopped down on the bed and grabbed the remote. "I'm going to see what's on ESPN, cool?"

"That's fine." She sat on the bed next to me. "What happened in the three minutes that passed when I went to the kitchen?"

"Nothing." I grunted and stared at the screen.

"You are so annoying." She groaned and stood up. "Let me think, you were standing over here." She walked over to the side of her bedroom and looked around, her face deep in concentration. I tried to ignore her, but I couldn't stop myself from watching her. There was something about Clementine that you couldn't ignore. Especially when she was wearing her cheerleader shorts. I knew that it was wrong of me to stare at her legs as hard as I was, but I couldn't help myself. She looked at me then and her eyes narrowed. My breath caught as she stared at me. Had she realized I was staring at her bare legs? They seemed so much longer than I remembered. And tanner too. Had she been laying out?

"What?" I frowned as she continued staring at me.

"Shh. I'm thinking." She stared at me and then looked around again. She looked at the wall and then stopped in front of the photo I'd been staring at. I froze as I realized she'd figured it out. I was upset because I'd been looking at a photo of my mother. How clichéd was I? Typical man with mommy issues. I waited for her to bring it up and start the conversation about my mother. I lay there staring at the ceiling, waiting for her to broach the subject. It was inevitable. Clementine was one for getting everything out in the open. "So, what do you want to do?" She walked back over to the bed and I stared at her through narrowed eyes.

"Huh?" I watched as she joined me on the bed again.

"What shall we do?" She smiled at me and took a swig of her beer and grimaced. I wasn't sure why she drank beer, as she hated the taste of it.

"What do you want to do?" I sat up, suddenly feeling relaxed again. "And please don't say you want to give me a lap dance. I'm not sure I can handle two in one night."

"You wish." She rolled her eyes at me and I laughed. I looked down at her long legs again for a brief second and looked away.

"Not particularly, I can't imagine you'd be very good."

"Excuse me?" Her voice rose.

"I mean that's not a bad thing." I gave her my signature Rhett smile. "It's just a fact. You don't really know much about moving your hips."

"You're an asshole." She shook her head.

"Better an asshole than depressed, right?" I winked at her and I watched as her eyes softened.

"If you ever want to talk about it, you know I'm here, right?" She grabbed my hand and squeezed it softly.

"I'm fine, Clemmie."

"I know. You da man, Rhett. You're stronger than He-Man."

"I'm glad you recognize it." I took another long chug of the beer.

"Wanna watch a movie?" She put her beer bottle down on the bedside table and lay down.

"As long as it's not a chick flick." I lay back next to her and I felt our shoulders rubbing together.

"I can't promise that there are no chickens in the movie." She switched the screen to Netflix.

"Can you at least promise that no chickens were hurt in the process of making the movie?" I joked.

"I can promise that I wasn't hurt in the process of making the movie."

"Well, that's good." I said seriously and we both laughed.

"Okay, what shall we watch?" She flicked through the titles and paused. "What about this?"

"'Date Night'?" I read the title on the screen. "Pass."

"It's got Steve Carrell."

"He's not funny."

"Fine." She groaned and paused again. "What about this?"

"Are you joking?" I gave her a crazy look. "No way in hell am I watching a movie called 'Beauty and the Briefcase'."

"You don't appreciate fine art," she mumbled and I started laughing.

"You're not seriously trying to suggest that a movie called Beauty and the Briefcase is a work of art, are you?" I glanced at her and raised an eyebrow. "Next thing you'll be saying is that 'Zack and Miri Make a Porno' should have won an Oscar."

"Very funny, Rhett." She shook her head at me, but I could see a hint of a smile on her face.

"Would you make a porno?" I asked her thoughtfully as she continued flicking through the movies.

"What?" She looked at me like I was crazy. "Hell no."

"Just asking. No need to bite my head off."

"Would you make a porno?"

"No." I shook my head and then grinned. "I'd make a sex tape though."

"Rhett." She groaned. "Of course you would."

"Come on now. Don't knock it." I laughed. "I think it would be pretty hot to watch me getting it on."

"I wouldn't be watching it."

"I wouldn't mind." I laughed and stared at her. "I don't have any secrets from you."

"That's one secret I wouldn't mind you keeping."

"So you wouldn't watch my sex tape?"

"Hell no." She shuddered. "Would you want to watch mine?"

"I don't know." I muttered and felt a pang of something in my stomach even thinking about it. "Likely not." I frowned at her, images of her in bed having sex with someone crossing through my mind. "That would be gross."

"It's gross for me to have a sex tape, but not for you?" She crossed her legs and I watched as her shorts rode even higher up her thighs.

"Let's not talk about sex tapes." I grabbed the remote from her. "Let me find a movie."

"Hey," She squealed. "I was looking."

"You're being too slow."

"No, I wasn't. I only paused because you asked me a question."

"Well, I'm not asking any questions right now." I kept scrolling. "Hey, what about 'The Expendables'?"

"Nope," she exclaimed immediately.

"Fine." I sighed. "I'm sure you'll enjoy it."

"I'm sure I won't." She retorted.

"Dude, Sly Stallone's in it."

"Dude, I'm not a dude and I don't care about Rambo or Rocky or whoever he was."

"He was Rambo and Rocky."

"Whatever." She laughed. "He could have been Barney for all I care. Not interested."

"What about 'The Transporter'." I stopped and grinned at her. "This is a good one. I've seen it already."

"No thanks." She shook her head and we stared at each other for a few seconds in silence.

"You're so difficult." I said finally and she reached over and tried to grab the remote back from me.

"Stop." I held the remote up high as she grabbed my arm.

"Rhett." She moved over and kneeled next to me. "Give me the remote."

"Nope." I laughed as she tried to pull my arm down.

"Rhett." She said my name in a softer tone now. "Please."

"Nope." I grinned and pushed her away.

"Rhett!" Her voice was more adamant and she grabbed my arm with both of her hands. "Come on." She moved even closer to me and I felt her breasts pressing lightly against my shoulder.

Knock knock.

"What's going on in here?" Linda walked through the door without waiting for an answer.

"Hey Linda." Clementine moved away from me slightly. "I'm just trying to get the remote from Rhett. We're about to watch a movie."

"In your room?" Linda looked at the two of us and her eyes narrowed.

"Yeah," Clementine answered her, not noticing the look Linda was giving us.

"You wanted something, Linda?" I looked at Clemetine's roommate and gave her a smile. Linda was one of those girls that was mad at the world for everything, but she always seemed to soften when I turned on the charm. I knew she had a thing for me. She made it pretty obvious, but I had absolutely no interest in her.

"I was just wondering what's going on." She smiled at me and batted her eyelashes. "I heard Clemmie squealing, so I wanted to make sure she was okay."

"I'm fine."

"You guys can watch the movie in the living room if you want."

"We're fine in here." Clementine responded.

"Hmm." Linda paused. "Are you sure you guys want to watch it in here? Your bed is so small." She looked at us. "Plus, it's a little weird. People might get the wrong idea if they knew you guys watched movies in bed together." She made a face. "And that he stayed over so much. Not that it's my business, but it's weird that you guys share the bed if you're not hooking up."

"We've been friends for almost fifteen years, Linda." Clementine sighed. "We've shared baths before."

"Not recently?" Linda's eyes widened in shock.

"Well, if you count last month as recent." I spoke up and smiled wickedly.

"What?" Linda gasped and Clementine hit me in the arm.

"Rhett's joking, Linda." She laughed. "We haven't had a bath together since we were little kids."

"I can still remember it like it was yesterday though." I winked at Linda and I watched as her face went red.

"Well, you know..." She swallowed. "If you ever want to you know," She smiled at me suggestively. "Just let me know."

"I will." I winked at her and watched as her face went bright red. It never failed to amaze me how easily it was to bring a woman to her knees. It didn't matter how shady she thought you were. Flirt, give her a sexy smile, and bam, all other thoughts went out of her head.

"Night, Linda." Clementine's voice was dry as she dismissed Linda from the room.

"Oh, night." Linda looked frustrated as she left the room and I felt Clementine staring at me as I lay back.

"What?" I questioned her.

"Why do you flirt with her when you know you're not interested?"

"It makes her feel good." I shrugged. "What's wrong with that?"

"It makes her feel like she has a chance." She sighed. "It's mean."

"How is that mean?"

"Because she doesn't have a chance."

"Well you never know..." I let my voice trail off and she hit me in the shoulder.

"You're gross."

"Hmm, I prefer easy."

"You prefer to be called easy?"

"I prefer to be called hot, but hey we can't always have what we want." I ran my fingers through my hair. "I can't help it if all the girls want me."

"Whatever." She rolled her eyes and grabbed the remote out of my hands. "Who's hot now?" She giggled as she scrolled through the movies.

"I let you get it." I shrugged and watched her laughing. I smiled as I leaned back and glanced at the wall again. I was grateful that Clementine hadn't asked me about my mother and my feelings. It had been years since I'd seen her and I hated talking about her. Clementine knew that it was something that I wasn't ready to really discuss. I appreciated the fact that she respected my wishes and I was grateful that she could always make me smile. "You can choose the movie." I said finally. "Just please, please, please, nothing with Channing Tatum."

"What?"

"I'll never be able to remove those moves from 'Magic Mike' from my brain." I shivered and made a face. "I don't want to watch a movie about male strippers."

"Yet you were fine with watching 'Showgirls'."
She rolled her eyes again.

"Uh, yeah. Hot topless women, having sex in the bar and the pool is fine with me any day of the week." I licked my lip. "Shoot, I'd love to have sex in the pool."

"Rhett." She groaned.

"Fine, we won't talk about sex, but if you play a chick flick I will proceed to tell you all about the time I had sex at the movie theater and..."

"Stop." She slapped her head to my lips and gave me a look. "We might be best friends, but I do not want to know all of your intimate details."

"But that's part of the fun of being best friends." I grinned and licked her hand. I laughed as she yelped and pulled her hand away.

"You're gross." She rolled her eyes and I laughed. I jumped off of the bed and pulled my jeans and t-shirt off and jumped back on the bed, wearing just my boxer shorts.

"You're way too comfortable with me, Rhett." She shook her head as she stared at my naked chest.

Rhett

"What?" I laughed and stretched. "You've seen me in boxers before."

"I know." She sighed. "But I was thinking about what Linda said. Don't you think it's weird that we still have sleepovers?" She paused. "And the fact that you sleep in only your boxers?"

"It would be weird if you were naked." I shrugged. "But, seeing as you're wearing shorts and a tank top, it's not really that weird is it?" I ignored the fact that my body was reacting to her in a way that was definitely not platonic.

"I guess." She sighed and nibbled on her lower lip.

"What is it?" I asked her softly.

"I just," She sighed and continued nibbling. "I just don't know if we're giving people the wrong impression."

"Wrong impression?"

"Like we're hooking up or something?" She jumped off of the bed. "Get up, I need to pull the sheets down."

"It doesn't matter what people think."

"Penelope thinks we act like an old married couple, yet we don't have any of the benefits." She sighed as she got under the sheets.

"What's that supposed to mean?" I crawled into the bed next to her.

"It means that we're intimate in ways that most people aren't, yet we're not really intimate."

"Lots of friends share beds, Clementine." I stretched my legs out and felt her smooth ones brushing against mine. "We're mature adults. Who cares what anyone else thinks?"

"It's just that maybe it's not healthy." She sighed and snuggled into the sheets.

"What's not healthy?" I put my arm around her shoulder and she snuggled into my chest.

"This." She looked up into my eyes as her arm crawled across my chest. "Maybe we shouldn't share a bed anymore."

"That's stupid." I glared at her and saw her face flushing. "If we're comfortable with it, then who cares what anyone else thinks?"

Rhett

"I guess." She sighed and I felt her breath teasing my nipple.

"Most people don't have a friend like us." I stroked her hair and relaxed back in the bed. "They don't understand that you can be close with someone, without sex. They're just jealous."

"I guess." She rested her chin on my chest and shifted against me. "I just don't know if we're too old to continue being this close."

"There's no age limit on a friendship, Clementine." I shifted my legs and slipped one between hers to get more comfortable. "People are just jealous of how close we are." I closed my eyes as I felt her fingers running up and down my chest. They felt soft against my skin and I felt relaxed holding her in my arms.

"Did you shave?" She asked me softly and I opened my eyes and saw her smiling at me widely.

"Huh?" I pretended to be ignorant.

"Did you shave your chest?" She grinned widely now. "There's no hair on your chest."

"I don't know what you're talking about."

"Oh my god, Rhett, you're so vain. You shaved your chest." She said and then giggled as she ran her hands across my chest.

"Oh my god, Clementine, you're so vain, there's no hair on your legs." I imitated her girly voice and ran my hands down her legs. That was a mistake. Her legs felt soft and supple to the touch and I found myself hardening as she shifted against me. Her hip was pressed against my groin and I tried to shift away from her as I became very aware of how close we were. My head started pounding as I moved my hands away from her legs quickly. This wasn't supposed to happen. I wasn't supposed to start seeing Clementine as a woman. I wasn't even sure why my body was reacting this way. It wasn't as if we hadn't shared the same bed hundreds of times before. Many times, she hadn't even worn shorts. I thanked God that she had shorts on now. I'm not sure what I would have done if she'd just been in her t-shirt and panties. Who knows what my hands would have done, where they would have gone.

"Ugh." She leaned away from me. "I forgot to take my bra off." I watched as she undid the bra and pulled it out of her t-shirt and threw it on the ground. I avoided looking at her chest. I didn't need to see her unsheltered breasts straining against her tank top. "Damn, I have to turn the light off." She sighed and jumped out of the bed. I stared at her ass as she walked to switch the light off. "Ready for the movie?" She grinned as she jumped onto the bed. I couldn't stop myself from watching her bouncing breasts as she moved and I stifled a groan as she cuddled up next to me again. Maybe her friends were right. Maybe we were getting too old for this.

"Yeah, sure." I muttered and stretched. "Though, I might just go to sleep. I'm feeling tired."

"So I can choose what I want to watch?" She peered up at me and grinned.

"Yay," I faked a yawn and closed my eyes. "I'm feeling sleepy."

"Night, sleepy head." She whispered and leaned up and kissed my cheek. I felt her breasts pressed against my arm as she kissed me and I clenched my fists to stop myself from grabbing her around the waist and pulling her on top of me. I frowned at myself. These were not the thoughts I wanted to be having about Clementine.

"Night." I whispered back and tried to control my breathing as she made herself comfortable next to me. All of a sudden I was aware of how close to naked we both were. Her body felt warm next to mine. Her scent filled my nose and her hair tickled my chest. All of a sudden, sharing a bed with Clementine didn't feel so innocent. It felt like temptation. And I didn't like it. Clementine was the last person I wanted to hook up with. It would ruin everything.

Chapter Three

"Shit! I didn't hear the alarm!" Clemmie sprung away from me and jumped out of the bed like a crazy person.

"So...?"

"I have a study group at eight." She opened her closet, grabbed a sweater and pulled it on. "Dang it, I can't even shower."

"I'll take an extra-long one. Just for you." I grinned and watched her running around.

"You're so thoughtful."

"I try to be." I stretched and grabbed the other pillow and put it under my head. "Ooh, now this is comfy."

"Jerkface." She turned away and ran her fingers over her hair to smooth it down.

"Is study group that important?" I checked my watch. "You've already missed most of the session."

"Argh." She frowned at me and grabbed her bag. "I can't miss the whole thing. I gotta go. See you later."

"I'll let myself out." I grabbed the remote and turned the TV on. "See you for lunch?"

"Can't." She shook her head. "I have to study for a test over lunch."

"Okay." I shrugged.

"With Penelope."

"I see." I stopped myself from groaning out loud. Of course, Penelope had to be involved. I was so annoyed that Clementine was cutting me out of day-to-day activities because she was hanging out with Penelope.

"Maybe tomorrow?"

"I have a date," I lied, feeling annoyed.

"Oh, okay."

"I'll call you later."

"Okay, ciao." She ran out of the room and I lay back in the bed. I didn't have any classes on Monday, but I was supposed to go into work. Though, I didn't have a starting hour at the company. My dad didn't really care when I came in. He was too busy making deals to bother with me. I grabbed my phone and checked to see if I had any messages. I had five missed calls from five different girls and eight texts. I checked them all, but didn't respond to any of them. I settled back into the bed and thought about the previous evening and how turned on I had been by Clementine pressing herself into me.

"You need to get a grip, Rhett," I muttered to myself, and jumped out of the bed. I looked at the tousled sheets and sighed. What the fuck was I doing? Was there something seriously wrong with me? Maybe Clementine and Penelope were right. I shuddered at the thought of agreeing with Penelope, but I was starting to wonder if I wasn't playing with fire. Maybe it wasn't smart to keep sharing the bed with Clemmie. It was still innocent and I still enjoyed the comfort of sleeping together, but I was starting to wonder if we weren't playing with fire. Were we using each other as placeholders for a real relationship? I sighed as my head started hurting. I didn't want to think about this at all. I grabbed my phone again and called Lily, a girl I'd met in my accounting class.

"Hello?" She answered the phone in a sultry voice.

"Hey Lily, it's Rhett. From accounting." I added in case she didn't remember who I was, though I knew that was highly unlikely.

"Oh, hi Rhett." She said smoothly, but I could hear the excitement in her voice.

"Want to get breakfast?"

"I have a class in fifteen minutes." She sounded sad. "Maybe we can get lunch."

"The offer's for breakfast." I grabbed my jeans and pulled them on. "If you can't make it, that's fine."

"No, no. I can make it." She spoke quickly, not wanting to miss her chance at a date with me.

"Meet me at IHOP?"

"IHOP?" She repeated.

"Yes, IHOP." I spoke slowly. "I'll be there in fifteen minutes."

"Okies." She agreed. "Thanks, Rhett. I've been wanting to..."

"See ya." I hung up as she spoke and rolled my eyes as I pulled my shirt on. I really didn't want to hear what she had to say. I hope she didn't think this was the beginning to some beautiful relationship. I wanted someone to eat breakfast with. I wanted someone to take my mind off of the questions spinning around my brain surrounding my friendship with Clementine. I sure as hell didn't need someone trying to make this seem like more than it was.

I walked into Clementine's bathroom and washed my face quickly. I stared at my reflection in the mirror and studied my features. My eyes seemed even bluer in the morning light. I smiled at my reflection and gave myself my signature Rhett smile. Clementine always laughed when I tried to use it on her. I frowned at the thought. Why couldn't I stop thinking of her? I grabbed her toothbrush and rinsed it and then used it to brush my teeth. I knew she'd be pissed if she knew I was using it, but I wasn't scornful of using it myself. I brushed my teeth quickly, spat out the toothpaste and walked through her apartment quickly.

I got to the IHOP within ten minutes and saw Lily waiting for me at the front of the restaurant.

"Hi, Rhett." She grinned at me widely, her green eyes pleased to see me.

"What's up?" I smiled and opened the door for us to go into the restaurant.

"Pretty good." She licked her lips. "Did you just shower?"

"No." I shook my head. "I spent the night at a friend's house and so I just washed my face and brushed my teeth. With her toothbrush." I stared into her eyes, unflinching. She looked taken aback but still she continued smiling.

"Oh." She bit her lower lip. "Was that your girlfriend?"

"Girlfriend?" I laughed out loud. "No."

"Oh. Friends with benefits?"

"She doesn't give me any benefits." I put my arm around her waist, eager to move the conversation away from Clementine. "That's why I called you."

"Oh." She blushed and smiled at me.

"Let's have a seat." We sat down in a booth and I sat in the seat next to her. "Are you hungry?"

"Yeah." She nodded and her eyes widened as my hand moved to her leg. She was wearing a pair of short shorts and I allowed my palm to rest on her thigh.

"Me too." I moved my hand further up, so that it was close to her wetness. Or what I assumed was growing wet as we sat there.

"I, uh," She looked at me with eyes full of lust. "You have beautiful eyes. Has anyone ever told you that before?"

"No," I lied. "Thanks." I moved my hand from her legs and opened the menu. "I think I'll get pancakes and coffee." I closed the menu and sat back. I looked around the restaurant and then turned back to her. "So what do you want to do after we eat?"

"Well, I have another class." She mumbled and shifted in her seat.

"You don't really want to go to class, do you?" I raised an eyebrow at her.

"Well, depends on what your offer is." She smiled and looked down at my pants suggestively.

I grinned at her. I liked a woman who got straight to business. "It depends on what you want it to be." I winked at her and ran my fingers through my hair. "I'm pretty down for whatever."

"Good." She looked around the restaurant quickly and then I felt her fingers on my crotch. She undid my zipper quickly and pushed her hand into my jeans and grabbed my cock through my boxer shorts. She moved her fingers back and forth quickly and I shifted in the seat, not feeling turned on at all. "Hmm." She frowned as she played with me, but I didn't grow hard.

"What?" I muttered annoyed, not understanding why I wasn't turned on.

"I just..." She sighed. "Hold on." She dropped her napkin on the ground and quickly got under the table. I stared down at her in shock. Not because she was about to give me a blowjob under the table, but because she was going to give me a blowjob under a table with no tablecloth. I felt her pulling my cock out of my jeans and then I felt the warmth of her mouth as she took me inside of her and bobbed up and down. I felt her tongue licking me as she sucked on the tip of my cock, and yet I still couldn't get hard. I sighed and closed my eyes and tried to concentrate. There was no way that I wanted her to think I couldn't get it up. My mind immediately flew to Clementine and the previous evening when she'd pulled her bra off. I wasn't sure why that image was so ingrained in my mind. She'd done the same thing so many times before, but I had never paid attention to the bounce of her breasts before, or the way her hard nipples felt pressed against me. I groaned and shifted as I felt myself finally growing hard. I knew that Lily was pleased at the fact because she increased her actions and started nibbling on the tip of my cock. I felt myself growing soft again as I thought of Lily. I frowned to myself. I wasn't sure why I wasn't feeling Lily and her blowjob. She was hot, in a nondescript way. Not that that had ever bothered me before. I didn't go out with all these girls because I wanted anything from them. All I cared about was having a good time. I wasn't like Clementine. I didn't believe in true love. I didn't believe in soul mates. She was a fool for believing in that shit. I couldn't believe that she was saving herself for marriage. Silly girl. An image of her lying on a king sized bed, naked and waiting for her husband to take her virginity filled my mind and I felt a swirl of jealousy in my stomach. Then I remembered her legs wrapped in between mine, so soft and silky. Shit, she was sexy. I allowed myself to imagine that it was Clementine sucking me off for just a brief second. I felt myself growing hard again, but this time, I could feel my body heat rising. I pictured Clementine's face and reached below and grabbed Lily's hair, imagining that I was pulling Clemmie's silky brown locks. Shit! I sat back and tried to stifle a groan. I was going to cum. I felt Lily's lips moving back and forth furiously and I imagined Clementine looking up at me with her laughing brown eyes as she sucked on my cock. I couldn't take it anymore. I exploded in Lily's mouth and pulled her hair hard. I opened my eyes slowly, feeling guilty and ashamed of myself. I couldn't believe that I'd actually had to think of Clementine in order to cum. I was angry and quickly zipped up my pants as Lily quickly moved back to the seat from under the table.

"Breakfast has been good so far." She licked her lips and reached for my arm. I stared at her in distaste and pulled away from her. Looking at her face turned me off. Didn't she realize that I'd been thinking of someone else while she'd been under the table? "I think I'm going to have an omelette for a second course." She shifted in her seat. "Then maybe we can go to your place and you can have dessert." She grabbed my hand and put it between her legs. "I'm ready to see if your tongue can work as hard as mine."

"Yeah, about that." I smiled down at her and jumped up. I pulled a couple of twenties out of my pocket and flung them on the table. "I just remembered something. I gotta go, but here's money for breakfast and lunch. I'll call you." I looked at her hurt expression and gave her another quick smile. "See ya." I hurried out of the restaurant quickly and jumped into my car, feeling slightly disgusted at myself.

"Get your shit together, Rhett." I grunted at myself as I started the engine of my Mustang and pulled out of the parking lot. I was seriously losing my mind and I didn't know what to do about it. I decided to go to the frat house that Tomas belonged to and see what was going on with the guys. I knew that I needed to occupy my mind. I didn't want to think about what any of the craziness of the morning meant.

I went to bed and tried to sleep pretty early that night. I didn't want to go on any dates and I didn't want to talk to anyone. I'd nearly gotten into a fight at the frat house when one of the guys had started talking about Clementine and how he'd like to fuck her at a party. Tomas had had to restrain me as I'd grabbed the guy's shirt collar. I knew I was losing my mind, but I didn't know why. It didn't help that Lily had sent me a hurt text message asking me if I was mad at her and if I had lost respect for her. I wasn't sure what she wanted me to say. I wanted to ask her if she had respect for herself, but I didn't care enough to get into any long conversation with her. I mean, what did she really think? I sighed and grabbed my phone as I realized I wasn't going to get to sleep anytime soon. I automatically called Clementine to see what she was up to, but she didn't answer. I lay there for a few seconds waiting for her to call me back, but when she didn't I sent her a text message instead.

"What you doing?"

"Trying to sleep," she texted me back immediately.

"I tried to call you."

"I'm in bed."

"So you can't talk?"

"What do you want, Rhett?"

":("

"Not going to work."

":(with tears."

"That's pitiful. Haha."

"Are you laughing at the fact that I'm crying?"

"Rhett Madison, you're not crying. Smh."

"Call me."

"Tomorrow! :)"

"Want to go to breakfast?"

"No."

"What do you mean, no?" I frowned at the phone. Clementine never said no to breakfast.

"I'm on a diet. :)"

"What? Why?"

"I have a date next week."

I dropped the phone on my bed in shock. Clemmie had a date? I frowned. Was she joking? Who could she have a date with? She hadn't had a date in months. The beep of the phone distracted me from my thoughts. I grabbed it hoping to see the words 'joke' or 'psych'. Instead I saw, **"Did I shock you?"**

"Who's the date with? Do I know him?" I waited for what seemed like forever for her to respond.

"You don't know him," she finally responded.

Rhett | 81

"How did you meet him?" My fingers tapped against the phone as I waited for her to answer. **"And why didn't you tell me about this date last night?"**

"Damn it, Clemmie." I muttered under my breath and called her again. "Pick up the damn phone." I growled as the phone continued ringing.

"Why are you calling me again?" She answered the phone sleepily and I exhaled.

"Why didn't you pick up the phone?" I lay back in my bed, finally relaxed.

"Because I'm about to go to sleep. I need eight hours a night, you know."

"You never needed eight hours before."

"It's part of my new beauty regime."

"You don't need a regime," I sighed, starting to feel agitated again. "Who is this idiot you're going on a date with, anyway?"

She sighed and I waited impatiently for her to answer me.

"Clemmie?"

"It's a guy I met online,"

"Online where?" I frowned.

"On a dating site," she whispered.

"A dating site?" I exclaimed, shocked. "Why are you on a dating site?" I was pissed that she hadn't even told me that she was thinking of joining a dating site. Why the fuck was she on a dating site?

"To meet a guy, duh." She said sarcastically and I half-smiled at her tone. I knew she was making a face into the phone.

"Why are you trying to meet a guy online?" I asked again, letting my annoyance show. I hadn't even realized that she was seriously interested in dating. I thought she was just concerned about her studies.

"Because I don't meet any winners in real life."

"True, I'm the only winner you know." I joked.

"Real modest, Rhett."

"What?" I laughed. "It's true."

"Anyway, I need to go to sleep now, so I can look fresh for my date tomorrow."

"Is your date in the morning?" I didn't want to hang up, not now that I had finally gotten her on the phone. And I wanted to know more about her online dating. Had she met anyone already? What exactly was she looking for?

"No."

"So, uh, what does it matter what time you go to bed?" I said feeling annoyed.

"Because I have a lot to do." She sounded annoyed as I rolled over on my side.

"Like what?"

"Like I need to get a new outfit and I need a new haircut."

"Haircut?" I frowned as I pictured her long chestnut brown locks. "You can't cut your hair."

"Actually, I think I can."

"Let me come with you tomorrow. I'll help you choose an outfit and I want to see your haircut."

"*You*, help shopping?"

"I want to come help my best friend. Can't I do that?"

"You just want to be an ass." She groaned.

"No I don't. Let me come."

"Don't you have to work?"

"That's the great thing about being the boss's son. I can take off when there's an emergency."

"There is no emergency."

"I'm coming, Clementine."

"Oh, thank you, Mr. Madison!" she exclaimed in a sing-song voice. "I'm so thankful for your help."

"As you should be." I laughed. "And who knows, maybe I'll take you to dinner tomorrow night."

"I told you, I have a date."

"Well, maybe you'll come to your senses."

"I'm allowed to date, Rhett."

"I know that, but a loser you met online?" I made a face. "Does Nanna know?"

"Of course not," she sighed. "No one in my family knows."

"Okay." I said simply. Nanna was Clementine's grandma, but we both called her Nanna. She felt like my real grandma and had always treated me as her grandson since I had met her as a little kid.

"By the way, Nanna asked me if you can come to the family BBQ in two weeks."

"Well, duh," I laughed.

"She also said to tell you that you can bring your girlfriend."

"What girlfriend?" I groaned. "Clemmie, you know that I don't do girlfriends. I don't want a relationship."

"Don't you ever want to get married or have kids?"

"Kids, ugh. And marriage? Why?"

"For true love? For companionship?"

"I don't believe in true love and I have you for companionship."

"But what about the other stuff?" Her voice sounded embarrassed.

"You mean sex?" I laughed and adjusted myself. "Are we going to talk about sex now?" My voice was light, but I was uncomfortable. Part of me wanted to tell her what had happened this morning, but I knew that there was no way she'd understand. I didn't even understand.

"Whatever, Rhett." She sighed. "Have sex with nameless women and just continue being a player."

"Thank you, I will." I snapped back at her.

"Why did you call me, Rhett?" She sounded annoyed.

"I wanted to talk. Or is that a no-no now you're dating online?"

"It's midnight."

"Would you rather I say this is a booty call?" I asked, half-joking.

"Rhett!"

"What?" I laughed.

"I'm going to bed now."

"No phone sex?"

"You're gross."

"I'm touching myself now." I muttered into the phone, while I adjusted myself.

"Rhett!" She gasped. "I'm warning you."

"I'm joking," I laughed. "I'll see you tomorrow."

"Fine. Bye," she hung up and I closed my eyes. My hands reached into my boxers and I started jerking off. I imagined myself in a dark club fucking some nameless girl on the dance floor. I could feel myself growing harder and harder and as I came Clementine's face popped into my head. I grabbed the small towel at the side of the bed and cleaned up. I lay back down and frowned. I didn't want to think about picturing Clementine as the girl at the club. I needed to think about something else. I sighed as I thought about her going on a date. I was worried about Clementine. She was too nice a girl to be dating online. Those guys were going to eat her alive. I was going to have to make sure that she wasn't taken advantage of. I was just going to have to figure out how.

I woke up the next morning feeling annoyed and I didn't know why. I jumped in the shower and then headed out to pick Clementine up. I honked on the horn instead of getting out and going to the door, and waited.

"What the fuck!" I grumbled to myself as I realized I'd been waiting at least fifteen minutes. I pressed my hand against the steering wheel and honked again.

My phone beeped and I saw a text from Clementine. **"Yes, Rhett?"**

"If you know I'm outside, why don't you hurry your ass up?"

"I'm waiting for you to come to my door like a gentleman," she texted back and I glared at the phone. I swore she thought we lived back in the fifties and hadn't gotten the note that men didn't have to woo women anymore. Especially not guys like me.

"Do you really expect me to come to the door?"

"If this was a date, wouldn't you be on your best behavior?" She was right, of course. Both of us had gone to etiquette and then cotillion classes. We knew what was expected of fine young southerners, but I just wasn't in the mood.

"This isn't a date."

Rhett | 89

"I'll be waiting inside until you show your manners," she replied, and I could see the smug smile on her face in my head. Clementine O'Hara was loving every second of this conversation.

"I swear I'm going to drop that girl and get a new best friend," I sighed as I stepped out of my black Mustang.

"Clementine!" I shouted as I knocked on the front door.

"Oh, hi, Rhett." She opened the door slowly and grinned at me. "Imagine seeing you here."

"I've been waiting in the car for the last 30 minutes." I glared at her and she laughed.

"Don't exaggerate." She walked out of the door. "Let's go eat. I'm starved."

"What about your whole weight-loss thing to impress this guy?" I looked at her for a few seconds as we walked if the car. "I thought you didn't wanna go on your date looking like a fatass."

"Are you saying that breakfast is going to make me a fatass?" She paused and looked at me.

"If you're going to get pancakes, eggs, bacon, sausage, toast, and hash browns like you normally do, then yes." I winked at her and she laughed.

"You're so rude, Rhett."

"That's why I don't have a girlfriend." I grinned as we got into the car.

"Yeah, that's why." She poked me in the ribs. "You're not all skin and bones yourself."

"Hey, we can be fatties together."

"You're a jerk." She turned away from me and looked out of the window.

"You're not seriously mad at me, are you?" I sighed as I stared at the side of her face. "I was just joking."

"Uh-huh, Clemmie."

"Uh-huh." She still didn't look at me.

"I was just joking about the amount of food you eat." I reached out and touched her shoulder. "Don't be mad."

"I'm so angry." She started and then looked at me with twitching lips. "I'm going to..." She started again but started giggling.

"What?" I frowned as I watched her laughing.

"Gotcha." She made a face at me and continued laughing.

"Don't do that, Clemmie." I groaned. "I thought you were seriously upset."

"That's what you get for being an asshole."

"Hey, I don't mind that you've got a little extra weight." I winked at her. "And neither will other guys. It's just more cushion for the pushing."

"Rhett." She shook her head as she buckled her seatbelt. "You're gross."

"I'm a man, baby. Trust me. A little extra meat is much better than skin and bones."

"So why are all your dates' skinny as models?" She pursed her lips at me.

"No, they're not."

"Yes, they are. I haven't seen an extra inch on any of them."

"Well maybe that's why it's never worked out before. I need to find me a big-boned lady." I laughed at Clementine's expression.

"Now I'm big-boned," she shook her head and rolled her eyes as I started the engine.

"You're perfect." I looked over and her and spoke honestly. "You don't need to change a thing."

"Uh-huh." She turned on the radio. "You're such a liar."

"There is nothing I'd change about you." I spoke softly and I knew she didn't believe me, but my words were completely true. Clementine was my best friend and I wouldn't change a thing about her.

"Let's just talk about something else." She rolled her eyes and I knew she was a bit peeved.

"You're not seriously mad, are you?"

"When do I ever stay mad at you, Rhett Madison?" She raised an eyebrow at me. "No matter how obnoxious you get, I always forgive you."

"Obnoxious? Me?" I joked and we both laughed. "So tell me about this mystery guy."

"I'll show you his profile." She exclaimed excited. "Well, maybe I'll show you when we get to the restaurant." She laughed.

"Okay..." I paused and have her a quick look. "So his name is? How old is he? Etc.?"

"His name is Elliott and he's the same age as us."

"So he's 21."

"That's the same age we were the last time I checked."

"What is he, some kind of loser?" I made a face. "Why is a 21-year-old guy looking for a girl online?"

"I guess he's a loser like me, then," she said tartly, and I felt my face growing warm. I'd put my foot in it again.

"My bad, Clemmie. That's not what I meant." I made a face. "So tell me more about this idiot."

"His name is Elliott, Rhett."

"Yeah, yeah."

"He likes to bird watch."

"Boring." I yawned.

"It could be fun." She came to his defense. "Plus that means he likes nature and silence."

"Clementine, you chat a mile a minute and you're not really a nature girl."

"I like camping," she protested.

"Clemmie, the last time we went camping with Jake, you complained the whole time about bugs and being scared a bear was going to come get us."

"I was just joking." She made a face at me. "Anyway, I can grow to love it."

"So tell me more about Mr. Country."

"He's not Mr. Country, city-slicker Rhett." She groaned.

"He lives in South Carolina and likes to bird watch. Trust me, he's country. Does he catch gators too?" I looked at her face flashing red and started laughing. "Oh my god, he does, doesn't he? He catches gators too. Does he ride?"

"We ride, Rhett." She glared at me. "And the last thing I knew we both live in South Carolina as well. In fact, I kinda remember seeing some cowboy boots in your closet and a big ol' pickup in your garage."

"That's cool country." I shrugged. "He's hick country."

"You're a snob."

"I'm just being honest." I licked my lips as we pulled into the Cracker Barrel parking lot. "Someone needs to ask you the hard-hitting questions."

"You haven't asked me any hard hitting questions. You asked some basic questions, made some assumptions and you sound like a jackass."

"Okay, I guess you'd rather sit in silence and wait for the bears to approach you and live in a trailer."

"Elliott doesn't live in a trailer." She paused as we got out of the car. "He's actually from Philadelphia. He came down here for school and lives on campus."

"Whoa, and big boy can't find a girl on campus." I gave her my shocked look. "What a loser."

"Rhett, you're an asshole."

"I'm just looking out for you. I don't want you dating a serial killer. You know Ted Bundy was up in Tallahassee killing all those girls."

"I think I'm fine."

"Do you want me to come with you?" I grinned. "I can go to the restaurant and sit at another table and look all incognito and shit. I'll wear my Ray Bans and John Deere cap, to cover up my face."

"No thanks. And why would you need a disguise? He doesn't know what you look like."

"Maybe he Facebook stalked me."

"Why would he do that?"

"When you told him about me, maybe he was curious as to what I looked like, so he Facebook stalked me."

"Rhett, he has no idea who you are." She laughed. "I haven't mentioned you."

"What?" I frowned as we sat down. "How is that possible?"

"Why would you come up?" She gave me a weird look.

"When he asked you about your friends or your best friend." I paused.

"He didn't ask me about my friends and I didn't bring you up. So don't worry, he hasn't Facebook stalked you."

"Well, you better mention me soon." I opened the menu and looked at my options for breakfast. I was starting to feel aggravated inside and I didn't know why. I wanted to tell Clementine to cancel her date with Elliott. He sounded like a loser and I didn't think she should even waste her time with him, but what did I know? I looked up and stared at Clementine as she studied the menu and made the small little noises she always made when deciding what to eat. I smiled to myself as her eyes studied each item carefully.

"What are you having?" I asked her after a minute.

"No idea." She groaned. "I don't know if I should get breakfast or lunch,"

"Hard decision." I nodded at her. I never knew what to get when I came here, but I knew Clementine loved the biscuits.

"Maybe I'll get a chicken-fried steak and gravy and some biscuits on the side." She grinned.

"Sure, big Bertha." I winked at her and she glared at me. I laughed as I stared at her face. I felt my heart stop as I stared at her. Everything about Clementine was familiar to me. Being with her was so natural. I was scared that she was going to meet someone else and everything was going to change. I didn't want anything to change. I wanted everything to remain exactly as it was.

Chapter Four

"I'm sure you look gorgeous." I spoke into the phone as Clementine waited on her date to show up at the restaurant. "The dress you bought looked great." I muttered as I thought about the slinky dress she'd bought at the mall. I hadn't been pleased about the purchase. It had looked a bit too slinky for me, but she hadn't cared what I thought. I was pleased that I'd stopped her from cutting her gorgeous hair off. "Call me when you're done and let me know how it goes."

"Sure," she whispered into the phone. "Oh, Rhett, I'm so nervous."

"You have nothing to be nervous about, Clemmie."

"What if he doesn't like me?" she mumbled, and I shook my head.

"It'll be fine." I muttered, starting to feel apprehensive. What if he really liked her a lot? What was going to happen between Clementine and myself? Then I felt myself growing angry again. What did I care if Clementine got a boyfriend? Maybe it would be better for both of us.

"Okay, I think he's coming. Talk to you later, Rhett."

"Bye." I mumbled into the dead phone. I felt out-of-sorts and wasn't about to hang around like some loser to hear how her date went. I quickly dialed Tomas's number.

"What up, bro?"

"What you up to?" I walked to my car.

"About to go to the bar. Wanna come?"

"Sure. Where you going?"

"Q bar." He laughed. "I got the bartender's digits the other night, figured I'd go back and say hi."

"Dirty dog." I laughed.

"Dude, I wanna see if her big ol' titties are real or plastic."

"They're so plastic." I laughed, knowing exactly who he was talking about. "She's way too skinny to have tits that big."

"Shit, I wanna suck on them big ol' titties." He exclaimed. "Fake or real."

"Guessing you and Sally aren't an item, then?"

"Dude, I fucked her, but she didn't even know how to move her hips," he responded nonchalantly. "You go all the way with her friend? What was her name again?"

"I can't even remember, and no." I laughed.

"You gotta get laid tonight, bro."

"Yeah, I'll see who's at Q." I agreed, I needed some pussy. Shit, I could do two pussies tonight. If I was fucking a pussy and eating a pussy, I'd have no time to be thinking about stupid Clementine on her online date.

"The big titty bartender had a hot friend that was at the bar last time. Maybe she'll be there tonight."

"Yeah." I grinned. "Or maybe I'll go for big tits myself."

"You wish." He chuckled. "She ain't turning down a Latino stud for no blond baby face."

"We'll see." I laughed.

"Yeah, we'll see. I'll be there around ten."

"Okay, I'll see you there then." I grinned and hung up. I jumped in the shower and blasted my shower radio to get myself in the mood. I was going to get laid tonight, come hell or high water.

"Yo, yo, yo! Give me and my boy another shot of tequila." Tomas slapped a twenty on the bar and leaned towards the bartender, whose name was Yvette. "Get one for yourself as well." He winked at her and she grinned back at us. I studied her clinically. She was possibly one of the hottest women I'd ever seen. She was petite, about 5'4, super skinny, with huge breasts, a tiny waist and long black hair.

"Make that double shots." I grinned and put another $20 down on the bar. "Let's get fucked up." I shouted and Tomas slapped me around the shoulder.

"I like the way you think, bro."

"Here you guys go." Yvette placed the shot glasses down in front of us and flashed us both a wide grin. "And thanks for the shot." I watched as she downed the shot quickly and flicked her hair back.

"Nice." I nodded and stared at her breasts. I still couldn't tell if they were real or not. They looked a little too perky to be real.

"Cheers to a great night." Tomas grabbed his shot glass and downed his tequila. I picked up my shot glass and checked the clock on the far end of the wall again. It was 11:00. I frowned and pulled my phone out. No missed calls. I put the phone back in my pocket and downed the shot quickly. I felt the burn through my throat hit my stomach and a warm feeling spread through me.

"Here's to a fucking good night." I grabbed another $20 and put it on the bar top again. "Three more shots." I looked at Yvette and then leaned forward and smiled. "Also, I have another $20 in my pocket if you're willing to tell us if your tits are real or not." I watched her face as she stared at me and smiled slyly before running her fingers over her breasts.

"Make it $40 and you can see for yourself." She placed a hand on her hips and stared at me. "What do you say, big boy?"

"I say you're on." I laughed. "This covers me and my boy?" I placed $40 on the bar.

"Sure." She nodded and grabbed the money. "Meet me down at the end." She nodded towards the end of the bar. "I'll get your shots when we get back."

"Come on." I grabbed Tomas and we walked towards the edge of the bar.

"Follow me." She nodded at us and walked towards the restrooms. We followed her into the ladies room and I laughed as a bunch of girls stared at us in aghast. Yvette pulled her top up and reached behind and unclasped her bra until her breasts were staring at us.

Rhett | 105

"Have at 'em, boys." She grinned and I didn't hesitate to reach out and grab her breasts. They felt hard and stiff as I squeezed them between my fingers. I ran my finger over her hard nipple and saw her eyes softening as she enjoyed the touch of my fingers on her. "You can use your mouth as well, if you want." She smiled at me, but I shook my head. I had no interest in sucking on her fake tits. I took a step back and watched as Tomas grabbed both of her breasts and squeeze them, his fingers playing with both of her nipples. A girl came out of one of the stalls then and I saw her eyes widen in shock.

"So what do you think, Tomas?" I asked him loudly and he grinned at me.

"Those are fake ol' titties." He grinned and I nodded.

"Plastic, baby." I laughed.

"Saline, actually." Yvette made a face and did her bra back up. "It's not that obvious."

"Girl, you couldn't even feel my fingers until I was rubbing your nips." I gave her a wry look. "It's very obvious."

"Whatever." She flicked her head. "No one's ever complained before."

"Shit, I wouldn't complain." Tomas ran his fingers over her breasts again. "I'd titty fuck you any day of the week."

I laughed and then walked out of the bathroom quickly as I realized my phone was vibrating. Finally, Clementine's date was over. That was long enough. I grabbed the phone and frowned as I realized that it was a text from Lily and not a call from Clementine. Where the fuck was she?

"Dude, you okay?" Tomas came out of the bathroom and frowned at me.

"I'm fine." I snapped. "Why?"

"You just walked out." He shrugged.

"You didn't need me in there to titty fuck her, did you?"

"No." He grinned. "Let's get our shots."

"Yeah." I nodded. "Then I gotta go."

"Already?" He looked surprised.

"Yeah, I gotta go somewhere."

"Oh." He grinned at me. "Booty call, huh?"

"You know it." I grinned back at him and checked my phone one more time before putting it back in my pocket.

"You okay to drive?"

"I'm always okay." I nodded. We walked back to the bar and got our shots and downed them quickly. Both of us walked away from the bar after that, which seemed to disappoint Yvette, but we'd gotten what we needed from her. Her tits looked great under the clothes, but naked they just seemed like balls of cement. "I'm out, okay?" I tapped Tomas on the shoulder as he danced his way over to a cute redhead.

"See you later, bro." He nodded and I watched as he continued dancing and then started grinding up on the redhead, who seemed very receptive to his movements. I laughed and left the club in a hurry.

"What the fuck, Clementine." I grabbed my phone and called her as I got into my car. "Where are you?" I muttered under my breath as the phone rang. What was taking so long? Who went on a first date that lasted hours like this? I threw my phone on my car seat as it went to voicemail and drove over to Clementine's apartment. I noticed immediately that her car was not in her parking spot, so that meant she was definitely not in. I parked my car and waited for her to get home. As the minutes passed, I got angrier and angrier. She was so irresponsible. Who met a guy online and stayed out all night with him?

I suddenly became alert as a Mercedes pulled up. I leaned forward and watched as a guy got out of the car and then ran around to the passenger seat and opened the door. I watched as Clementine got out of the car slowly, holding onto the guy's arm. My eyes narrowed as I watched them. Clementine's dress looked even shorter than I remembered and I felt myself growing heated as I stared at her long legs and red pumps. Since when did Clementine wear heels? I frowned as they walked a few yards and stopped. Clementine was grinning from ear to ear and I could see him whispering something in her ear. The dirty dog was trying to get into her pants. I was sure of it. I was about to jump out of the car when I saw the guy lean down and kiss her. I was frozen as I watched them kissing for what seemed like an eternity. Then I saw Clementine pull back and say something. The guy nodded and she leaned up and gave him a kiss on the cheek. I felt myself exhale as I realized that the guy was leaving. At least she had some common sense. I watched as the guy got back into his car and pulled out of the parking lot. Clementine stood there waving as he left and then walked to her apartment door. I sat back feeling absolutely furious. What did she think she was doing kissing a guy on the first date? Was she crazy? I finally jumped out of my car and ran to her apartment door and banged.

"Did you forget something?" She asked sweetly as she opened the door, and then I watched her huge smile turning into a frown. "Rhett? What are you doing here?"

"Do you know what time it is?" I asked as I pushed my way inside the apartment.

"No, why?" She looked confused.

"It's midnight." I walked straight to her bedroom. "You met him at what, seven?"

"Huh?" She followed me to her room. "What are you talking about?"

"You were supposed to call me when you got back from your date. I was worried about you." I sat on her bed and frowned at her. "You went and met some stranger and you've been out all night. I had no idea what happened to you."

"Nothing happened to me, Rhett." She shook her head and I watched as she pulled her hair up and put it in a ponytail.

"You didn't call me." I stared as she removed her long dangly earrings.

"I just got in." She turned away from me and slipped off her heels.

"Since when do you wear heels?"

"Since I started going on dates." She sighed and looked back at me. "What is this? Twenty questions?"

"I was just curious." I looked away as she stared me in the eyes, her brown eyes flashing in annoyance.

"What are you even doing here?" She frowned and walked towards me. "Have you been spying on me?"

"As if." I rolled my eyes. "I was out with Tomas and just popped by to see if you were okay, because you didn't call."

"I'm fine." She glared at me and leaned forward. "Have you been drinking?" Her eyes narrowed and she sniffed near my mouth.

"I had a couple." I shrugged.

"And you drove?" She looked angry.

"I'm fine."

"You're staying over." She sighed and shook her head. "I'm not letting you drive home drunk."

"I'm not drunk."

"You're not driving home." She bit her lower lip. "You can sleep on the couch."

"What?" I looked at her in shock. "What are you talking about?"

"I don't think it's appropriate for us to sleep in the same bed anymore." She paused and licked her lips nervously. "I don't think Elliott would like that."

"You just met Elliott." I jumped up and grabbed her arms. "Are you joking with me right now?"

"Rhett." She sighed. "I already told you that..."

"We slept in the same bed last night, Clementine." I pulled my shirt off. "It's no big deal."

"I just don't think it's..." She stopped and stared at me as I tried to unbuckle my belt. "Need help with that?" She smirked as I fumbled around.

"I've got it." I looked down, but all of a sudden I felt drunk as all the tequila shots hit me.

"No, you don't." She sighed and I felt her fingers reach my belt buckle. "I swear, Rhett Madison, you're a big baby."

"No, I'm not." I mumbled as her fingers deftly untied my belt and then undid my zipper. My body stilled as she pulled my jeans down. All of a sudden I was aware of how close she was to me and how good she smelled.

"Pick your feet up." She kneeled down and pulled my jeans off of my body. She stood back up and stared at me, standing there in my boxers and frowned. "Fine, you can share my bed tonight, but this is the last time, I swear, Rhett."

"You can't just turn your best friend away." I smiled at her and collapsed on the bed. "That wouldn't be cool."

"Uh-huh." She rolled her eyes and I watched as she grabbed a t-shirt. "Close your eyes." She mumbled and I pretended to close them as she pulled her dress off quickly. I stared at her standing there in her bra and panties and felt my body stilling. She was so gorgeous. I wanted to groan out loud at the sight of her body. "Are your eyes closed?" she muttered.

"Duh." I grunted back and put my hands in front of my eyes. I watched as she pulled her bra off quickly and I felt my cock hardening in my boxers as I caught a quick glimpse of her breasts before she pulled her t-shirt on. She then turned the light off and walked back over to the bed.

"Move over real quick, so I can pull the sheets up." She muttered and I rolled over. She pulled the sheets to the side and I rolled back over so she could pull the other side up. She pulled the other side up and them jumped into the bed next to me. I felt her warm body next to mine and I tried to pretend that she was Tomas.

"So did you and Tomas have fun tonight?" She turned toward me and spoke softly.

"Yeah, I guess." I shrugged and looked into her eyes. "We got to feel a pair of plastic titties."

"What?" She frowned at me.

"Just some hot chick with big breasts." I mumbled and paused. "But never mind that, what about your night?"

"It was great." She smiled at me widely, her eyes dancing with excitement. "Elliott is such a gentleman. The night was perfect."

"Uh-huh." I mumbled, not wanting to hear about how perfect the douchebag was.

"He ordered dinner for both of us and got this bottle of wine that was so amazing," she continued excitedly as she stared at me.

"Okay." I answered shortly and sighed. "I'm uncomfortable."

"Okay." She looked at me with a question in her eyes. "What do you want me to do?"

"I don't know." I shrugged. "Shift? Move over?"

"Okay." Her voice was soft and she rolled onto her side. "Is this better?"

"I guess." I sighed and turned onto my side as well, so that my chest was facing her back. "I need to put my arm here." I muttered and lifted my arm up so it was over her waist.

"That's fine." She mumbled and snuggled back a little bit.

"Good." I muttered and moved a bit closer to her. That was a mistake and I froze as I realized her t-shirt had ridden up and her ass was pressed against the front of my boxers. The only thing stopping us from having naked one-on-one contact were her silky panties and my boxers. I stifled a groan as she moved back and forth slightly against me.

"You okay?" She looked back at me with a concerned look.

"I'm fine. Just tired."

"Oh okay." She sounded disappointed. "I wanted to tell you more about my date."

"Go on, then." I said reluctantly, not really wanting to hear anymore.

"It was so great. After dinner he took me to the park and we swung on the swings and looked up at the stars." She gushed and I found myself growing angry. "And he even kissed me."

"Oh yeah?" I grabbed her waist and pulled her back into me, so that she could feel my hardness against her ass. I didn't know why I did it, but I just didn't want to hear about this guy anymore.

"Yeah." She mumbled and I felt her attempting to move forward, but I kept my grip on her waist tight.

"Was he a good kisser?" I muttered into her ear as I pressed my back against her. Her body felt warm and I felt her shiver slightly as my breath tickled her.

"He wasn't bad." She sighed. "It wasn't a magical moment."

"That's a shame." I smiled for the first time since she'd started telling her story. "That's a real shame."

"Yeah." She sighed and I felt her body relaxing. "I was a bit disappointed."

"I bet." I released my grip on her waist and rested my hand casually just below her breasts and closed my

Rhett | 117

eyes. "That's a pity, but I'm sure you'll find someone better soon."

Clementine didn't answer and I felt myself drifting off to sleep with her snuggled back against me. All of a sudden I felt content again. Everything was as it should be. The date had gone okay, but I knew a bad kiss would be the end of it. Hopefully, Clementine wouldn't go on any more dates anytime soon and we could remain as we always had been. I didn't have time to keep worrying that she was possibly going on a date with a psycho.

Chapter Five

"Tomorrow's Elvis night down at the club, do you want to come?" I looked at her casually, starting to feel annoyed that she didn't seem to want to hang out me. I hadn't seen her all week since the night she'd gone on her date and I was beginning to feel frustrated and rejected. The only reason I was seeing her now was because I'd showed up at her apartment.

"Nah." She shook her light brown hair and didn't look up from her desk and books.

"What do you mean 'nah'? You love Elvis and you love Elvis night!" I frowned. The only reason I had gotten two tickets was because I thought she wanted to go. We always went together. Since we were ten years old.

"I've got other plans." She looked up at me then and shrugged.

"What other plans?" I stared at her, not believing my ears. Clementine never had plans. I could always count on her to be there for me when I needed her. And if she said she had plans with Elliott, I was going to be mad.

"I have a date." She smiled then and her eyes twinkled. "That's why I need to study hard now. I can't afford to get anything but an A on my finals next week."

"So bring your date to the club." I muttered, not even believing I was actually telling her to bring someone else to our night.

"You sure you wouldn't mind?" She nibbled her lower lip and I smiled inwardly. So she did know that it wasn't really cool to ditch me and then bring someone else to Elvis night.

"I mean, Elvis night has always been a night we celebrate together." I shrugged. "And I always take you.

I've never taken a date, but if you want to bring some guy you just meant online, feel free."

"Rhett." She frowned at me. "Does it really mean that much to you that we go together?"

"It's kinda like a tradition." I shrugged. "But fine, bring whoever and I'll just find someone else to go with."

"Fine, I'll go." She rolled her eyes. "Heaven forbid, you take one of your many girls with you."

"I don't want to go with anyone else; unlike you." I paused and gave her a look. "I mean, we've been going as friends for years."

"I know, I know." She groaned. "Fine. We'll go together. I'll tell Elliott I can't make it."

"Elliott?" I made a face. "You're still seeing bad kisser?"

"He's not a bad kisser." She made a face. "Anyway, it might have been nerves."

"Uh-huh." I rolled my eyes.

"This is the start of something beautiful." Her eyes lit up as she spoke excitedly. "Aren't you excited for me, Rhett?"

"Of course." I lied as I stared into her wide brown eyes. "I mean, if you're sure this is what you want to do. Who am I to be a Debbie Downer?" I shrugged and looked away. How could I tell her that the start of her something beautiful was the start of my nightmare? I wasn't sure what was going on and why things seemed to be changing so quickly, but I did know that all I wanted was for everything to stay the same.

"This is what I want." She nodded. "I think I'm ready for my first proper boyfriend."

"Whatever." I pulled out my phone. "Anyway, I just popped over to make sure we're still on for tonight. I've gotta go. I got a date tonight."

"Oh okay." She nodded and looked disappointed. "Maybe we can watch a movie later."

"You mean you won't be with Elliott?"

"He might have to study." She shrugged and I rolled my eyes. "But, all three of us can watch one if he doesn't."

"I'll see what happens tonight. I might be getting laid." I shrugged my shoulders and turned away, feeling angry. All three of us, my ass. "I'll text you and see what's going on."

"Okay, sounds good." She smiled. "See you later, Rhett."

"Yeah, see ya." I walked out of the room and sent a mass text to about fifteen different girls. **"What you doing tonight? Wanna get a drink?"** There was no way that I was going to spend another night alone thinking about any bullshit.

"So I told Monica that there was no way that I was going to go on a date with Aiden." Veronica spoke rapidly as she told me another story about her best friend and all the guys that supposedly wanted to date both of them.

"His loss, my gain." I leaned in towards her and pretended to be interested, before taking another long chug of beer.

"I was so glad when I got your text message this morning." She grinned. "I was wondering if you were ever going to call."

"I texted." I corrected her. "I didn't call."

"Well, I was glad when I got your text." She grinned.

"Why?" I studied her face for a second. "Why were you glad?"

"Because you're hot." She didn't hesitate in her response.

"What do you think is going happen tonight?"

"I don't know?" She shook her head as her face went red. "I just wanted to see you."

"You wanted to go out for a drink?"

"Yeah, sure." She played with her glass.

"Anything else?"

"No." She looked down and I went in for the kill.

"Are you hoping to ride me tonight?"

"What?" She looked shocked, but her eyes lit up at my words.

"I guess you're not saving yourself for marriage." I commented and took another chug. "No worries that you're not. Only fools save themselves for marriage."

"Uhm. Okay." She paused and looked at me in confusion. I knew she was trying to figure out whether I had just called her a fool.

"Don't worry. I'm down for some fun tonight. You're a beautiful girl." I said smoothly and watched her start smiling again. I could have patted myself on the back. It was so easy with women. Give them a few compliments and smiles and they were like putty in my hand. Everyone aside from Clementine. It was like she was immune to my charm. It had never bothered me before, but now it was fucking annoying me. Why wasn't she more into me and hanging out? Why had she never been into me? I frowned as I thought back to high school and the moment when I'd turned into the boy all the girls wanted. Clementine had never started acting all girly on me. I'd never seen her writing my name. Or drawing hearts or even giving me looks of love. I didn't get it. Was she immune to my blue eyes? I paused as I remembered one night in eleventh grade when I'd thought something was going to happen.

"Did you hear me? Veronica interrupted my thoughts and I frowned.

"Sorry what?"

"I said we can go back to my place after this, if you want. My roommate's staying over at her boyfriends."

"Oh, yeah. Sure." I shrugged and my mind went back to eleventh grade. We'd been at Nanna's house and Jake was watching wrestling on TV. I'd grabbed a cookie from her hand and stuffed it in my mouth and eaten it quickly. She had jumped on my back and we'd rolled around on the ground play fighting. Everything was all fun and games until she'd ended up sitting on top of me, her hair falling in my face as we'd laughed. Then she paused and for one second, it was just me on my back and her on top of me and we weren't best friends playing around. There'd been a look in both of our eyes and I'd seen her face going red as we just stared at each other. I'm not sure what would have happened if Jake hadn't jumped down and joined in the fun.

"I said I'm ready." Veronica touched my hand.

"Ready for what?" I frowned and looked at her.

"To go back to my place." She looked taken aback. "I was just saying that I got a new nightie from Victoria's Secret." She smiled sexily. "For a special occasion like this."

"I see." I gave her a small smile, but I knew there was no way I wanted to go back to her place.

"And I got some toys as well." She leaned forward and licked her lips suggestively. "Some very naughty toys."

"Oh?" I feigned interest and she grabbed my hand and stroked my palm. I grabbed her fingers and was about to push her away when I got a text message. I grabbed my phone and read the message. It was from Clementine and read, **"Elliott just got here, want to come over and watch a movie? We were thinking about Love Actually. We can wait on you if you want."** I read the text message and I could feel my lips curling in disgust. Was she fucking high? Did she really think I wanted to come and watch some sappy movie with her and her loser friend? I didn't consider him her boyfriend at all. I put my phone back in my pocket without texting her back. Love Actually, I thought to myself again. What a fool Elliott was for agreeing to watch that piece of shit.

"You ready?" I jumped up and grabbed Veronica's arm. "Let's go."

"Oh okay, sure." She almost purred as we walked to my car.

"So what are these toys you got?" I asked her as we got into the car.

"Well, I got handcuffs." She grinned. "And I also got a rabbit. I think you can help me with it if you want."

"Sounds good." I pulled out of the parking lot quickly. *Boring.*

"I just want you to know this isn't something I normally do." She said softly. "Normally, I wait until I'm in an official relationship…" She paused and I could feel her eyes on me.

I wanted to laugh at the absurdity of the situation. She wasn't seriously trying to hint that we should be in a relationship? Didn't she realize I couldn't give two shits about her? I was going to fuck her just to fuck her, not because I actually wanted to be with her.

"I was waiting for marriage." She started again and I froze.

"You're not a virgin are you?" I looked at her quickly. There was no way this girl was a virgin, was there?

"Well, not anymore." She giggled. "But I had hoped to wait for marriage."

"My best friend is a virgin." I muttered. "Trust me, I don't think she's having as much fun tonight as we're going to have."

"Unless she meets the right guy." Veronica laughed. "It's funny how quickly the right guy can talk any girl out of their panties."

"What?" My voice was hoarse and I slowed down a bit.

"I mean, I don't know her, but there are plenty of guys who can touch and talk real smooth and before you know what hit you, you're in bed with your legs spread and his tongue in places, you never thought could feel so good." She giggled again. "Just saying is all."

"Yeah." I felt my skin growing cold as I thought about her words. Maybe it wasn't such a smart idea to let Clementine spend the night alone with Elliott at her apartment. She was too trusting and I didn't know what sort of punk he was. He might try and make a move on her and she might not have a clue what to do or say. I thumped the steering wheel as I realized that I needed to go to Clementine's apartment to make sure that Elliott didn't try to take advantage of her.

"Take a right here." Veronica exclaimed as I kept driving.

"Hey, we have to make a pitstop." I didn't look at her.

"Oh?" She sounded surprised. "Where are we going?"

"I need to make sure a friend of mine is okay, I won't be long." I muttered and frowned as we hit a red light. Of course, I was going to hit every red light now that I was on the way to Clementine's. I was angry that Clementine had put me in this position. What smart girl had a guy she just met over to her apartment? What was she thinking? Now I had to interrupt my date to go and make sure she was okay. She really owed me, big time.

"What?" Veronica sounded put out. "How long is that going to take?"

I ignored her and concentrated on the road. There was an uncomfortable silence in the car as we drove to Clemmie's apartment. "Look, I'll make it up to you, I promise." I gave Veronica a big smile as I parked and got out of the car.

"Shall I come in as well?" She looked confused and annoyed.

"No." I shook my head and then paused. I was going to look like a loser showing up by myself, while Clementine sat there with her new man. "Actually, yeah, come on in."

"Okay." She got out of the car slowly and closed the door. "We're not going to be here long, are we?"

"No." I locked the doors and walked to Clementine's front door purposefully, leaving Veronica to follow behind me.

Bang, Bang. I knocked on the front door loudly. Bang, Bang. I knocked again impatiently.

"I'm coming," I heard Clementine's voice as she walked to the door and I could feel myself growing angry. How could she sound so nonchalant while putting herself in danger for a possible rape?

Bang, Bang. I knocked on the door again angrily. I heard Veronica approach behind me. I turned to look at her and I could see that she was visibly upset at having to walk across the parking lot in her heels without my assistance. I looked at her for a second and knew that I was going to have to make it up to her, but right now I needed to make sure that Clementine knew I wasn't impressed with her online dating safety measures.

"I said I'm coming." Clementine opened the door with a perplexed expression on her face that changed to surprise when she saw me. "Oh hey, Rhett, what's going on?" She looked at me curiously and then looked behind me at Veronica. "And hi," She smiled weakly. "I'm Clementine, nice to meet you."

"Okay." Veronica nodded and spoke in a pissed tone.

"Your name is okay?" Clementine asked softly and I looked her in the eyes. She raised an eyebrow at me as if to say, another bimbo and I frowned at her.

"My name is Veronica." Veronica spoke stiffly. "Who exactly are you? And why are we here, Rhett?" She touched my shoulder.

"Clementine, can we come in?" I stepped into her apartment without waiting for an answer. "Where's Elliott?"

"He's watching the movie." She frowned at me. "We just paused it."

"Tell me you're not watching it in the bedroom." I strode down the corridor and into the living room, feeling furious. "Oh, hi." I stopped as I saw Elliott on the couch eating popcorn. He looked up and gave me a small smile.

"Hi," His expression was friendly, but surprised. I looked him over and wanted to laugh. Elliott looked like a nerd. He couldn't have been taller than 5"10 and he looked like he had a pretty small frame. I knew that he didn't compare to my 6"2 stature and 200lbs of solid muscle. He had blond hair and doeful looking brown eyes. He was cute, I'd give him that, but he certainly wasn't a hunk. Not saying that I'm a hunk or anything, but I knew that if we both walked into a bar, there would be way more girls over me.

"I'm Rhett." I walked over to him and reached my hand out. "I'm Clementine's best friend and Knight in shining armor."

"Elliott." He jumped up and shook my hand firmly. "It's nice to meet a friend of Clementine's."

"Best friend." I gave him a deceptively innocent smile.

"Does that really matter now we're in our twenties?" His eyes narrowed as he continued smiling back at me.

"Does what matter?" Clementine walked into the room with Veronica following behind, looking out of place.

"The distinction of best when talking about friends." Elliott walked over to her and put his arm around her shoulder. "I just thought that was a pretty grade school thing, to classify friends as best." He shrugged and smiled at me. "I've never been one to have to stress how close I was to someone."

"Oh," Clementine laughed. "I guess Rhett and I still refer to each other as best friends." She gave me a winning smile, but I didn't smile back. What did she see in this douche?

"This is your best friend?" Veronica looked at me and then at Clementine, her eyes narrowed. I looked at Clementine through her eyes and I understood why she looked pissed. Clementine looked hot in her black skinny jeans and midriff top. Since when did she own a midriff top? Her long hair was flowing around her shoulders and her brown eyes were sparkling. I looked closer and I could see that she had eye shadow covering her eyes. When did she start wearing eye shadow?

"You look like a raccoon." I muttered at Clementine and she frowned at me.

"What?"

"We need to talk." I walked over to her and grabbed her hand and pulled her to her bedroom with me. "We'll be right back." I muttered to Veronica and Elliott as we left the room.

Rhett | **135**

"What's going on Rhett?" Clementine exclaimed as we walked into her bedroom.

"Do you know how irresponsible you're being?" I growled at her and leaned against the door so no one could get in.

"Huh?" She looked confused.

"You just met this guy online. He could be a psycho or a stalker." I shouted, furiously. "And after one date you already have him in your apartment, alone. How stupid are you?" I glared at her. "I had to leave my date to come and check up on you to make sure you're okay."

"Are you crazy?" She glared at me. "Elliott is not a psycho and you didn't need to come and check up on me." She shook her head. "What the fuck is your problem? You chose to bring that bimbo here."

"She's not a bimbo." I glared at her.

"Sure, okay is not a bimbo." She glared back at me.

"What?" I frowned, confused by her words. Then I couldn't stop myself from smiling. "Her name isn't okay. Her name is Veronica."

"Same difference." She grinned at me, reluctantly.

"She's hot." I shrugged. "Her name means nothing to me."

"That's so wrong." She sighed. "Poor girl."

"You don't care."

"I care about you." She bit her lower lip. "I want more for you than nameless encounters."

"This is about you, don't change the subject."

"Don't go all Papa Bear on me Rhett." She sighed. "I can take care of myself."

"What if he makes a move on you?" I frowned. "What are you going to do?"

"I can take care of myself and I can make my own decisions."

"You've never been in this situation before." I stiffened. "You don't know what guys are like."

"I know you." She smiled gently. "I know what you do with girls, I'm not some sheltered little princess." She sighed. "And I want to start dating. I want to get out there. I want a boyfriend. I want a life."

"I thought you were concentrating on your studies." I could feel my heart beating fast.

"My studies aren't going anywhere." She looked at the ground. "I've wasted so much time already. I feel like I've wasted so many years."

"You're 21, Clementine." I rolled my eyes.

"Yeah, but most girls my age have had a boyfriend before." She sighed. "Most girls went to Prom."

"You went to Prom." I protested.

"I went with Jake." She shook her head. "Going to prom with your little brother is no fun."

"You went with me too."

"Rhett, you had a date." She rolled her eyes. "You went with a date and I went with Jake. Yeah, we shared the same limo ride, but it wasn't fun."

"I thought you had a good time." My heart thudded. "I tried to include you, you know that."

"I know." She stepped forward and grabbed my hands. "You've always been here for me, Rhett. You're the best friend a girl could ask for, but I need more than that. I want a boyfriend. I want romance. I want a man to sweep me off of my feet. I want to be the only date of some guy. I want him to wake up and think of me. I want him to fall asleep dreaming of me. I want him to text me in the middle of the day just to say hello. I want him to love me with all his heart. I want his heart to be so full of love for me, that he can't believe he's so lucky." She gave me a short smile. "I know I sound sappy, but I'm ready for my true love."

"Clementine," I shook my head at her. "That shit doesn't exist. That's Hallmark cards and those crappy romance movies and books you watch and read. I don't know one guy that tells me his heart is so full of love for anyone." I reached over and stroked her hair. "I'm not trying to be a jerk, but I don't want you to spend your life searching for something that doesn't exist."

"I think it does exist." She bit her lower lip.

"I'm telling you it doesn't."

"Well, you live your life that way." She stepped back from me. "But I'm going to live my life this way."

"So you want to live in a day dream?"

"I want to live with hopes and dreams, yes." She nodded. "And I'm going to search for my true love, but I can't do that, if I don't date or put myself out there."

"So you think that Elliott is your Prince Charming? Even though he's a crappy kisser?"

"Rhett," Her eyes widened and she pushed her hand against my mouth. "Shhh."

"What? I'm just saying?" I smiled at her innocently.

"I don't know what's going to happen with Elliott, but I like him and I'd like to see where it goes." She spoke softly. "Thank you for being concerned, Rhett, but I think I can handle this by myself. I don't need you to play bodyguard."

"Uh-huh." I frowned and looked at her bed. "Fine."

"Veronica seems nice enough." She looked at me curiously. "Do you like her a lot?"

"She's fine." I snapped and stepped forward. "I guess we can go back in the living room."

"Rhett." She touched my arm. "Are you okay?"

"I'm fine." I pulled away from her and walked back into the living room. "You ready?" I walked over to Veronica and ignored Elliott. She looked up at me with an annoyed expression.

"I've been ready." She replied with a sour look on her face.

"Let's go." I looked back at Clementine and raised an eyebrow at her. "Gimme a call, if you need me." I stared at her for a few seconds and I could see from her expression that she was upset. Good, I thought. Let her think about what she's doing. I walked out of the living room and through the front door without looking back. I could hear Veronica running behind me, but I didn't slow my pace down.

"Are we going to my place now?" Veronica asked softly as she got into the car.

"I'm taking you back to your place, but I'm afraid I can't stay the night." I muttered as I pulled out of the parking lot.

"What?" Her voice was high. "What do you mean?"

"I mean you'll have to use that rabbit on yourself." I shrugged. "Or I have a friend you can call, if you really need to have some help. Tomas would be down I'm sure."

"You're a jerk." She exclaimed pissed and I laughed.

"Trust me, you're not the first girl to say that and I'm sure you won't be the last."

I pulled up to her apartment and dropped her off, not even bothering to make sure she made it to the door before pulling away. I was so pissed that I could barely think straight. I didn't know where to go or what to do. I didn't want to go home. I couldn't go to Clementine's. I didn't want to see any of my guy friends. I didn't wanna hook-up with any of the girls I had in my phone. I just wanted to be by myself in nature somewhere. I just needed to switch my brain off. I drove and drove for about an hour, before I decided to go to an old park that I used to go to as a kid. It was one of the only positive memories I had of my childhood and my mother.

I parked my car and got out and walked to a bench that was a couple of yards away from the children's playground. The night air was warm, but there was a cool breeze. I closed my eyes for a second and sat back. The earth seemed to be moving beneath me and I was finding it hard to breathe. I took a couple of deep breaths and then opened my eyes and looked at the sky. The stars were shining brightly and I looked around at the playground as if seeing it for the first time. I could picture my mother's face as she watched me from the bench, her face looking like an angel as she stared at me with pride and love. Her hair had been long and blonde and her big blue eyes were always warm. Or they'd always been warm, until everything changed. I'd loved coming to the park. We'd always pack a picnic lunch and my mom would swing me around and around until both of us felt slightly dizzy.

I gripped the seat beneath me as I remembered my mother's laughing face and her loving eyes. Her loving eyes had lied to me though. She didn't love me. She'd never loved me. If she had, she wouldn't have left. She wouldn't have loved the alcohol more than me. It had been ten years since I'd seen my mother. Ten long years of wondering why she'd stopped loving me. Ten years of wondering what I could have done differently. I could feel my eyes growing heavy and my heart aching as I sat there.

I hated that she could still do this to me. I hated that there was never a day that went by that I didn't feel that slight ache inside. The ache I couldn't reach. I hated that sometimes late at night, I woke up and all I could think about was her. I didn't understand it. I didn't want to feel this way. I wasn't that guy. I didn't get emotional. I didn't care. I didn't let anyone get too close or affect me. The only person I loved was Clementine. And she was my best friend. I knew that she was the only one I could count on to always be there for me. I couldn't risk that friendship. Not for anything. I frowned as I realized my thoughts had changed from my mother to Clementine. I sighed as I sat there, feeling so tired and confused. I sat there in the silence, enjoying being by myself. This was what my life was now. It was just me. Clementine would find someone and leave me. It was inevitable.

Beep Beep. My phone vibrated as I received a text message and I pulled the phone out of my pocket.

"Hey." It was Clementine. I was about to put my phone back in my pocket, but decided to text her back.

"Hey." I didn't have anything else left to say.

"Movie was good."

"That's nice."

"Elliott left."

"Okay."

"Don't be mad."

I didn't respond.

"Veronica and you having a good time?"

"I dropped her home."

"Oh."

I didn't respond again.

"I thought about it and you were right." She texted me again after two minutes.

"About what?" I texted back.

"It wasn't smart to invite Elliott back to my apartment after one meeting."

"Told ya." I smiled to myself.

"He's not a psycho though."

"We'll see."

"What you doing?"

"Relaxing."

"At home?"

"No."

"Oh."

"I came to relax."

"Oh. I see."

I didn't respond again. Instead, I stood up and walked over to the playground and looked around.

"Can I come?" She texted back again.

"If you want." I responded slowly. There was no response from Clementine after that and I walked back to the bench and sat down again. About ten minutes later, I saw a car pulling into the parking lot. I watched as Clementine got out of the car and walked towards me with something in her arms.

"Hi." She smiled at me softly.

"Hi." I nodded and tried not to stare at her beautiful face.

"I brought this for you." She handed me a sweater. "I knew it was pretty cool out and I knew you just had on your t-shirt."

"Thanks." I took it from her gratefully and pulled it on. "How'd you know where I was?"

"How could I not know?" She smiled and sat down next to me.

"Yeah." I sighed and leaned back, my shoulders rubbing hers.

"That's what best friends are for." She rested her head down on my shoulder and we both sat there in silence just watching the stars. These were the times that I loved. These were the times I craved. Sitting in silence with someone. With her. It reminded me that while I felt alone, I always had her. Even in my darkest hours. Even when I didn't want to talk. Even when I felt like the world was caving in on me. Clementine was always there. She was the light at the end of the tunnel. I closed my eyes and thought about my mom. There was a point in my life that I had thought she'd always be there as well. There was a point when I thought that I was her world. But I'd been wrong. I felt my body tensing as Clementine rested next to me. What if Clementine left me as well? What if her forever was temporary as well? Would I ever be able to get over losing my best friend?

Chapter Six

"What time is the barbeque?" I watched Clementine as she pottered around in my kitchen.

"I told Nanna, we'll be there around noon tomorrow." She opened the fridge and pulled out some butter and cheese. "Want a grilled cheese?"

"Sure." I nodded and sat on one of the stools that she had helped me choose out. "Don't burn the bread."

"When have I ever burned the bread?" She turned to me and raised an eyebrow.

"Well there's a first time for everything."

"There's a first time for me to stab you with this knife." She rolled her eyes at me and I laughed.

"Just don't burn the bread."

"Don't just sit there watching me cook." She grabbed a frying pan and put it on the stove.

"What else should I be doing?" I jumped up and walked over to her.

"Go and watch TV or something."

"You're the TV fiend." I reached over and grabbed a slice of American cheese and started eating it.

"Rhett!"

"Yes?" I grinned as I nibbled on the cheese.

"You're going to ruin your appetite."

"Yes, mom."

"Whatever." She punched me in the arm. "Get out."

"In case you forgot this is my kitchen."

"What's yours is mine." She grinned at me and I groaned.

"Never." I shuddered.

"Thanks, Rhett."

"Sorry, but that makes me think of weddings and forever and evers." I made a face and she gave me a look.

"There's nothing wrong with forever and ever and happily ever afters."

"They don't exist." I opened the fridge and grabbed a coke. "Unless you live in a fairytale."

"Not true." She shook her head. "There is someone out there for everyone, even you."

"Even me?" I laughed and took a long swig of coke. "I don't want anyone."

"Don't you ever wonder what will happen though, Rhett?" She looked at me curiously. "Don't you want to grow old with someone?"

"I have you." I laughed and she smiled at me softly.

"But I'm going to get married and have kids, what then?"

"You'll still be my best friend." I frowned and tried to ignore the pang that hit my heart at her words. What would happen if Clementine met someone and fell in love? What if she got married and had a bunch of kids. What would happen to us?

"I will, but my husband won't like me hanging out with you every day."

"You guys can adopt me." I grinned.

"I'm being serious, Rhett." She frowned. "We won't be able to hang out every day. You can't just come over. You can't call me at all hours of the night. You can't expect to just be in my life like you are now."

"What are you trying to say, Clemmie?" I frowned now. "Are you mad at me or something? Are you still upset about the other night?"

"No." She sighed. "I'm just saying you have to realize that everything isn't going to stay the same."

"I want us to stay the same." I grabbed her around the waist and picked her up.

"Rhett, put me down." She squealed as she squirmed against me. "Rhett."

"What?" I laughed and carried her through to the living room and dropped her on the couch.

"You can't just pick me up like that." She sat up and glared at me, her face a red flush.

"Why not?" I grinned and winked at her.

"Because it's not appropriate."

"Since when have you cared if something is appropriate or not?" I sat on the couch next to her. "You've worn my boxer shorts to sleep in. That's not appropriate."

"That's only because I slept over and didn't have PJ's." She glared at me.

"You could have slept naked."

"Yeah, that's going to happen." She rolled her eyes at me and I laughed. All of a sudden an image of a naked Clementine in my bed appeared in my mind and I stifled a groan. I hadn't had sexual thoughts of her in a few days and I thought I'd controlled them, but I guess I was wrong.

"So you going to come to the truck race with me next week?" I said and then grinned as she flipped the sandwich in the pan.

"Not sure." She grabbed a plate from the cupboard. "Maybe."

"Dude, what do you mean maybe? It's the beginning of summer. We always go together."

"I said maybe," She spoke softly. "We have a lot of traditions, Rhett and I can't keep up with all of them. Sometimes things change and life gets in the way."

"Uh-huh." I rolled my eyes and ignored the tenseness in my shoulders at her words. "Nothing has to change if we don't want it to."

"Rhett, you made it." Nanna walked over and gave me a huge hug as I walked in the door.

"Of course, I wouldn't have missed it." I grinned back at her and looked around. "Where's Clementine?" I asked, feeling irritated.

"Oh, she's in the back with her brothers playing softball." Nanna smiled. "She brought her friend Penelope as well."

"Yeah, I gathered." I responded politely. "I thought Clementine and I were going to ride over together. That's what we always do." I frowned as I stood there.

"I think her friend Penelope needed a ride." Nanna rubbed my shoulders. "Now come, let me give you some lemonade and you can go out and join everyone."

"Thanks Nanna. The ribs nearly done?" I looked at her hopefully and she laughed.

"You always did have an appetite, didn't you Rhett?" She laughed. "There'll be ready soon, I promise. Did you bring anyone with you? I told Clemmie to tell you that you can bring your girlfriend."

"I don't have a girlfriend, Nanna." I grinned at her and made a face.

"Well how do you like that? You and Clementine both young, single, free, and disengaged and the neither of you has a girlfriend or a boyfriend." She shook her head. "I don't understand you kids today."

Rhett |

"We like being alone, Nanna." I shook my head at her expression and laughed. "Anyway we're too young for serious relationships."

"Y'all are nearly college graduates. I ain't never seen a college graduate that was too young to get married."

"Married?" I looked at her in shock. "I thought we were talking about boyfriends and girlfriends. I'm sorry Nanna, but I'm never getting married."

"When you meet the right girl you will." She patted my shoulder.

"I don't think so." I shook my head and shuddered." No way am I doing that to myself."

"No way you're doing what to yourself, Rhett Madison?" Clementine walked into the kitchen with a huge smile and gave me a hug.

"I'm mad at you." I frowned as I hugged her back. I tried to ignore how snug her white t-shirt was across her chest and how short her shorts were. When did she go and get a pair of long tan legs and decide to show them off?

"Why?" She tilted her head and paused. "Another date go wrong and you want to blame me?"

"Very funny." I made a face. "I thought we were coming to the barbeque together." I frowned.

"Oh really?" She shrugged and poured herself a glass of lemonade. "My bad, I thought I told you I had to go and pick up Penelope."

"No, you didn't." I shook my head irritated, feeling like a jealous little kid.

"Well you're here now." She rolled her eyes. "Nanna, you got any brownies?"

"Not now, Clementine." Nanna laughed. "Plus, you sure you wanna be eating brownies. A minute on the lips is a lifetime on the hips."

"I'll take my chances." Clementine grinned at me. "Anyway for me it's hips and waist, so who cares?" She laughed and rubbed her stomach. I stared at her movements and laughed along with her, even though all I was thinking about was her taunt stomach.

"Is that a baby I see sticking out?" I grinned and reached over and rubbed her stomach as well. My fingers ran across the softness of her stomach gently and all of a suddenly she tensed as I touched her. Our eyes met for a few brief seconds as I continued to rub her stomach and then I stepped back, feeling hot and awkward.

"You ready to go outside?" Clementine looked away from me and turned around. "We're playing softball."

"Am I ready?" I choked out a laugh, though I still felt slightly tense. "Dude, I was nearly signed by the Red Sox."

"I thought it was the Yankees?" She laughed.

"I don't wanna be no damn Yankee." I retorted and we both laughed.

"You two never change." Nanna stared at us both as we left the kitchen. "Both of you are as blind as bats." She muttered quietly as she started getting the coleslaw together.

"Rhett, my main man." Clementine's brother Jake hollered at me. "We've been waiting on you to get this party started."

"I'm here now." I grinned and high-fived some of the cousins. "Hi, Penelope." I gave her a quick smile. I wasn't sure why we'd never hit it off. I'm sure it had something to do with the fact that Clementine didn't always come to me first like she used to before she met Penelope. It annoyed me knowing that sometimes she valued Penelope's advice more than mine. I also wasn't pleased that sometimes when I wanted to hang out, they already had plans. And well the guy thing pissed me off. I had no idea why Penelope was trying to push Clementine into getting a boyfriend. I felt like she was using that as an excuse to push me out of Clementine's life! Imagine telling her I was the reason guys didn't approach her! What the fuck? She was such a bitch.

"Hello, Rhett." She smiled back at me with a thin smile. "I see you made it."

"Of course I made it. This is my family too. I've been coming to the barbeque since I was in grade school."

"Uh-huh." She rolled her eyes and turned around. "Funny you never feel fit to bring someone with you."

"Who would I bring?" I gave her my 'are you stupid look'?

"Maybe a girlfriend." Her eyes narrowed. "But I suppose you're only interested in girls for a night."

"Wish you were one of them do you?" I gave her a slow wink and watched as her face burned bright red and then turned away. "So you want me to pitch?"

"Duh." Jake shouted back with a huge grin. Jake was 18 and a recent high school graduate. I'd always felt like he was my little brother as well and I did my best to make sure he stayed on the straight and narrow. I tried to hang out with him at least once a month and was planning on letting him room with me when he started college in the fall.

"How'd your date go with that girl?" I shouted to him.

"Which one?" He winked and we both laughed.

"Rhett, I wish you wouldn't turn Jake into your mini me." Clementine shook her head.

"Hey, the girls love him. What can I say?" I grinned at her and she groaned.

"Okay, do we have teams?" I looked around and counted how many people we had. "I want Jake. Clementine and Penelope can be on the other team."

"That's not fair." Clementine put her hands on her hips and shook her head. "How are the two best players going to be on the same team?"

"I thought that was fair." I ran over and ruffled her hair. "The two best players on one team and the two worst on another. I've already got the team names picked, the winners and the losers."

"You're a loser." She stuck her tongue out at me.

"Don't let the wind change on you now or that's the face you'll end up with."

"You'll still be stuck with me, tongue out and all." She grinned and I pulled her towards me and grabbed her as I fell into the ground.

"Try and get rid of me."

"Guys, you're being so childish." Penelope's voice was irritated as she walked over to us. "Clementine, this is what I mean. Guys who see you acting like this with Rhett are going to get the wrong impression."

"What impression is that?" I looked up at Penelope and then jumped up, pulling a giggling and guilty looking Clementine up with me.

"That you guys are either dating, sleeping together or have some other weird relationship. Or," and she looked at Clementine. "That you're both really immature."

"Clementine is immature." I shrugged with a straight face.

"Shut up, Rhett." She punched me on the shoulder. "Penelope, Rhett is my best friend, he's like my brother, and we're always going to be close and goofy. The guy that comes into my life will have to accept Rhett."

"No guy is coming and staying as long as Rhett's around." Penelope shrugged. "But hey, maybe that's what he wants."

"Penelope." Clementine exclaimed and gave me a look. I shook my head and walked over to Jake.

"Hey bro, let's decide our team." I rolled my eyes at him. "Your sister and her new friend are debating our friendship."

"You know Penelope doesn't get you guys." Jake laughed. "I think she's has the hots for you."

"Who?" I froze, my heart thudding fast. "Clemmie?"

"No." Jake gave me a weird look. "Penelope. That's who we were talking about."

"Oh yeah." I made a face. "No thanks."

"Not even for one night?"

"Not even for ten minutes." I laughed.

"What about a million dollars?" He grinned at me and I grinned back.

"That's the beauty of being rich. Not even for a million dollars."

"Show-off." He laughed. "I'd make out with her for ten bucks."

"Jake, don't lie. You'd make out with her for free."

"True that." He threw the softball at me. "You want a glove?"

"Nah." I shook my head. "Where are the 'rents?"

"Grocery store." Jake rolled his eyes. "Dad wanted more beer and mom wanted some nuts, but she didn't trust dad to get the right ones."

"Ha, sounds about right." I threw the ball back at him. "You talk to them about staying with me next year?"

"Dad thinks it's great." Jake nodded. "Mom not so much."

"Why not?" I frowned.

"She said Clemmie doesn't think it's a good idea."

"What why?" My frown deepened. Clementine hadn't said anything to me.

"She thinks it's too much." Jake shrugged. "She says it's not right to live with you for free." He made a face.

"Are you joking?" I looked back at Clementine as she talked to Penelope and my eyes narrowed. I bet I knew why Clementine didn't think it was a good idea all of a sudden. "Don't be ridiculous, you're my brother from another mother." I gave him a look. "You're staying with me."

"It's a great savings." He nodded. "Dad's already worried about having both of us in college at the same time." He looked around and chewed his lower lip. "Clementine's even looking into transferring to a school where she can get a scholarship." He made a face. "I'm not meant to say anything."

"Why hasn't she told me?" My heart dropped. "I had no idea."

"Yeah, it's pretty recent." He shrugged. "I guess her new friend told her about it."

"Penelope?"

"No, her boyfriend, that guy she's seeing."

"What guy?" My voice rose. "Clementine doesn't have a boyfriend."

"Yeah, I guess it's new. Some guy called Elliott."

"Elliott?" I frowned and immediately thought back to seeing Clemmie kissing him the other night. "Not that loser she met online?"

"I dunno." Jake looked like he regretted bringing the subject up. "I guess you'll see tonight. He's coming."

"She invited him to the barbecue?"

Jake nodded and I frowned.

"Excuse me a second." I threw the ball back to him and ran over to Clementine. "Hey, we need to talk." I grabbed her arm.

"Huh?" She looked at me in confusion.

"We need to talk!"

"Now?" She looked at Penelope and then back at me. "We were kinda in the middle of something."

"That can wait," I looked her in the eyes. "We. Need. To. Talk. Now."

"Listen to your husband, Clem." Penelope rolled her eyes. "Oh wait, he's not your husband or your dad."

"Clementine," I gave her the look. It was something we had come up with as kids so we could let each other know that it was imperative we talk right away.

"Fine, excuse us." She gave Penelope a quick smile and grabbed my arm and dragged me into the house. "What's going on, Rhett?" She sighed as we walked up the stairs and went into one of the spare bedrooms that Nanna always had ready and waiting for guests.

"Transferring?" I stood there with my arms crossed and raised an eyebrow. "What's that about?"

"Oh." She chewed on her lower lip and sat on one of the two twin beds in the room.

"Yes, oh." I sat on the other bed directly in front of that. "Though, I'm thinking OH."

"It's not for sure," she gave me a weak smile.

"I didn't even know it was a thought."

"It's just something I've been thinking about to help dad out. He can't afford to pay for me and Jake and I don't want Jake to take out loans and well he's not going to get any scholarships."

"We always said we were going to graduate from State." I tried not to look angry. "And we're graduating in just over a year." My voice rose. The news had turned me on my head and I was not happy.

"Well that was the plan, but plans change."

"Where did this come from?"

"Nowhere." She looked down at the ground.

"So Elliott had nothing to do with it?"

"Jake has got a big mouth." She muttered.

"Why didn't you tell me?"

"There was nothing to tell."

"You don't think it's news to tell me you might be moving. Where are you going? Chapel Hill? Duke? That's a long drive you know."

"I was thinking Harvard or Yale."

"What?" My jaw dropped. I stared at her in shock as my stomach dropped. There was no way I could make weekend drives to Boston or New Haven.

"I figure if I'm transferring, I should go to the best."

"Harvard?" I ran my hands through my hair and stared at her in shock. "What are you talking about?"

"You know I got in for freshmen year."

"But you didn't wanna go and hang out with those snobs."

"I just need to do what's best for me and Jake." She sighed. "It's not like I want to leave you guys, but I'll see you still."

"What the fuck." I felt a certain satisfaction as I watched her eyes expressing their dismay at my choice of words. Clementine hated the fact that I used the f bomb so much.

"Nothing's going to change, Rhett." She got up and sat next to me. "I'll still be here for you."

"What are you talking about?" I glared at her. "I'm talking about something we agreed upon years ago."

"Sometimes things change." She put her arm around my shoulder and I shrugged her off of me.

"I know that."

"Have you seen your mom recently?" She asked softly and I frowned as my stomach lurched.

"No and I don't want to." I frowned. "This has nothing to do with her."

"I was just asking." She sighed and lay back. "I know you don't like to talk about her, but I think it would be helpful."

"It won't be," I looked down at her and tried to ignore the stirrings in my heart as I stared into her wide concerned eyes. Clementine was my rock. She was the only person I knew who truly loved me and had my best interests at heart. I had no idea what I would do if she left me.

"It might be good for you as well." She offered me a weak smile and I stared at her lips as she spoke.

"What might be good?" I frowned as I realized my eyes had fallen to her chest. I wasn't sure why I was so interested in her breasts all of a sudden. I felt uncomfortable admiring her body. I tried to look away, but I couldn't keep my eyes off of the swell of her breasts and the imprint of her nipples as they pushed against her t-shirt.

"Me going away." She sat up and her hair swung in front of her face.

"How will that be good?" I gave her a look.

"Maybe it will help you..." Her voice trailed off.

"Help me how?" My voice rose.

"Find someone to be serious with." She bit her lower lip and shrugged. "Maybe you can have a real relationship."

"I like how everything is now." I lay down and stared at the ceiling. "I don't want anything to change."

"We'll still be best friends, Rhett." She lay down on her side and stared at me.

"So why do you want to leave?" I turned over and stared at her.

"I don't," she shook her head and her nose crinkled. "But we have to face up to it sometime. One of us is going to move away sooner or later."

"No, we don't have to face up to anything." I reached over and played with her hair. "You need a trim."

"Thanks, another one?" She rolled her eyes and grinned. Then she reached over and played with the hair at the front of my face. "So do you."

"You're not cutting it." I winked at her and we both laughed as we thought back to the time in tenth grade she had given me a Mohawk.

"Hey," she laughed. "Maybe I was just jealous of your blond locks."

"Uh-huh." I grinned and stared at her for a few seconds in silence. "I don't want this to change." I sighed.

"I know," she bit her lower lip. "But people don't understand our relationship now. They think we must be dating or something."

"Eww no." I shuddered and she laughed.

"Thanks, Rhett."

"No offense or anything, but dating?" I stared at her and ignored the sudden rapid beating of my heart. "Hell no."

"I know you don't do relationships." She giggled and rested her hands on her arms.

"We'd ruin our friendship if we tried to be more than friends." I spoke slowly. "Not worth it at all."

"Don't worry, Rhett. I don't want to date you either." She grinned and I felt a pang of some unknown emotion in me.

"Now you have Elliott huh?" I frowned, feeling angry again.

"No." She made a face.

"Why is he coming anyway? I thought he was a crappy kisser?"

"He's not that bad."

"Oh!" I attempted a smile, though I wasn't feeling very happy at her words, and moved towards her. "Want to know what a better than not bad kiss feels like?"

"Huh?" She frowned at me and looked confused.

I wasn't really sure why I decided to kiss her. It shocked and surprised both of us as I pressed my lips against hers and kissed her lightly. Her lips felt soft and moist beneath mine and I felt myself deepening the kiss as her lips pressed against mine firmly. My arms instinctively reached towards her and brought her into my chest. I felt her breasts pressed against me and I felt something in me loosen up as I internally groaned at the same time. I was sexually attracted to her and I wasn't sure what the fuck I was going to do.

"Rhett," she breathed against my lips. "What are you doing?" She pulled away from me with wide eyes. I stared at her for a few seconds wanting to kiss her again, but instead I started laughing.

"I wanted to show you how a real man kisses, so that you have something to compare a great kiss to."

"I see." She frowned. "I don't know why you did that."

"I was playing around." I jumped off of the bed and smiled at her as if it were nothing.

"You can't just do that." She stood up slowly.

"Sorry, it was a joke."

"I see." She touched her lips gingerly and she had a dazed expression on her face.

"What did you think of the kiss?" I asked her softly, unable to resist.

"I've had better." She grinned and I watched as she walked out of the room. Better, my ass! I thought to myself as I followed behind her. She was lucky she was my best friend or I would have gone back for seconds to show her that there was no one better than me.

"So, who's ready for some baseball?" I walked into the yard and flexed my muscles as if I hadn't just been kissing Clementine and enjoying it.

"Let's get this party started." Jake hollered back at me and I grinned.

"Winners vs. Losers baby." I ran over to him and held my hands out for him to throw me the ball.

"Where you been?" He looked at me curiously.

"Nowhere." I laughed, guiltily and looked over at Clementine who was tying her shoes. I turned away and pretended that I hadn't just overstepped a boundary. It was just in fun. It didn't mean anything to either of us. It was just a kiss. Nothing more and nothing less.

"Elliott." Penelope's voice was loud and happy. I looked up and stared at Elliott as he made his way into the backyard. Of course she would like him. I frowned as I watched Clementine walking over to him with

Penelope. Both of them were smiling widely at him and I felt my face growing hot.

"Hey guys." Elliott waved to all of us and he gave me a short smile as our eyes connected. My eyes narrowed as I looked at him and I turned away without acknowledging him.

"Ass." I muttered under my breath.

"What?" Jake asked me curiously.

"Nothing." I shook my head and looked back over to Clementine and Elliott. I felt my face growing heated as I watched him giving her a bouquet of flowers. "Really?" I mumbled under my breath, feeling angry. "What a suck up." I muttered. Why was he bringing her flowers? He was really trying to play a strong hand. I watched as Clementine smiled and gave him a kiss on the cheek after taking the flowers. She looked happy and pleased and I frowned at her expression. Was she really falling for his crap?

"You guys ready to play or are we going to stand around in the sun all day?" I shouted out and I saw Penelope turn towards me with a smug smile.

"We're ready." She gave me a look and then turned back towards Elliott.

"Clementine." I called out to her. "Can we get this game going?"

"Yes, Rhett." She stepped back from Elliott. "Let me go and put these flowers in a vase. I'll be right back."

"I'm going to get a drink." I turned to Jake and followed Clementine into the house.

"Wait up." I ran up behind Clementine.

"What's up?" She turned to me with a small smile.

"Just wanted another drink before the game. I can't wait to kick you guys asses."

"Okay." She nodded and turned away from me.

"Also, about earlier. It didn't mean anything. I was just playing around."

"It's fine." She mumbled and I saw her face flushing.

"I know I'm an ass." I tried to joke about it. "I was just being goofy."

"It's fine, Rhett." She sighed. "Hey Nanna, do you have any vases? Elliott got me these peonies."

"Oh beautiful, of course Darling." Nanna rushed over with a tall vase. "How thoughtful of him." She bent down and sniffed them.

"Careful, Nanna, you don't want a bee to sting you." I muttered.

"Oh, Rhett." She smiled at me gently, her eyes glinting. "They smell wonderful, darling." She rubbed Clementine's shoulder. "I'll have to sit down and have a longer chat with him later."

"Chat about what?" I frowned at her.

"His intentions with my granddaughter." She replied promptly.

"Nanna, no." Clemmie groaned and I could see her face going red again.

"Isn't it a bit fast for that?" I walked to the fridge and opened it slowly, feeling myself growing agitated.

"It's never too early to find out a man's intentions." Nanna's voice was soft. "If he's serious about you, it's important for him to know that you have a family that is looking out for you."

"Nanna, we just started dating." Clemmie's voice was weak. "Do not say anything to him."

"Say anything to who?" Mr. O'Hara bellowed out as he and Mrs. O'Hara walked into the house with some shopping bags. "Are you and Rhett finally dating now?" He grinned as he dropped the bags onto the floor. "Here we go momma." He kissed his mother on the cheek.

"Dad." Clementine rolled her eyes. "You know Rhett and I are not dating."

"What she said." I gave Mr. O'Hara a small smile as he gave me a quick hug.

"Good to see you, Rhett. We haven't seen you in a couple of weeks." He patted me on the back and stepped back as Mrs. O'Hara gave me a hug.

"You must come to dinner next week, Rhett. We want to hear how finals went."

"They were fine." I made a face.

"And how is your dad?" She asked me softly and looked me over with an interested face.

"Same as usual." I shrugged.

"You're looking very handsome, Rhett." Mrs. O'Hara ran her fingers along my shoulders. "Such a handsome man, you've grown up to be."

Rhett | 179

"Surprised?" I said and laughed.

"I always knew you'd be a handsome man." She shook her head and smiled at me sweetly. "Even when you were a troublesome little boy."

"That we did." Mr. O'Hara nodded. "We always worried about what was going to happen when you and Clemmie became teens. We thought we'd have to ban you from seeing each other."

"Dad." Clementine rolled her eyes and gave me a small smile.

"But we had nothing to be worried about." Mrs. O'Hara patted her husband's shoulder. "You two have always been so good. We almost forgot you were friends of the opposite sex."

"Almost." Her dad laughed. "I wasn't about to let you guys have sleepovers once you hit puberty."

"We still had sleepovers dad." Clementine made a face.

"With the door open." Her dad laughed. "And trust me, I didn't want to let you have them."

"We've been friends since we were little kids, dad." Clementine rolled her eyes. "Nothing happened."

180 | J.S. COOPER

"I know." Mr. O'Hara grinned at me. "I thank God, that Rhett is a gentleman."

"Thanks, Mr. O'Hara." I smiled back at him.

"Though, I'm not sure why neither of you have dated?" He looked at us curiously. "Is one of you gay?"

"Dad!" Clementine exclaimed and Mrs. O'Hara rolled her eyes.

"Come on, Hank." She grabbed her husband's arm. "Let's go and see Jake and the others, while momma finishes cooking."

"What did I say?" He laughed as they walked out of the kitchen.

"Dad is too much." Clementine shook her head and spoke to Nanna. "I hope he doesn't say anything crazy to Elliott." She bit her lower lip. "In fact, I think I better go outside and make sure he doesn't ask when he's going to propose or something crazy." She hurried out of the kitchen and I watched her go, before looking at Nanna.

"What?" I frowned as I realized she'd been staring at me.

"I don't normally like to get involved in other people's business." She stepped towards me and looked up into my eyes with a serious expression.

"What do you mean?" I stared back at her with a puzzled expression. What was going on here?

"You and Clementine have been best friends for a long time." She said softly and handed me a plate of brownies.

"I thought we had to wait 'til later to have a brownie?" I smiled at her as I grabbed one off of the plate.

"I'm going to let you have one now." She smiled and sat at the table and patted the chair next to her.

"Thanks, Nanna." I grinned and had a seat. "So what did you want to talk about?"

"Elliott seems like a nice boy." She started and I frowned.

"He's seems okay." I shrugged and took a huge bite of the brownie.

"He really seems to like, Clementine."

"I guess." I muttered, unenthusiastically.

"Clementine is ready to grow up." She spoke softly. "I've been waiting for this day to happen. It's come slower than I thought it would, but I suppose in the circumstances it's understandable."

"What day? What's slower than you thought?" I frowned confused.

"Clementine is a true romantic." She nodded to herself. "She gets it from me. I've told her stories about me and Hank Sr. and how he wooed me. He was my true love you know."

"I know." I nodded. Nanna's husband had died five years previously, but I could still remember what a great guy he had been and how he'd doted on Nanna.

"She's been waiting for her Prince to come find her since she was a little kid." She smiled. "She wants the fairytale love."

"It doesn't really exist though." I mumbled and she shook her head at me.

"Oh, Rhett. Typical bitter man."

"I'm not bitter."

"You know that things will change between the two of you once she gets serious with her young man."

"You think she'll get serious with Elliott?"

"I wouldn't be surprised." She smiled at me gently. "I don't want to see you getting hurt, Rhett."

"Why would I get hurt?" My eyes narrowed. "I don't want to be with her. We're just friends."

"Things will be different between you, once they get serious."

"We'll always be best friends."

"Yes, yes." She sighed. "What I'm trying to say is. Sometimes we don't realize what we have until it's gone."

"You think she'll stop being friends with me?"

"You guys have a very special friendship." She sighed. "I've never seen two people closer in my life. You both play very important roles in each other's lives. I don't think ya'll realize just how important." She reached out and took my hand. "Sometimes the things we run away from are the things we already have."

"I'm not running anywhere, she's the one that's trying to find a boyfriend. I'm happy with our friendship. I don't need a girlfriend."

"Maybe because you get everything you need from a girlfriend from Clemmie already." Her eyes softened as she stared at me with a loving glance.

"We don't sleep together, Nanna." I laughed.

"Sex while important is not the be all and end all of a relationship, Rhett."

"It's a lot of fun though." I grinned and she shook her head.

"It's not for me to ask if you're attracted to Clementine and I don't want to stick my nose in where it's not wanted, but I don't want you to lose someone that could be everything you never knew you wanted." She paused. "Sometimes God makes two people that are perfect for each other in every way. It's always a shame when they miss the signs."

"I don't know that God always gets everything right." I gave her a weak smile and stood up. "I mean what's love really? And what's perfect? Maybe his plans don't always go to plan? My mom loved my dad more than her own life. She always told me that. She also used to tell me that I meant more to her than the moon and sun combined. And where is she now?" I shrugged. "Sometimes God's plans don't always work out."

"I think he got his plans for you perfectly right." She whispered behind me as I walked out of the kitchen and towards the backyard. I wasn't sure what she'd expected me to say. Did she really think Clementine and I were perfect for each other? I stopped at the back door and watched Clementine running to catch a ball and throwing it to Jake. She was laughing about something and her hair was flying everywhere. I stared at her for a few minutes and watched as she moved and started chatting to Penelope. My breath caught as I watched Elliott walking over to her and I saw him giving her a quick hug. My body tensed as I realized that I was in serious trouble of losing my best friend and I didn't know what do to. I wasn't what Clementine wanted. I didn't believe in happily ever afters. I didn't want a girlfriend. I didn't believe in true love. And I didn't know how she felt about me. Maybe she didn't even like me like that. I could feel a headache coming on. I watched them talking and I felt loneliness creeping in. Elliott was already replacing my role in Clemmie's life. Her family already seemed to like him and I knew that a boyfriend would have precedence over a friend. I'd be inched out of this family, just like I'd been inched out of my own. I pulled my phone out of my pocket and sent a few texts. "Want to grab dinner tomorrow?" I sent to a few different girls. I had to stop relying on Clemmie so much. I needed to keep going out. I needed to occupy my time with other women. I knew that if I was getting my needs met by them, I would stop thinking about being with Clemmie. I wouldn't want to kiss her and I certainly wouldn't fantasize about being with her. I put my phone back in my pocket, plastered a big smile on my face and ran out into the yard.

"Who's ready for a game?" I shouted exuberantly and flashed my million dollar smile as I made my way to the grass, ignoring the look I was getting from Clementine.

Chapter Seven

"We're going to go to Outback." I smiled at Jenny as we walked to my car. "I hope you like steak."

"I'm a vegetarian." She made a face as I opened the door for her.

"They've got salads." I closed the door and walked around to the driver's seat, feeling annoyed and thinking about Clementine going on another date with Elliott tonight. "Ready?"

"I guess so." She sighed and played with her fingers.

"What's wrong, Jenny?" I turned towards her and gave her my Rhett smile. "Aren't you excited about our date tonight?"

"I just don't think you care about my needs." She pouted her lips.

"What needs?" I took a deep breath. I was not in the mood for another serious talk.

"I told you I like a guy to call me every day and to ask me out on a date, at least three days before we're going to go out." She gushed out. "You've never called me and you texted me last night for this date tonight."

"I don't see the problem." I shrugged and started the car. It had been a mistake to text Jenny. The only reason why I'd asked her on the date was because I knew she was eager and Clementine had blown me off yet again. I was going to have to have words with Clemmie about letting Elliott take over her life. It was starting to interfere with my life.

"And I don't eat meat." She mumbled. "Why would you take me to Outback?"

"You can get salad anywhere." I answered her, not bothering to hide my annoyance. "I can't get steak at a salad bar."

"We could have gone for seafood." She mumbled back.

"I wanted steak." I reached over and turned on the radio. I was starting to feel angry. Part of me wanted to drive Jenny back home and then call Clementine and argue with her. Maybe she'd even cancel her date. I just didn't trust Elliott. I felt like he was bad news. He was taking over her life, trying to alienate her from her best friends. I was fuming by the time we reached the red light and I pulled out my phone.

"*We need to talk when you finish your date.*" I text her angrily. I waited for a response, but nothing came.

"The light's green, Rhett." Jenny touched my arm and I frowned at her.

"I'm going." I revved the engine and slammed on the accelerator.

"You're going too fast." She squealed as I swung around a corner, but I ignored her. "Rhett, please slow down."

"We're here." I snapped as we pulled into the Outback parking lot. I jumped out of the car and checked my phone. There was still no response from Clemmie.

"*Hope you're having fun.*" I sent her another text and pushed the phone in my pocket. I looked around for Jenny and realized that she was still sitting in the car. "Girls." I muttered to myself as I walked around to open the door for her. I watched as Jenny got out if the car, she was wearing a short black dress that exposed a lot of cleavage and a lot of leg. Her long blonde hair was hanging down her back and her big blue eyes were framed by luxurious black eyelashes. She gave me a hurt look as she stepped out and pouted her bright red lips again. I tried not to roll my eyes as I closed the doors. She was so obvious. I knew that even though I had put no thought or concern into the date, I could close the deal pretty easily. Maybe even in the back of the Mustang if I wanted. It would be easy as pie as I was pretty sure that Jenny was even easier than that.

"Ready?" I gave her a short smile, already ready to take her home. I had no interest in sex or a make out session with her. Her kisses had been pretty weak and wet the first time and I hadn't really cared about getting a second date with her.

"I guess so." She batted her eyelashes at me. "Though I'm feeling pretty cold." She grabbed onto my arm. "Keep me warm, Rhett." She cuddled up to me and pressed her body into my side. I didn't respond as we walked into the restaurant, though I wasn't my normal jubilant self.

"A table for two please." I asked the hostess politely and gave her a huge smile. "And your number." I winked at her.

"Haha." The redhead grinned back at me as we made eye contact. I felt Jenny drop my arm and stiffen next to me. I smiled to myself. This was the easiest trick I knew to let a girl know I wasn't interested. Only the desperados stuck around for another date when I openly flirted with another girl in front of them. "It'll be about ten minutes, is that okay?" The hostess continued as she played with her hair.

"That's fine." I nodded. "The names Rhett, by the way."

"I'm Candy." She grinned back at me.

"I love to suck on Candy." I slowly licked my lips and watched as Candy blushed. Then I heard Jenny gasp and I turned to her with a frown. "You okay?" I asked in a barely caring voice.

"No, I'm not okay." She glared at me. "You Sir, are a rude, un…."

"Hi, a table for two please." I recognized Elliott's voice right away and froze. I turned around slowly and saw Elliott and Clementine standing behind me. Clementine was dressed in a short skirt and tight top. My eyes narrowed as I took in her appearance. She looked sexy as hell and that made me even more annoyed.

"Clementine." I said her name softly and I saw her eyes widen in surprise and happiness for a brief second as she smiled at me.

"Rhett." She walked over and gave me a hug. "Fancy seeing you here."

"Date night." I nodded towards Jenny and Clemmie gave her a small wave.

"Same here." She grinned. "We're so mature now. Going on date nights."

"Uh-huh." I nodded, but didn't feel as happy about it as she looked. "Hi, Elliott." I nodded at the other guy as he gave me a small nod. "Why don't we have a double-date?" I asked her quickly and then turned to Candy before Clementine could respond. "Hey, Candy, make that a table for four please." I grinned. "We're all going to sit together."

"Sure." Candy gave me a weak smile. I could tell she was put out that I seemed to be close to another girl.

"That's cool, right?" I looked back at Clementine and she nodded.

"Yeah, how fun." She smiled at me and I had a sudden urge to reach out and run my fingers down her pink cheeks. "That's cool with you, right Elliott."

"Sure." He responded, looking anything but cool about it.

"Hi, I'm Clementine and this is my friend Elliott." Clemmie introduced herself to Jenny.

"I'm Rhett's girlfriend, Jenny." Jenny narrowed her eyes and smiled fakely at Clementine.

"Oh, I didn't know he had a girlfriend." Clementine grinned at me. "You sly dog."

"Jenny's not my girlfriend." I laughed and Jenny glared at me. "No offense, Jenny, but let's not get the date off on a false pretense."

"You're a jerk." She muttered and I could see her giving me the evil eye.

"Trust me, he knows." Clementine responded and I pinched her. "Hey."

"That's what you get for calling me a jerk." I smiled at her and we both laughed. All of a sudden, I felt better than I had in days. I knew the awkward tension had gone from our relationship and we were back to acting like we had before all the silly drama had started.

"I'll get you back for that." Her eyes glittered into mine and I leaned towards her and whispered in her ear.

"Promise?" I blew slightly as I whispered and she giggled. She was sensitive to air in her ears and it always made her laugh.

"Just wait, Rhett Madison."

"I'm here all night."

"I'll get you when you least expect it." She winked at me and I stared at the long expanse of her neck and then below to her glistening chest and bosoms.

"What are you wearing?" I spoke softly as I stared at her sexy outfit.

"Clothes."

"Barely." I raised an eyebrow and she blushed.

"So how are you doing, Rhett?" Elliott stepped towards us and tried to assert his masculinity.

"Good, you?" I gave him a cursory glance.

"Good, though not as good as you." He looked over at Jenny. "On a date with another girl, I see."

"Good eyesight." I gave him a broad smile and took a step closer to him, so that he was looking up at me.

"Thanks." He smiled at me again, but I could see from the glint in his eyes that he knew I didn't like him and I could tell that he didn't like me either.

"Rhett, I'm hungry." Jenny walked up to me and batted her eyelashes.

"We'll be seated soon."

"I thought we were going to sit by ourselves." She gave Clemmie a sour side-glance and then looked back at me. "I thought we could have a nice private dinner."

"It will be more fun with friends." I smiled at her and then looked back at Clementine who was watching us with interest. I gave her a quick smile and she winked at me.

"Your tables ready, Rhett." Candy called us over and I ignored the number she tried to slip me as another girl guided us to our table.

"That girl was trying to give you her number." Clementine whispered to me as we walked to the table.

"I didn't take it though."

"You're such a player." She shook her head and frowned. "I don't know how you can date so many women."

"I don't know how you can date one loser."

"Rhett." She pursed her lips and I sighed.

"Sorry, he's not a loser." I rolled my eyes as I apologized.

"It's fine." She smiled and we sat down. I took the seat next to her in the booth and Jenny and Elliott sat on the other side. I could see that they both looked put out by the seat assignments, but I didn't care.

"Wanna split a Ribeye and a filet?" I asked Clementine as we studied the menus.

"Sure," she nodded. "Let's get the blooming onions as well."

"Sounds like a plan to me." I grinned.

"Okay then." Elliott looked at us and frowned. "I suppose that's you two set."

"Oh, sorry." Clementine blushed. "Sorry, Rhett and I always come to Outback and we always split meals."

"Not just at Outback." I smiled at him. "Pretty much every time we eat out."

"Which is a lot." She laughed. "We eat out a lot."

"Because we're pigs." I agreed.

"You're the pig, Rhett Madison. Not me." She rolled her eyes.

"Sure, you only stuff your mouth every other meal." I poked her in the stomach. "Not every meal."

"Stop," she squealed and moved away from me.

"Are you two done?" Elliott shook his head and gave Clementine a look. I could feel her tensing up in embarrassment and I was annoyed that he was trying to make her feel guilty.

"What you getting, Jenny?" I looked over at my date. She was glaring at me and she wasn't even trying to hide her anger. "See any salads you like?"

"They only have a Caesar salad." She looked pissed. "I wanted a Greek salad."

"Oh that sucks." I shrugged and looked at Clementine. "You getting any alcohol?"

"No," She shook her head. "Not tonight."

"Good." I smiled at her. "I don't want you drinking when you go on dates with strange guys."

"Rhett." She gave me a look and I shrugged. I wasn't going to keep my mouth shut in front of Elliott. I wanted him to know that he better not try anything with her or I'd be on his ass.

Rhett | 199

"Let's just order and enjoy our food." Elliott shook his head and spoke in an aggravated voice. "Next time, I'll make sure to take you to a more up-class restaurant, Clementine. That way we can avoid hanging out with the trash." The table went quiet then, but I saw Clementine rolling her eyes and I smiled to myself. This idiot wasn't going to last too long, I thought to myself.

I dropped Jenny off in silence. I felt her glaring at me all through the ride home and I knew that I might as well delete her number. There was no way in hell that she was going to go on another date with me. Not that I really cared. She was boring and a whiner and I knew there were too many women in the world to waste my time with her. I pulled my phone out as soon as I dropped her home and called Clementine.

"What you doing?" I asked as soon as she picked up the phone.

"I just got home. Where are you?"

"Driving home."

"No bow-chicka-wow-wow tonight?"

"No." I laughed. "Where's Elliott?"

"He went home." She sighed. "He was upset."

"Why?"

"He thought we were being rude at dinner." She paused. "And he wanted to stay over."

"Stay over?" I frowned. "He wanted to spend the night?"

"Yeah."

"What the fuck?" My voice rose.

"I said no, Rhett." She spoke softly. "He said he wanted to watch a movie. No biggie."

"He wanted to do more than watch a movie, trust me." I pictured Elliott's face and my fist hitting it.

"Well, he went home. And angry."

"I'm sure he was more than angry." I muttered. Dude most probably had blue balls.

"He said that he thinks we have a weird friendship." She continued. "He said that he doesn't think we should spend so much time together."

"Really?" I spoke in a low tone, not wanting to show my anger.

Rhett | 201

"Yeah. So I told him I won't go to the truck show with you. I'm going to come with him. Is that okay?" She sounded hesitant and it was all I could do to stop myself from shouting, "of course it's not fucking okay."

"Whatever." I said finally.

"You know I would go with you normally." She sighed. "I'm sorry, Rhett. I just don't want him to think that I'm putting you over getting to know him better."

"Heaven forbid."

"Rhett." She groaned. "Come on now."

"It's fine." I pulled outside my house. "You know how I feel about it."

"So we'll see you there okay?"

"Fine."

"I'm going to invite Penelope to come as well."

"Oh great all my favorite people." I rolled my eyes as I walked into my house.

"Stop." She giggled.

"I'm stopping, trust me." I walked into my bedroom and flopped down on the bed.

"What are you doing?" She asked me and I grinned to myself.

"You know when a girl asks you that question late at night, it's like an invitation for phone sex."

"Rhett." She groaned and I laughed.

"It's true." I spoke in a deep voice. "What are you doing is the gateway word to getting naked and masturbating over the phone."

"You're gross."

"It's true." I propped myself up on the bed. "You ask me what I'm doing, I say I'm playing with myself and then ask you what you're wearing. Then you tell me a bra and panties and I groan into the phone and start playing with myself harder as I picture you in bed, with your hand down your panties."

"You're gross, Rhett." She muttered. "I do not want to hear about your fantasies."

"I don't have any fantasies that involve you with your hand down your panties playing with yourself." I whispered into the phone and stifled a groan as I pictured her on the bed. Shit, I thought to myself. Why did I bring this up? I was starting to feel hard and it was making me feel guilty.

"Well, I'm glad to hear that." She giggled. "Cos my hand isn't down my panties, it's in my bra."

"Clementine O'Hara." My jaw dropped as she spoke. "I had no idea you were such a dirty girl."

"There are many things you don't know about me Rhett Madison."

"So what are you wearing?" I whispered into the phone, unable to stop myself.

"I'm wearing my t-shirt and panties." She laughed. "I'm getting into bed now."

"So you really did take your bra off?" I whispered, picturing her snuggling up next to me, pushing her ass against me. I shifted in the bed as I thought about her next to me.

"Duh, I always take my bra off when I go to bed." She yawned. "It's not comfortable sleeping in a bra."

"Yeah, I know." I sighed as I pictured the quick glimpse I'd seen of her breasts the other night. "Makes sense." I muttered as I pulled my jeans down.

"It's so constricting." She sighed. "I wish they made bras that were more comfortable at night."

"Why?" I closed my eyes and reached into my boxers. My hands found my cock already semi-hard.

"Because wearing a bra at night helps to stop your breasts from sagging. At least that's what Penelope told me."

"Oh yeah?" I spoke slowly as my hand moved up and down on my cock. I was barely listening to her as my hand moved. All I could think about was her lying next to me in bed and rubbing her ass over my cock as I squeezed her tits.

"Yeah. I guess when you have larger boobs you gotta do everything you can to stop the sag." She giggled and I groaned at the sound.

"Clementine." I whispered into the phone. "This is not appropriate conversation."

"I thought I could tell you anything, Rhett."

"You can." I whispered, imagining her lips on my cock.

"Don't laugh, but Elliott asked if he could go down on me tonight."

"What." I froze mid-jerk and my eyes flew open. "Are you joking?"

"He said he wanted me to know what it felt like." She whispered into the phone. "He was shocked no guy had ever eaten me out."

"He's a pervert." I frowned into the phone. "What did you say?"

"I said no of course." She mumbled. I knew she was blushing just from the sound of her voice.

"Good."

"I was curious though." She admitted.

"Curious?" I spoke deceptively low.

"Yeah, I wanted to know what it felt like." She sighed. "What exactly he was going to do."

"I can tell you if you want to know. You don't have to let him do that." My voice was rough.

"No." Her voice rose. "That would be weird."

"Why?" I asked softly.

"I don't know. I mean yes, we're best friends, but you're a guy."

"I can't tell you about sex because I'm a guy?" I sounded annoyed. "Listen, it's better to come from me."

"What? Why?"

"Because you can trust me and I'm going to tell you the truth."

"I guess."

"Do you want me to tell you about oral sex, Clementine?"

"No." She whispered, but I could hear the hesitation in her voice.

"Are you sure?"

"No." She sighed. "Maybe you can tell me the basics."

"Okay. Hold on." I dropped the phone on the bed, pulled my jeans all the way off and threw my shirt on the chair before getting into bed and grabbing my phone. "You there?"

"Yeah."

"Where are you? In bed?" I asked softly.

"Yeah."

"Lights out?"

"Yeah, why?"

"Just curious." I bit my lower lip.

"Okay…"

"Have you ever touched yourself?"

"No." She exclaimed and I laughed. "Why?"

"No reason." I took a deep breath and rubbed my forehead. I'd been about to tell her to touch herself at the same time, but I knew that would be pushing it too far. Get it together, Rhett.

"Okay." She sounded confused.

"Okay, so when a guy goes down on a girl, she usually always orgasms." I muttered, not sure how in-depth I should go.

"Oh wow." She exclaimed and I closed my eyes.

"Yeah." I paused. "Basically, a girl takes off her panties and spreads her legs."

"Okay." She whispered into the phone and I found my hand moving to my still hard cock. "What then?"

"Well then he uses his tongue and his lips to tease her."

"How?" She asked and I stifled a groan as I pictured her lying on the bed with her legs spread.

"Well, he'll lick her pussy, suck on her clit, fuck her with his tongue." I spoke crudely and quickly.

"Oh wow." She sounded like she was shocked at my language.

"Then, he'll lick her juices up as she orgasms on his face." I continued, moving my hand faster. "Some girls pull your hair or push your face deeper into their pussies. Some close their legs so you can't move."

"That's crazy." She answered me and I felt my body building up to climax.

"Hold on, a second." I muttered and put the phone down. I kept my eyes closed and imagined Clementine sitting on my face and riding me as I fucked her with my tongue. I could picture the look in her eyes as she came. I'd grab her hips so she couldn't move and she'd scream as I made her orgasm. I groaned as I felt myself cumming in my hands. My body jerked for a few seconds and I opened my eyes slowly before reaching over for my washrag and wiping off my hands and cock. I picked the phone back up and spoke slowly.

"Hey, sorry about that." I yawned into the phone, suddenly feeling tired.

"You okay?" She sounded concerned.

"Yeah, I'm fine. Just a bit tired." I felt guilty talking to her on the phone, knowing I had just jerked off to thoughts of her riding my face.

"Oh okay. I'll let you sleep. Thanks for telling me about what happens when a guy goes down on a girl."

"No problem." I whispered into the phone. "You can come to me for anything."

"Thanks, Rhett."

"Night, Clemmie."

"Night, Rhett." She hung up the phone and I lay back in the bed and groaned. I wasn't sure what I was doing? Why was I suddenly obsessed with thinking sexual thoughts about Clementine? Part of me wanted to tell her that I could do more than tell her about oral sex. If she wanted, I could also show her what she'd been missing as well.

Chapter Eight

"I like the neon lights." Tomas walked around my vintage red 1986 Chevy pickup truck.

"Yeah, I thought it gave it the modern look." I grinned at him.

"You got a nitrous express kit as well?"

"Nah, just upgraded the engine, transmission and fuel."

"Oh you taking more octanes?"

"You better believe it." I zipped up my leather jacket and grinned at him.

"Dude you look like James Dean." Tomas looked me over. "Very cool."

"I might just be the coolest dude in Charleston."

"Not cooler than me." He shook his head and then paused. "Whoa, mamacita. Isn't that Clementine? She's like sexy as shit." His eyes bulged as he looked to the right of me. I turned around and looked to see her. My heart stopped beating as I stared at her walking in a pair of tight black leather pants and a white top. Her hair was curled and she was grinning from ear to ear. I stared at her body and shifted as I felt myself growing hard. Then I saw Elliott next to her and frowned.

"Who's the dude?" Tomas sounded taken aback.

"Some asshole." I muttered as my eyes narrowed. This guy was seriously getting under my skin.

"Yo, you need to take care of him." Tomas hissed. "He looks like a papi chulo."

"He looks like a douche."

"Man I think I know him." Tomas frowned. "What's his name?"

"Elliott." I grunted, not able to stop myself from staring at Clementine.

"Yeah, that's him." Tomas nodded. "He dated this chick I used to mess with last year. Apparently he's packing." He made a face. "Not that I know personally, but this girl, Jackie, she said he was into some kinky ass shit."

"Like what?" I frowned and looked at him.

"He likes fucking up the ass." Tomas made a face. "And he's into that bdsm shit."

"Huh, okay." I frowned. "Clementine's not down for that."

"Dude, you know these bitches. They down for everything. You know how many chicks tell me they don't suck cock? You know how many chicks I got sucking my cock at every traffic light?" Tomas raised an eyebrow at me. "I'm not trying to raise no trouble. I don't know what you and Clementine got, big Elliott ain't no sheep. He looks all innocent, but that dude be fucking at sex clubs and all sorts of shit."

"Sex clubs?" I looked at Tomas in disbelief and then back at Elliott and Clementine. "Really?"

"I'm just telling you what I heard." Tomas shrugged and I felt myself tensing up again.

"Hold on, stay by the truck. I'm going to go and get them. I'll be right back." I made my way over to Clementine time and touched her on the shoulder. "Hey you." I smiled at her as she grinned at me.

"Hey." She reached out and gave me a big hug. "I've been looking for you."

"I'm over there with Tomas." I pointed to the corner of the parking lot and grabbed her arm. "Come and see the truck."

"Elliott's here as well." She nodded behind her and smiled widely. "He was excited to see all the trucks."

"Sure he was." I said slowly and nodded in his direction. I knew that Elliott had no interest in vintage pickup trucks. He just didn't want to see me and Clementine go anywhere without him. "Come." I grabbed her hand and led her across the packed parking lot. There must have been at least 35 trucks and about two hundred people there already. Everyone was talking loud and fast and someone was blasting some Kenny Chesney through their car speakers.

"Are you hungry?" I asked as we made our way to my truck. I could see some guys staring at her with lewd stares and it was pissing me off.

"A bit." She shrugged. "I think Elliott and I are going to go and eat afterwards."

"Oh where are you going? Maybe I'll come too."

"Oh." She bit her lip and looked behind. "I don't know."

"You don't know what?" I gave her a quick look and noticed she was nibbling her lower lip.

"I think Elliott wanted us to have a private dinner."

"Oh I'm sure he won't mind me coming along." I smiled widely. "Right, Elliott?" I looked behind and gave a big smile. "You're a champ aren't you?"

"What?" He gave me a dirty look and I saw him staring at my hand on Clementine's arm.

"Nothing." I smiled at him. "We can talk over dinner."

"Rhett." Clemmie shook her head at me. "You're horrible."

"I'm not so bad." I leaned over and gave her a kiss on the cheek.

"What's that for?" She gave me a surprised look.

"For being my rock." I grinned. "Thanks for coming out, even if it wasn't with me."

"I wouldn't have missed it for the world." She grinned at me and reached over and flicked something off of my face. "You had a bug on your cheek." She whispered and we stared at each other for a few seconds.

"Thanks for being my bug protector as well."

"You're a goof." She rolled her eyes. "Hey Tomas." She smiled at Tomas as we stopped at the car.

"Hey ms sexy."

"Tomas." She giggled. "Stop." She paused and then grabbed a sour looking Elliott. "Elliott this is Tomas. He's one of Rhett's good friends."

"Hi." Elliott nodded.

"Nice to meet you idiot." Tomas spoke in a highly accented voice and I snickered.

"It's Elliott." Elliott frowned.

"That's what I said." Tomas spoke slowly. "Idiot."

"Whatever." Elliott rolled his eyes. "I'm ready to go whenever you are honey." He put his arms around Clementine's waist and pulled him towards him. "Oh you're cold." He rubbed her shoulders and I bit my lower lip and looked away.

"Just a bit." She nodded. "Hey, Penelope's coming by the way."

"Oh?" I made a face. "Yay."

"Don't be mean, Rhett." She gave me a stern look.

"I'm never mean." I smiled at her and she smiled back.

"So doesn't she look great?" I pointed at the truck.

"She looks gorgeous." Clementine nodded and admired the truck. "You've outdone yourself this time, Rhett."

"This time?" Elliott spoke up. "You've done this more than once?"

"This is the fourth vintage truck I've fixed up."

"Oh." He didn't look impressed. "I guess you don't study much, so you have time."

"Yeah, that's it." I rolled my eyes and turned to Tomas. "Dude, I need a beer. You got any?"

"Here you go." He threw me a van of bud light. "I bought a 24 pack so I got you covered."

"Thank you." I grinned at him and opened the beer. "Want some?" I handed the can to Clementine and she nodded and chugged.

"Thanks." She handed it back to me with a smile.

"That's not very hygienic." Elliott frowned at us.

"You think not?" I laughed. "I used her toothbrush a few weeks ago. I'm guessing that's way worse."

"Rhett." She made a face at me. "That's gross."

"Hey, what's some shared food particles?" I grinned at her and she shook her fist at me while Elliot's eyes narrowed at me. I took another chug of beer and let out a large burp. "Why, excuse me?" I winked at Clementine and she laughed.

"I swear he's not normally like this." She looked over at Elliott and I could see him frowning and whispering something. "We can't leave yet." She whispered back. "Penelope isn't even here yet."

I turned to Tomas and raised my eyebrows at him. "I'm done, gimme another."

"Here you go bro." He threw me another can and opened another one himself. "Dude, did I tell you that bartender called me the other night."

"Oh yeah?"

"I titty fucked her all night." He grinned.

"Nice." I grinned at him.

"Really guys?" Elliott sounded pissed. "That's not appropriate talk in front of a lady."

"My bad." Tomas apologized. "Would you rather talk about how you like to take them up the ass?" He paused and took another chug of beer as Elliott's face grew red. "What I wanna know is why you like it up the ass more than the pussy? Actually don't tell me, it's cos you can't impregnate them up the ass, isn't it?" He took another chug of beer and grinned at me. We all stood there in silence and I could see Elliott fuming. I looked to see if Clementine was upset, but felt a warm feeling spreading through me as I saw her lips twitching, that's my girl I thought. She hasn't lost her twisted sense of humor.

"It's Penelope." Clementine pulled her ringing phone out of her pocket. "Hold on, I'm coming to get you." She shouted into the phone. "Stay at the front." She gave me a quick look. "I'm going to go and get Penelope. I'll be right back."

"I'll come with you." Both Elliott and I exclaimed, but she shook her head.

"You guys stay here. I'll be fine by myself. I'll be right back." She quickly left the group and walked away with all three of us staring at her pert ass as she walked away.

"Damn, but she's fine." Tomas exclaimed and threw me another beer.

"Yeah, she is." Elliott exclaimed and smiled. "I'm going to enjoying feeling up on her ass tonight."

"What did you say?" I froze and looked at him with hatred in my eyes.

"I said I'm going to enjoy feeling up on her ass tonight." He repeated with a tight smile. "And sucking on her nipples." He licked his lips. "She's got some big ol' titties." He grinned. "Maybe she'll let me titty fuck her." He looked over at Tomas. "Thanks for the idea. I know she's a Virgin, so I might not be able to fuck her for a few weeks, but I can wait. Her pussy is sure to be sweet and tight." He stared right at me. "But who knows, she might let me titty fuck her tonight instead."

"I swear if you lay a hand on her, you jackass." I grabbed him around the neck and pulled him towards me. "I will fuck your sorry ass up, mother fucker."

"I'm so scared." He spit out, but I could see that his eyes were afraid of what I was going to done next. I was so angry that I was about to hit him, but then I saw Clementine walking back towards us with Penelope. I didn't need to give them any more reasons to make me look bad. I let go of his shirt and stepped back and opened a new can of beer and chugged it all down.

"We're back." Clementine walked over to me and looked me in the face. "You okay?"

"I'm fine." I looked away from her.

"Hmm." She frowned. "You don't look good."

"I'm fine." I looked at her briefly and I could see the worry in her face. "I'm fine, trust me."

"Okay." She sighed and looked over at Elliott who was talking to Penelope. "Do you want a beer guys?"

"No thanks." They both shook their heads. I stared at Penelope. She was wearing a black strapless dress with no bra. Her titties were practically popping out the top of the dress. She wasn't leaving much to the imagination and I saw Tomas staring at her as well.

"Nice dress." I called over to her and looked down. It barely covered her ass and I wondered if she'd worn it deliberately hoping to get laid tonight.

"Thanks." She nodded and looked away from me with a small smile. I stared at her for a second and remembered what Jake had said. Maybe he'd been right. Maybe she was so pissy towards me because she had a thing for me. She wouldn't be the first one to fall for my baby blues.

I watched as Clementine walked over to Elliott and he stood behind her and put his arms around her waist. He started kissing her neck and I saw his hands moving up and down her stomach and dangerously close to her breasts. I started breathing heavier as I watched them. What the fuck was Clementine doing allowing him to touch her like that? I saw him whispering something in her ears and she stared laughing.

Tomas walked closer to me and handed me another beer. "Damn I hate to say it bro, but looks like he wasn't lying. She looks like she's minutes away from allowing him to squeeze her titties."

"Tomas, I'm warning you." I shook my head at him and took another long sip of beer.

"Yo I know she's your friend from childhood and all, but looks like she's finally growing up." He shrugged. "She's fucking hot as hell. I can't say I wouldn't be trying myself if he wasn't with her. I don't know how you've resisted all these years." He continued talking and I found myself growing cold. I didn't want to hear about Clementine being hot. I didn't want to see her letting that douche feel her up.

"Hey Clementine, wanna go and..." I started and she stopped my head before I even finished my sentence.

"Sorry Rhett." She shook her head. "Elliott is not feeling so good so we're going to go back to his place."

"Go back to his place?" I froze. Was she for real?

"Yeah, we're leaving now." Elliott grinned at me. "Have fun with the trucks. We'll be having our own fun." He winked at me and I felt my face growing hot. "Clementine." I walked over to her. "I need to talk to you."

"We can talk later, Rhett." She shook her head. "You've for Tomas and Penelope here. I'll talk to you later."

"Clementine." I grabbed her arm. "We need to talk now."

"Not now Rhett." She frowned and shook her head. "Elliott and I are leaving now."

"Fine." I turned around and shook my head. "What the hell ever." I watched as they left and I felt empty inside.

"So what you up to tonight?" Penelope walked over to me and gave me a small smile.

"Not much." I shrugged and took another chug of beer. I looked at her and gave her a small smile. Then I made the mistake of looking down and gazing at her huge almost exposed breasts. "That's a really nice dress." I stared at her tits for a few more seconds and then back at her.

"Thanks." She blushed. "I figured you'd notice it."

"Why are you such a bitch to me?" I sipped some more beer and asked her honestly.

"I don't know." She shrugged and looked down.

"Hey guys, my bartender friend just texted me." Tomas interrupted us with a huge grin. "I'm out."

"See ya." I pat him on the back and watched him walking away. "Guess he's going to have a good night."

"We could have a good night too." She licked her lips and leaned towards me.

"Oh?" I looked into her eyes with interest, wondering what she was propositioning. I needed to keep my mind off of Clementine and Elliott.

"I don't know, take me out in the truck and we can see where it leads us."

"I'm not going to be able to move this truck for hours." I shrugged and looked around. "It's packed in the lot tonight."

"Maybe we can just sit in the back and talk then." She asked softly.

"Okay." I nodded and downed the rest of my beer. "Hold on." I grabbed my phone and checked to see if Clementine had text me to apologize for just leaving without talking. There was nothing. I put my phone back in my pocket and grabbed her arm. "Come." I opened the door and let her get in first. She slid down in the back seat and I crawled in after her and closed the door. "So what do you wanna talk about?" I stared at her through tired eyes. All I wanted to do was go to bed and try to sleep off my anger. Then I wanted to call Clementine and go off on her.

"I don't want to talk." Penelope said quietly and I looked over at her and saw that she'd pulled the top of her dress down.

"Alrighty then." I nodded and smiled. "So what do you want to do?"

"I don't have any panties on either." She grabbed my hand and pushed it up her dress. She pushed my fingers against her naked pussy and I felt her wetness.

"You don't shave?" I asked curiously and pulled my hand away, a bit turned off by how easy she was being.

"Do you really care?" she moved towards me and tried to kiss me. I avoided her lips and moved to the side. I felt her hands rubbing the front of my pants and I closed my eyes. I stared feeling like shit, but then I remembered Clementine and Elliott and the hurry they were in to leave. I felt Penelope unzipping my jeans and pulling my cock out. Her face fell to my lap and yet I couldn't get hard. I sat back and tried to relax, but I just wasn't feeling her. I tried to imagine it was Clementine's face in my lap and I felt myself hardening.

"Oh yeah big boy." Penelope whispered as she sucked me off and I pushed her head down. I didn't want to hear her voice. If I heard her voice my mind would know it wasn't Clementine. She bobbed her head up and down on my lap and I reached down and grabbed her tits and squeezed. She moved back to sit on my lap but I pushed her down.

"Not yet." I shook my head and adjusted myself so I was in front of her. I grabbed her tits and pushed them together and moved my cock up and started titty fucking her. Her eyes widened and I turned my face away from her. I didn't want to see her face. Looking at her made me feel guilty and I could feel myself growing soft as my body realized I was with her and not Clementine. After about a minute, she must have realized that my cock was no longer hard and she reached out and started rubbing it again, but it didn't help. I pulled away from her and shifted on the seat.

"Sorry, I must be too drunk." I lied as I looked at the disappointment on her face.

"Let me blow you again." She leaned forward and reached for my cock. "I'll get you hard with my mouth and then I can ride you."

"I don't have any condoms." I lied and shrugged. "My bad."

"Oh." She sat back and looked at me with an anxious face. "You can go down on me if you want or you can suck my tits." Her voice trailed off and I stared at her trying to hide my disgust. What were we doing here? How had it come to this? I'd much preferred her when she was being a bitch.

"Maybe next time." I shook my head and looked away. "Maybe you should pull your dress up." I opened the door and got out of the truck. I felt my phone vibrating in my pocket and grabbed it quickly.

"Sorry I couldn't talk before I left. Elliott has been a bit jealous over our friendship, so I figured I should just go. :("

My heart warmed at Clementine's text. **"It's fine. Just don't do it again."** I hit send and waited for a response.

"What you doing?" Penelope got out of the back of the truck and I looked up at her.

"Nothing." I looked away, barely able to look her in the face. Her boobs were still almost popping out and all I could think about was my cock shriveling up as I'd tried to titty fuck her.

"Do you want to go back to your place?" She walked over to me, pleading in her eyes. "I can drive us."

"Nah." I shook my head and text Clementine. **"What are you doing?"**

"Going home, it's a long story."

"Oh no!" Yes! I thought to myself.

"I'll talk more later. Ttyl." She text back and I bit my lower lip wondering what was going on.

"So what do you want to do?" Penelope asked me softly.

"I'm about to peace out." I shrugged. "I think we should both catch a ride home. To our separate homes."

"Am I going to see you again?" She bit her lower lip and I cursed myself mentally. Why had I attempted a drunken hookup with Clementine's friend?

"Sure." I nodded and wondered how I was going to tell Clemmie I had messed around with her friend.

"Okay." She smiled. "Maybe we can go on a double date with Clementine and Elliott." She ran her hands through her hair. "I think that will be fun."

"Uh-huh." I smiled weakly at her.

"It's a pity you were drunk." She giggled. "You really seemed to enjoy my mouth though."

I shuddered as I stared at her and I felt myself stilling. I had only grown hard because I had been thinking about Clementine going down on me. I groaned as I realized this was the second time I had needed to think of Clementine before feeling horny. What was happening to me? I groaned inwardly as I thought about how jealous I felt about Clementine and Elliott. I fucking had a hard-on for Clemmie. I knew that every fiber of my body wanted to be in her. I needed to taste and touch every inch of her. Only then would I be able to function as I used to before. I sighed as I realized what a precarious position our friendship would be in if we fucked. I didn't want to risk it. She was worth more than sex to me.

"You okay, Rhett?" Penelope frowned at me and I shook my head.

"Nah. I gotta go home." I closed my eyes as I realized just how fucked up everything was. "I gotta go home."

Chapter Nine

"When we were young, we never wondered who we were. When we were young, we never cared about no one. When we were young, we thought the world was at our feet. When we were young, we thought we were destined to be it. Now we are old, we know not what we do. Now we are old, we think about only you."

I lay in bed singing the song that Clementine and I had written when we were 16 years old. It made me smile and frown both at the same time. I missed my easy friendship with Clementine. I missed the way we used to finish each other's sentences and just assume that the other person would be available to hang out and talk. I missed how comfortable we used to be with each other.

Rhett |

I missed writing songs with her. When I was about eleven years old, there was a game that Clementine and I used to play called sing that song. We would create lyrics to a song and try and come up with a melody to the song and sing it together as if we were in a band. It wasn't anything serious and we didn't create songs that were super profound or lyrical, but it was something that bonded us together. It was something we both had in common. It was something we both loved to do. "When we were young, we never wondered who we were." I sang the lyrics again and smiled to myself. How true those words hard turned out to be.

I grabbed my phone and sent her a text message: **when we were young, we never cared about no one.** I typed fast and pressed send. I lay there staring at the phone, wondering if she would bother to text me back. I wouldn't have been surprised if she had ignored me. I knew she was angry at me and what was going on with her and Elliott. I knew she was mad that things had changed between us. I knew she felt confused. I didn't blame her. I felt confused as well. I didn't understand why I was acting the way that I did. I didn't want her like that. I didn't want to date her. Yet, I didn't want her to be with Elliott. It annoyed me to think about her with him. Some might even say I was jealous, but I didn't do jealousy. I was just concerned about her. I didn't want her to lose herself in a relationship that wasn't right for her and I knew that Elliott was not the guy for her. He was boring and he could never make her laugh like I did. I also knew that he was a jerk. After what he'd said last night about titty fucking her, I knew he was no better than me or Tomas. He only pretended to be a nice guy.

I also knew that he didn't really like me. I knew that he didn't think I was a great friend. Just like Penelope. Though, I didn't want to think about her. I was hoping that she would forget what had happened last night. I felt embarrassed and ashamed for both of us. I still didn't really like her as I knew she had tried to ruin my relationship with Clementine. I was fed up of people coming into Clemmie's life and trying to break us apart.

Beep beep. My phone went off as I received a text. *"When we were young we thought the world was at our feet. Now we are old, we know that*

Rhett | 235

nothing's meant to be." I read Clementine's text and frowned before calling her.

"Hello?" She sighed as she answered the phone.

"Why did you change the lyrics?"

"Things change all the time." Her voice sounded sad. "I thought the lyrics needed to be updated."

"What's that supposed to mean?" I sat up in my bed and frowned. "What are you doing? You sound sad."

"I'm fine." She sighed again.

"Clementine O'Hara, what's wrong?" I growled.

"Nothing is wrong."

"Clemmie." I purred her name and waited for her to answer me. "I know your moods, what's wrong?"

"Nothing is wrong." She paused. "Elliott and I broke up."

"What do you mean you broke up?" My voice was annoyed, though my heart was jumping. "I thought he wasn't your boyfriend."

"He wasn't." She snapped. "However, we were seeing each other and he doesn't want to see me anymore."

"Why not?" I asked softly, not wanting her to hear how elated I felt.

"No special reason." She mumbled.

"Can I come over?" I asked softly. "We should talk in person."

"Do you want to see Linda?" She answered smartly and I groaned.

"Not really, but I can risk it."

"Let's just chat on the phone." She sighed.

"Can we talk in person?" I jumped out of bed and grabbed a sweater and pulled it on. "Please."

"I'm in bed."

"So was I."

"You can't come over and I'm not driving to your place."

"I'll come and pick you up."

"Why?" She sounded annoyed.

"Don't be mad at me, Clem. We need to talk in person."

"You're like a girl, Rhett. We have nothing to talk about." The phone went silent after she spoke and I stood there rigidly. She had hung up on me. I knew that I was pushing it and if it was anyone other than Clementine I wouldn't even care. But she was my best friend. She was the only constant in my life. I cared about her more than anyone in my life. I wasn't sure what my life would be like if it wasn't for her. As corny as it sounded, she made me a better person. I knew that I still had a heart because of her. If she wasn't in my life I'd be completely cynical.

I called her again and as soon as I heard her answer the phone, I started singing. *"When you feel like crying, just think of me."* I sang softly. *"When you feel like lying, just dream of me. When the whole world feels like it's crashing, remember me. Call me when you need me. Need me when you can't be, alone."* I could hear her breathing softly into the phone as I sang the friendship song she had created for me for my 17th birthday. I'd pretended to be embarrassed as she'd sung it to me. She'd been so earnest and adorable and I'd been so macho and untouchable. I had rolled my eyes and pretended that I thought it was sappy and totally girly, but it had meant the world to me. I'd thought of the song many times, even in my darkest hours, and it always comforted me.

"You can't sing." She said softly and I smiled. She was coming around.

"I'm going to come and pick you up and we'll come back here."

"We're too old for sleepovers, Rhett."

"We're never too old, Wendy." I joked and she laughed gently. "And anyway, its day time, so it's not a sleepover."

"You're always going to be my Peter Pan, aren't you?" Her voice was soft and slightly jaded.

"As long as you'll have me." I whispered back, my heart feeling empty. Clementine had always compared me to a lost boy and I understood why. It was because I'd felt abandoned by my parents and I knew the emotional part of me had never really grown up. I'd never gotten over my childhood traumas. Even with

Rhett | 239

Clementine's family in my life. Even with everything else that I had, I'd never understood why my parents hadn't cared.

"I'm always here for you, Rhett." She sighed. "That's the problem."

"What does that mean?" I paused, my heart stilling. Her voice sounded resigned and a part of me felt like everything was changing around me and I had no control to stop it.

"Nothing," she sighed. "Just come and pick me up."

"I..." I started and paused. I wanted to tell her that she meant the world to me. I wanted to tell her that I didn't want anything to change between us. I wanted to tell her that I wish we could go back to high school. I wish we could go back to the days where all she cared about was studying and talking to me. Those were the days when everything was perfect. Or almost perfect. I had football. I had my truck. I had the cheerleading and dance team dying to date me and I had Clementine to call and hang out with when I needed to just chill. I knew it was selfish of me to want everything to remain the same, but that was what had made me happiest.

"I'll be waiting Rhett." She said softly and then hung up. I grabbed the keys to my mustang and headed over to Clemmie's apartment.

"You didn't have to wait outside." I frowned as Clementine jumped into the car as soon as I pulled over. "I would have come to the door." I looked over at her tired face as she got into the car.

"I didn't want Linda to know you were here." She shrugged and did her seatbelt up without looking at me. The air felt awkward between us and it wondered if I'd ruined everything by kissing her again.

"She'll get over me." I muttered as I pulled away from the curb.

"It's not so easy for everyone to get over someone they have a crush on." She muttered under her breath and I laughed.

"There is no reason for her to have a crush on me." I sighed. "I've never given her any reason." Unlike Penelope, I thought to myself and frowned.

"You're mean." She sighed and then giggled slightly.

"Are you mad at me?"

"What do you think?" She snapped and finally looked at me.

"Are you mad at me for kissing you or are you upset because you and Elliott broke up?"

"I don't understand what's going on." She spoke softly and I felt myself tensing up. "I don't get why you kissed me. I don't know why you were upset about Elliott."

"I wasn't upset." I protested too loudly.

"Penelope thinks you were jealous." She continued and sighed.

"Jealous of what?" I turned onto my street. I could feel myself growing angry and worried. What else had Penelope said? "I wish Penelope would just shut up and keep her thoughts to herself."

"Rhett," her voice was angry. "Penelope is my friend."

"She's not your best friend." I sighed. "She's never liked me. It's obvious to me that she doesn't want me in your life."

"She does like you." She sighed.

"I don't care about her. I don't want to talk about her. I want to talk about us. I want to talk about why you've been ignoring me. I want to talk about what's going on." I shouted feeling angry. "And I'm pissed that I sound like a little pussy wanting to talk about anything."

"Rhett," she touched my arm. "Are you okay?" Her voice was soft and I gave her a quick glance. I saw concern in her face and I felt a part of me softening. Even after everything that had happened, she was still worried about me. It made me angry. I wanted her to harden up. I wanted her to tell me to fuck off. I wanted her to tell me that she'd had enough. I wanted to see her turn her back on me. I wanted it and didn't want it at the same time. A part of me wanted it because it would prove to me once and for all that nothing was forever. Not love and not friendships.

"I'm fine." I growled and moved my arm away from her. I didn't want her touching me. I didn't want her concern. I wanted so much more from her. My body craved carnal knowledge of her, even though my brain told me that it would be a mistake.

"I can't believe you're angry at me." She sighed. "It's me that should be upset."

"Can't we just forget all of it?" I sighed. "Let's go home and watch a movie and forget everything."

"That's fine by me." She shrugged and a part of me relaxed. Everything would be okay if we could just forget everything that had happened recently.

"So you wanna watch a movie?" I pulled up to my house and she smiled at me hesitantly.

"Yeah." She nodded. "Chick flick?"

"Hell no." We both laughed as I shook my head.

"Fine." She sighed and I looked at her carefully. I could see the traces of tears in her eyes.

"What's wrong?" I frowned as I turned off the engine and turned to her. "Why are you crying? Are you upset because of Elliott?"

"No." She shrugged. "I don't know."

"What happened?"

"Nothing." She looked away from me.

"What happened, Clementine?"

"He tried to tell me we couldn't be friends." She sighed. "When we left the truck show, he told me I had to pick between you and him. Then he tried to touch me."

"What?" I frowned. "Where the fuck is he right now?"

"It's okay, Rhett." She grabbed my arm. "He tried, but I didn't let him."

"Where did he try to touch you?" I growled, feeling angrier than I'd ever felt.

"On my breasts." She bit her lower lip. "He said he wanted to play with my tits and do something else." Her voice dropped.

"Do what?" My eyes narrowed.

Rhett | 245

"I don't wanna say." She shook her head.

"Clementine, tell me." I took a deep breath, imagining what he had said.

"He said he wanted to titty fuck me." She whispered and I froze. I wasn't sure what to say. I was furious, but I felt like a hypocrite. How could I get angry at what he had tried to do, when I had technically titty fucked her friend the previous evening. It wasn't like I was any better than him. Maybe even worse. He actually liked Clementine. I couldn't give two fucks about Penelope.

"Say something, Rhett." She groaned and I looked up at her red face.

"Sorry, I was just thinking." I sighed. "He's a pig and you're better off without him. Let's go inside, okay."

"Okay." She nodded. "I can't believe how different he was."

"What do you mean?" I asked her as we walked into my house.

"He seemed so nice, like he liked me, but all he cared about was sex."

"What can I say?" I shrugged, not wanting to tell her that was basically every guy. I didn't want to give her any excuse to go back to him. "He was a jerk."

"Yeah he was." She frowned. "I'm so pissed at myself. I can't believe I treated you like shit and he was such an asshole."

"It's okay." I rubbed her hair. "All's forgiven."

"I'm so glad you're not like him." She shuddered. "You would never pretend to be into a girl, just to get laid. You're straight up about it from the beginning."

"Well, I don't sleep around that much." I frowned.

"I know." She smiled at hooked my arm. "What movie do you want to watch?"

"I don't know. Let's see what's out." I opened the front door. "Bedroom or living room?"

"Let's go to the bed." She smiled. "I didn't sleep well last night, so I want to relax."

"Sounds good." I nodded and we walked to my room. "Could you imagine if Elliott could see us now?" I laughed. "He'd go crazy."

"Penelope as well." She laughed. "She doesn't think it's healthy that we're so close."

"Oh, have you heard from her?" I kept my voice light.

"Not since yesterday." She shrugged. "Why?"

"No reason." I shook my head and we hopped onto the bed. "Okay, let's see what we have." I turned Netflix on my TV and flicked through movies. "Okies, what about a comedy?"

"That's fine." She jumped off of the bed and I watched as she walked to my closet. "Hey, can I borrow a t-shirt?" She glanced at me as she opened the door. "I'm not super comfortable in these jeans and tank top." She grinned at me and I nodded. "Thanks." She pulled a white t-shirt out and I watched her as she undid her jeans. "Turn around, Rhett."

"Okay." I turned towards the TV, but I couldn't concentrate. All I could think about was that Clementine was taking her clothes off in my room. It had never felt like this before. I'd never felt so tense and stiff. All of a sudden, it didn't seem so innocent any more.

"Oh this is much better." Clementine spoke and I turned to look at her. I froze as she walked towards me and jumped on the bed. I wasn't sure if she realized it, but I could see her nipples clearly through my white t-shirt. Her breasts bounced as she moved and I groaned inwardly as my t-shirt rode up her legs as she settled onto the bed.

"Well, you look comfortable." I smiled at her gently and turned back to the TV.

"I am." She relaxed back into the bed. "We need to spend more days like this." She squirmed on the bed as she got comfortable. "I miss the days when we just used to lie in bed and watch TV all day."

"Yeah, me too." I nodded and shifted as I felt myself hardening.

"Are you going to change as well?" She asked innocently as she poked me in the back.

"Of course." I jumped up and pulled my sweater and jeans off and sat back on the bed in just my boxer shorts.

"Ooh, sexy." She giggled and I smiled at her weakly.

"Okay, let's see what's on." I flicked through and she squealed.

"Ooh stop."

"What?" I frowned and looked back at her.

"I heard that movie Nine and a Half Weeks was good."

"You want to watch Nine and a Half Weeks?" I sighed. I was in no mood to watch a sexy movie.

"Yeah. Let's start with that one."

"Okay then." I pressed play and sat back on the bed next to her. We sat next to each other, shoulders pressed together as we watched the movie. Everything was going well until the first sex scene.

"Oh wow, hot." Clementine squirmed on the bed.

"We can change it if you want."

"No, it's fine." She whispered and lay back. I sighed and sat stiffly and continued watching the movie. "Wow," Clementine turned to look at me. "This movie is dirtier than I thought."

"Yeah, it's almost a porno." I agreed and lay down so I could look at her properly.

"You know what I was thinking about this morning?" She spoke softly and I shook my head.

"No, what?"

"I was wondering what would have happened if I'd let Elliott go down on me."

"Really?" I frowned and looked into her eyes. "Trust me, he wasn't worth it."

"I didn't necessarily want him." She blushed. "I just wanted to see what it felt like."

"I see." I frowned and shifted. What was she doing to me?

"Does that sound bad?" She wrinkled her nose and I smiled at her.

"Of course not."

"Okay good." She bit her lower lip and then looked back at the TV screen. I continued to stare at her and I could tell that she was thinking about something, not related to the movie.

"What are you thinking, Clemmie?"

"What do you mean?" She looked at me and blushed.

"I know you're thinking something." I gave her a look.

"No, I'm not."

"Clementine, tell me what you're thinking." I grabbed her hip and pulled her towards me.

"I'm embarrassed." She shifted and the t-shirt rose even higher. I looked down at her legs and realized that if it rode any higher, I would see her panties.

"Tell me." I sighed.

"Don't laugh."

"I won't laugh."

"So you know how you told me about oral sex the other night."

"Uh-huh." My eyes narrowed and I watched her lips as she spoke.

"Nothing." She shook her head and looked back at the screen.

"Okay." I let it go and settled back and watched the movie. I moved closer to Clementine and put my arm over her waist. She lay back into my chest and we watched the movie snuggled together. I let my hands move along her stomach softly and she shifted against me so that her ass was resting against the front of my boxer shorts. Her t-shirt had now ridden all the way up and I could see the pink of her panties. My hand ran down to her leg and I traced a trail down her thigh.

"What are you doing?" She whispered in front of me.

"Nothing." I whispered and stopped moving my fingers.

"You don't have to stop." She whispered back and I moved my fingers back to her stomach and held her. I closed my eyes and lay back wondering what I should do. I really wanted to make a move on her, but this was unchartered territory. I didn't know what to do. My body was aching to touch her, but I didn't want to risk our friendship. My fingers didn't listen to the hesitation in my voice and I found them trailing her leg again and running up over the side of her panties. All of a sudden I felt, Clementine stilling next to me.

Rhett

"Is this okay?" I whispered in her ear and she nodded. That was all I needed to continue. I ran my fingers up underneath her t-shirt and caressed her stomach and upper abdomen, stopping just under her breasts. I could feel and hear her breathing get heavier as I touched her and it was making me feel horny as hell. I then started moving my fingers up a little higher and traced the sides of her naked breasts. I could feel my breathing growing heavier as well as I ran my fingers down the sides of her breasts. Then I went in for the kill. I moved my fingers over her nipples slightly, rubbing them gently with my palms before moving my fingertips to them and squeezing them gently. At first, Clementine stilled and then she started moving against me slowly. I could hear her moaning and I stopped.

"Are you okay?" My fingers lay still on her stomach and she nodded.

"Yes." She whispered and paused. "It feels good."

"I don't want to do this, if you don't want me to."

"I want you too." She moved back against me and I felt her hand moving mine back up. "Touch me, Rhett." She didn't need to tell me twice, my fingers moved back up to her breasts and I squeezed them together, loving the feel of her breasts in my hands. I pinched her nipples again and grinned at how hard they were. "Oh, Rhett." She moaned as I played with her breasts and I moved in closer to her, so she could feel how hard I was. I groaned as I played with her and moved my hand down to her stomach again. "Don't stop." She groaned.

"Do you trust me?" I whispered in her ear and moved my fingers down slowly.

"Yes." She nodded.

"Are you sure?" I moved my fingers down to the top of her panties and I felt her stilling.

"Yes, I'm sure." She whispered and I felt her squirm against me as I slipped my fingers into her panties and down into her pussy. She was wet to the touch and surprisingly hair free.

"You shave?" I asked her in surprise.

"Uh-huh." She giggled and I groaned as she closed her legs on my hands. I groaned and pulled her back against me and ran my fingers along her slit and clit.

"Oooh." She moaned and I felt her legs open up again. "Ooooh, Rhett." She groaned as I rubbed her clit back and forth slowly, enjoying the feel of her wetness on my fingers.

"You're so wet for me." I groaned in her ear.

"It feels so good." She moaned and I increased the pace of my fingers. "Oh my God, Rhett." She exclaimed as I moved faster. I grinned as I felt her pussy getting even wetter. I moved down and quickly pulled her panties off. She looked down at me with a sweet smile and flushed.

"Is this okay?" I asked her again, wanting to make sure I didn't do anything she wasn't comfortable with.

"It's more than okay." She nodded and I moved up and kissed her. Her eyes widened in surprise as my tongue entered her mouth and she sucked on my tongue eagerly. I kissed her hard and passionately, enjoying the feel of her fingers in my hair as I tasted her properly for the first time. Her lips tasted sweet and soft and I knew that I could kiss her for a million years and not get tired of it. I pulled her up slightly and pulled her t-shirt off so that my chest was crushing down on her naked breasts.

I kissed down her neck and then took her nipple in my mouth and sucked on it as I played with the other one. She wiggled on the bed beneath me and I smiled as she cried out when I started nibbling on her nipple with my teeth.

I moved my hand back down to her pussy and spread her legs, playing with her clit for a few seconds before pushing my index finger inside of her. She froze for a second and I watched as her eyes widened at the feel of me inside of her.

"You've never had anything inside of you, have you?" I groaned against her breast as I fingered her. Her pussy was so wet and her lips were closing in on me as I entered a second finger inside of her and moved in and out.

She shook her head and closed her eyes as she moaned on the bed beneath me.

"Ooh," She moaned as I moved my fingers back and forth faster.

"Come for me, Clementine." I kissed back up her body and whispered against her lips. "Relax and come for me." I groaned as her eyes went wild and her body started shaking. I grinned as I felt her pussy contract and then release and all her juices poured down on my fingers. "Good girl." I kissed her softly and she moaned against my lips.

"Wow." She grinned up into my eyes.

"Wow, indeed." I smiled down at her and kissed her on the lips hard. "I'm going to make you come again."

"Again?" Her eyes widened in surprise and I grinned at her.

"This time with my tongue."

"Tongue?" She grinned at me and blushed.

"What is it, Clemmie?"

"I was going to ask you earlier." She paused. "You know."

"No, what?" I smiled down at her, knowing what she was going to say.

"I was going to ask you to show me what it was like." She grinned up at me and I laughed.

"Well, I'm about to show you." I kissed her quickly on the lips again and then kissed down her body.

I reached my fingers in-between her legs and started rubbing gently again, so I could get her wet. I smiled as she got wet again right away. I spread her legs and then kissed down her pussy and straight to her clit. My tongue licked up her juices eagerly and I groaned as I tasted her. I should have known that her pussy would taste just as sweet as her lips. My mouth found her clit and I sucked on it eagerly. I moved my hands to her hips and brought her pussy down on my face harder. I licked her eagerly, wanting to taste every piece of her. She moved against my face eagerly and I realized that it was even better that my fantasies had been. She came as soon as my tongue slid inside of her, though that didn't stop me from fucking her with my tongue. I slid in and out of her eagerly and I was rewarded for my efforts by feeling her body quaking and shuddering for a third time. Her juices flowed out quickly I licked up every last drop of her. I was as hard as her by the time I finished eating her out and I knew that I needed to go to the bathroom and finish myself off. I didn't want to scare her by masturbating in front of her.

Rhett | 259

"Enjoy it?" I grinned at her as I kissed back up her body. She nodded and I could see her eyes were still dazed from the three orgasms I had given her.

"Oh yes." She smiled and then she shocked me by pushing me down on the bed. I watched as she rolled her naked body on top of mine and I reached up and grabbed her breasts.

"What are you doing?" I asked softly as she positioned herself on top of me.

"Nothing." She grinned and I groaned as she pulled my hard cock out of my boxers.

"Clementine." I groaned and shook my head. "No." I grabbed her waist and she frowned.

"Come on, Rhett." She gave me a pouty look and I felt her pussy on top of my cock.

"No, Clemmie." I groaned as she rubbed back and forth on my cock. "We're not going to have sex."

"I just want to feel it." She moaned and moved her pussy back and forth even faster. I groaned as I felt her juices on my cock as she teased me. All I wanted to do was lift her up and slide my cock inside of her.

"Clemmie, I don't know how long I can take this." I groaned as she smiled down at me wickedly.

"Sshh." She laughed and leaned forward, rubbing her breasts over my face. I grabbed her waist and moved her back and forth on me faster, wondering if I could come just from rubbing against her pussy. I could feel my cock was close to erupting and so I allowed her to continue teasing me. It was getting harder and harder to resist the urge to enter her and I was pretty positive she had no clue just how close she was to losing her virginity. Though, I didn't want it to be like this. Not after she'd waited so long. I wanted it to be more special.

"This feels so good." She groaned. "I think I'm going to come again." She moved back and forth on me faster, grinding her pussy against the tip of my cock. I knew that I was hitting her clit each time and I knew that one slip and I'd be inside of her.

"Clementine," I groaned as she was getting wetter and wetter on the tip of my cock. I could feel her clit throbbing next to me and my fingers grabbed her ass cheeks. I closed my eyes and everything seemed to happen so fast. I could feel that I was close to orgasm,

Rhett | 261

but then she reached orgasm before me and I felt her stop moving against me as she came. I instinctively grabbed her hips and moved her back and forth on me and before I knew what was happening, the tip of my cock was entering her. Her eyes widened as she felt my cock inside of her and she jerked back. As she jerked back, my cock fell out of her pussy and rubbed up the slit of her. She rubbed back and forth on me two more times and I felt myself coming against her. She paused for a second in shock as she felt my hot cum against her and I quickly moved her off of me as I continued spurting onto the sheets. I groaned as I came and my body shuddered for about a minute as I came down for my high.

"Wow." Clementine finally spoke up as I opened my eyes and looked at her.

"Wow indeed." I grinned at her and pulled her face down to me and kissed her.

"You came." She smiled and looked down at my now soft cock.

"So did you." I winked at her and she blushed.

"You entered me." She ran her finger down my cheek. "Does that mean I'm not a virgin now?"

"No." I shook my head and reached over and played with her breasts. "The tip of my cock barely entered you. You're still a virgin. My whole cock would have had to have entered you, for you to have lost your virginity." I spoke as if I knew that to be truth, though I really had no idea.

"Oh okay." She ran her fingers over my chest. "Your sperm was warm." She grinned. "I think you sprayed it on me."

"Sorry, I didn't mean to do that."

"It's fine." She laughed. "It's not like you got me pregnant." She played with my nipples and I stilled at her words. "You weren't coming inside of me, so it's fine."

"Don't." I groaned as I felt my cock hardening. All I could think about was her pussy walls hardening on my bare cock. I closed my eyes and tried to ignore the urge to pick her up and place her on my cock. Even if she wasn't a virgin, it was a dumb idea. I never fucked without a condom. And I knew she wasn't on the pill. It would be a stupid risk. Though every part of me wanted to fuck her and explode inside of her.

"What?" She snuggled next to me.

"Nothing." I hugged her to me and ran my fingers down her back. "How do you feel?"

"I feel fine." She grinned. "Awesome even."

"Good." I smiled and held her closer to me. "This wasn't my plan by the way, when I asked you to come over."

"It's fine." She smiled. "I'm glad that we did this."

"Me too." I played with her hair and smiled. Though a part of me was already starting to grow worried. Would this change our relationship? I tried to ignore the warning bells in my head as I held her next to me.

"Why didn't you want to make love to me?" She whispered against my lips and I frowned.

"I didn't have a condom." I lied, thinking about the pack I had in my wallet and in my bathroom. The truth of the matter was I didn't want to be the one to take her virginity. Not really. It was too big a deal. And I didn't think I was good enough for her.

"Oh sad." She groaned and her hand reached down and touched my cock. "Who was the last person you had sex with?"

"I can't even remember." I answered honestly. "It's been a while."

"Who's the last person that touched your cock?" She whispered against my lips and I froze. There was no way in hell, I was going to tell her that Penelope had had me in her mouth the night before.

"I'm not really sure, that was a while ago." I lied.

"What?" She smiled happily at me. "A player like you?"

"I'm not that big a player." I smiled.

"You let women go down on you randomly though." She sighed and looked into my eyes. "Don't tell me." She shook her head. "I don't really want to know."

"Clemmie, it's never been as special with anyone elsc as it has been with you." I kissed her nose. "Trust me, the only person I want holding my cock right now is you."

"That's so corny." She groaned and rolled her eyes.

"It's true." I laughed.

"Oh my God." She shuddered. "We just became those friends."

"What friends?" I asked her curiously.

"The friends that hook up."

"There's nothing wrong with that." I kissed her softly.

"I feel like friends that hook up always fall out." She made a face.

"That's friends that have sex." I answered quickly. "Friends that have sex are easier to fall out, but best friends that hook up, that's fine. It's normal even."

"It's normal?" She raised an eyebrow at me and I laughed.

"Well, it's fine, I mean." And laughed as well. "Now, be quiet so I can regain my energy and make you come again."

"We're never going to want to go anywhere again." Clementine panted after I went down on her for the second time. "What could be better than this?" She held me in her arms and I grinned as I nibbled on her lips.

"You going down on me." I winked at her and she groaned.

"I've never done that before." She nibbled her lower lip.

"If you don't want to, it's fine." I brushed her hair back. "I don't need you do that Clemmie, I don't want you to do anything you're not comfortable with."

"I know." She nodded and chewed on her lower lip. "Can I ask you something Rhett?"

"Of course." I smiled at her.

"I want you to come somewhere with me tomorrow."

"Sure." I shrugged. "Wherever you want."

"I want us to go and visit your mom." She spoke softly and I froze.

"My mom." I frowned and pulled away from her.

Rhett | 267

"Please." She bit her lower lip and I could see her expression was pained. "If you trust me like I trust you, you'll come."

"I really don't want to go and see her." I felt my body tense just thinking about her. "I really don't want to go, Clemmie."

"I promise we don't have to stay if you're not comfortable." She grabbed my hand. "I'm not doing this to hurt you, Rhett."

"I know." I sighed and closed my eyes. "I just don't want to go and see her."

"It will just be for an afternoon." She leaned over and kissed me. "Please, for me."

"You're asking for a lot, Clementine." I shook my head and sighed. "And I mean a lot. This is even more than asking me to go down on you."

"You wanted to go down on me." She blushed.

"Only because you made us watch that porno." I teased her.

"I didn't know it was a sexy movie." She blushed and I paused.

"Clementine O'Hara, I do believe you're lying to me." My breath caught as I studied her face. "You knew that movie was sexy, didn't you."

"No." She shook her head and looked away from me.

"You totally knew that movie was sexy." I laughed. "You tried to seduce me."

"I didn't try to seduce you." She made a face at me and groaned.

"Clementine, tell me the truth and I'll go with you tomorrow."

"Fine." She buried her face in my chest. "Yes, I had heard that that movie was sexy and yes, I kinda wanted to know what it was like for a guy to go down on me. And yes, I wanted that guy to be you. After you told me about it the other night, I've been thinking about it." She paused. "I'm so embarrassed."

"Don't be embarrassed." I pulled her towards me and kissed her. "I think that's awesome." I held her close to me and closed my eyes. One part of me felt like I was soaring high and the other part of me felt like I was about to make one wrong step and trip down into hell.

Chapter Ten

"Hey, hey, hey." Clementine sang along to the radio as I drove down the highway on the way to Beaufort.

"You think you want me to drive you to the American Idol auditions instead?" I smiled at her as she continued singing at the top of her voice. She grinned back at me and I tried not to wince as she pulled her phone out of her pocket. Every time her phone rang or she got a text, I was scared it was going to be from Penelope. Not that I thought I was completely in the wrong. It's not like Clementine and I were official or I did anything to break her trust, but I just didn't know how she'd react. I knew deep inside that what I'd done was a bit shady.

"Well you know. I don't want Simon to fall in love with me and take me away from you." She giggled and I shook my head.

"I hope you wouldn't leave me for Simon."

"Ugh." She looked at her phone and changed the subject.

"What's wrong?" I gave her a quick glance and saw she was making a face at the phone.

"Elliott wants to talk about what happened." She sighed. "He says he owes me an apology."

"Ignore." I shook my head. "He's so predictable."

"Yeah." She sounded hesitant. "Are you excited about seeing your mom?"

"I wouldn't say excited, no." My tone changed and I felt my heart harden. "You know I don't want to see her."

"She's your mom, Rhett." Her voice was soft as she touched my arm lightly.

"So?"

"You'll regret it if you never see her."

"I don't agree." I turned the radio up and stared at the road in front of me. I wasn't sure why I'd agreed to come to Beaufort to see my mom. I hadn't even know she'd lived so close. I didn't even know how Clementine knew. I didn't care. I didn't want to care. I was so annoyed that she had talked me into coming. I knew I had only agreed because I was still feeling high from my orgasm. Only thing was, I didn't want to think about the orgasm either. I didn't want to think about touching Clementine. I was ashamed that I'd touched her and enjoyed it, knowing I could never give her what she wanted.

"Rhett." She reached over and turned the volume down. "You can't ignore her for the rest of your life."

"She's never contacted me." I spat out bitterly. "Not once since she left. No cards. No presents. No visits. No nothing. Why should I care about her?"

"Maybe she had her reasons."

"Maybe she did. I don't care." I sighed and reached to turn the volume back up, but Clementine grabbed my hand and stopped me. Her fingers felt warm

Rhett | 273

on me and I cringed and pulled my hand away. I didn't want her touching me, trying to make me think things I didn't want to think.

"I'm sorry." Her voice sounded hurt and I just kept my eyes forward. "You can turn the radio back up if you want to."

"It's fine. We can keep it off." I shrugged and swallowed. "You're going to have to give me directions in a bit. I have no idea where we're going."

"I put it in the GPS on my phone." She sighed. "Let me check."

"Fine." I mumbled.

"Okay, when we exit, we need to take the first right."

"Fine." I ignored the sudden lurch in my stomach as I realized that I was close to seeing my mom again. What would she look like? Would she recognize me? Would she cry or try to hug me? I shuddered as I thought about her touching me. I'd step away. I wouldn't want her to touch me. Not at all. "My dad would be surprised to know I was going." I laughed bitterly.

"He should have handled everything differently." She spoke softly. "He cheated on her and then kicked her out. He knew she had a problem with alcohol. He could have handled things differently."

"So it's his fault that my mom is a drunk."

"She's not a drunk anymore." She sighed.

"So now you're on her side."

"I'm not on her side. I just understand how devastating it must have been for her to find out her husband had been cheating on her."

"It happens." I rolled my eyes. "Everyone who gets cheated on doesn't turn to alcohol or drugs."

"Heartbreak is a hard thing for some people to deal with."

"Sex is sex. It has nothing to do with love."

"Some people only have sex with people they love."

"That's what they tell themselves so they don't feel guilty. People have sex because it feels good. They want to have an orgasm. They want to fly high for a couple of minutes."

"Sex means more than that, Rhett." Her voice was soft and I could tell she was feeling annoyed.

"Sex is sticking a dick in a vagina." I said bluntly. "And whatever lesbians and gays do."

"Rhett." She sighed.

"Don't tell me, you need me to tell you what they do?"

"No. I don't." Her words were abrupt and I knew she was getting angry.

"Just don't get it twisted, Clementine. Sex doesn't equal love. Shit, half the guys I know at school would fuck any girl that would have them."

"Thanks." She muttered.

"Don't act like you're surprised." I sighed. "And don't act pissed. I didn't fuck you because I know you need it to be all special and shit."

"You had oral sex with me." She said stiffly and I felt myself growing warm at the memory of her supple body beneath mine.

"I eat pussy good. Don't I?"

"You're a pig." She gasped.

"I'm just being honest."

"I know it didn't mean much to you, Rhett, but it meant something to me." Her voice broke and my heart stopped for a second.

"I'm sorry." I gave her a quick look and reached out and touched her shoulder. "It meant something to me as well. Ignore me. I'm being a jerk."

"It would hurt me if I found out you'd been with anyone else." She sighed. "Not before obviously, but now."

"What do you mean?" The words coming out of my mouth sounded distant to my ears.

"I mean, if you went and slept with a girl tomorrow, it would hurt me."

"I'm not going to be sleeping with a girl tomorrow." I gave her a quick smile. "Unless it's you."

"This is difficult." She sighed and nibbled on her lower lip. "Take the next left by the way."

"Okay." I got into the left hand lane and turned on my indicator. "What is difficult?"

"How do we navigate this?" She sighed and I could see her staring at me.

"Navigate what?" I could feel my face growing hot. She wasn't turning into that girl already, was she?

"I know you don't do relationships." She said softly. "I don't expect you to change for me. I just don't know what we do next? Do we continue to mess around and stay friends? Do we hook up and see what happens?"

"What do you mean and stay friends?" I pulled off to the side of the road and turned off the ignition and turned to face her. "We're staying friends, period. There is no option where we don't stay friends. Do you understand that?"

"I do." She nodded and looked at me with wide eyes. I could see the fear in her brown eyes. She was already having doubts about what we'd done. I couldn't say I blamed her. I wouldn't have wanted her to hook up with someone like me.

"Let's just see what happens." I shrugged and grabbed her hands. "Not much has to change. We'll just do what we always did, but when we sleep over now, we don't have to wear any clothes." I grinned at her and she gave me a small smile.

"You think it's going to be that easy." She licked her lips quickly and I couldn't stop myself from moving forward and kissing her. Her eyes widened as my tongue slipped into her mouth and my lips sucked on her tongue. I pulled back after a few minutes and nodded.

"It will be that easy." I grinned. "I have no problem sleeping naked with you."

"What about…" She mumbled and paused.

"What about what?" I frowned and tilted my head.

"What about sex?" She looked down and blushed.

"We don't have to do anything you don't want to do." I grabbed her chin and brought up her face to look at me. "We'll go at your pace."

"Why do I think you don't normally say that?" She smiled at me and I laughed.

"Maybe because I don't." I ran my hands through my hair and sighed. "I don't want anything to change between us, Clementine. I just want this to be another perk of our friendship."

"I see." She nodded slightly.

"Friends with benefits if you will." I nodded, pleased at the conversation. "Or rather, best friends with benefits."

"You're not going to mess around with anyone else are you?" She frowned and I felt myself starting to feel sick again. I wasn't sure why she wanted to have this conversation right now, but I couldn't just walk away and ignore her.

"I'm not going to hook up with anyone else."

"Good." She smiled. "It makes me feel better knowing you haven't been with anyone in a while as well. I know that sounds cheesy, but it helps that I don't feel like sloppy seconds."

"You could never be sloppy seconds." I ran my finger down her cheek and sighed inwardly. I felt like I should tell her about Penelope, but I wasn't sure how she would react. It was before we had hooked up, but not very much before. And Penelope was her friend. I didn't feel like she would appreciate the fact that we'd nearly had sex.

"I'm glad you're not going all crazy and into Rhett panic mode." She smiled and leaned forward and stroked the hair by my ears. Her eyes were warm and she looked happy and content. "I know this is new for both of us, but I really think that this could be good for both of us."

"Let's not talk about it anymore." I leaned forward and kissed her again. "I'd rather be doing something else." I reached down and cupped her breast and smiled as she squirmed against me.

"Rhett." She groaned against my lips as I pinched her nipple.

"Yes, Clementine." I licked her lips as my fingers moved to her other breast.

"I want to get out of this car." She moaned as she tried to move in the seat.

"We can go back home." I nibbled on her lower lip. "I can turn around now."

Rhett

"No." She moaned and pulled back, her eyes filled with lust. "No, we're going to go and see your mom."

"Fine." I sighed and pulled away. "Your loss."

"Maybe later." She bit her lower lip and looked away.

"Maybe later, what?" I froze and looked at her. I could see her face burning red and my cock hardened as I stared at her hard nipples.

"Maybe we can move to the next level." She turned towards me and smiled shyly.

"Next level?" My eyes narrowed as I looked at her. "Are you saying what I think you're saying?"

"Maybe." She smiled and nodded slightly. "But we have to go to a hotel. I don't want to do it in your house."

"Why not?"

"I don't want to do it somewhere you've done it with someone else."

"Oh." I tried not to roll my eyes. "None of those girls meant anything to me."

"I know." She looked away from me, her face growing red. "I just don't want to be another notch."

"You could never be another notch." I frowned and shifted. My entire body was buzzing with anticipation. I wasn't sure this was a good idea, but I knew I couldn't say no to her.

"I'm glad to hear that." She said softly and reached over and ran her fingers down the bulge in my pants. "It feels like you're excited as well." She giggled as I grabbed her hand and made her squeeze my cock.

"I'm hard as hell." I winked at her. "And yes you did that." I felt her squeezing me again and groaned as she moved her hand away. "Let's get this reunion over and done with. I'm ready to go and find a Marriott."

"You don't even want to see your mom, do you?" She looked at me with a sad look in her eyes and I shook my head. At the end of the day, Clementine knew me better than I knew myself and I wasn't going to lie and pretend that I thought this was going to be some life-changing moment.

"Let's get it over with." I started the engine again and pulled back onto the road. My thoughts drifted away

Rhett | 283

from Clemmie and back to my childhood. I could remember the day that I came back from school and realized something was different. I'd been young enough to not really understand what was going on right away, but old enough to feel the full extent of loss and loneliness. My father hadn't been of any help. All he'd said was that my mother had left us for alcohol. It didn't seem to affect him at all. Every night I'd waited for my mom to come home or to call me, but she didn't. I hadn't understood what had happened until I hit my teen years. And then my heart was already pretty empty and jaded. Love didn't exist to me, asides from Clementine and her family. They'd taken me in, when no one else had cared. They were like angels in my life and if it wasn't for them, I'm not sure what road I would have gone down. Clementine was the balance in my life. She was so loving, so caring, so open, so honest and genuine about everything. She'd been quiet when I needed silence, talked when I needed noise and filled the empty space in my life that had taken over. I didn't want to see my mom. I didn't want to acknowledge that there was still an empty space there. I didn't want to understand or forgive. I just wanted to forget.

"It'll be okay, Rhett."

"We'll see." I sighed.

"I'll be with you." She touched my arm. "I promise, it'll be okay."

I didn't cringe at her touch this time. I welcomed the fact that she was here. As my friend. I didn't want to think about all the other stuff. It was almost too much. Too close to home. Too scary. I didn't want to acknowledge how being with Clementine intimately had made me feel. It had shown me a side I hadn't thought existed. A side that let pain in, that let fear in. I didn't want to let those emotions in. I didn't want to love her as anything more than a friend. Everything in my life was changing too fast. I was on the roundabout of life and I just wanted it to stop. I wanted to reverse time and go back to six months ago. I wanted to go back to the time when Clementine was busy studying. I was busy working and we both made time to hang out and just be. *"But then you never would have tasted her."* A little voice whispered in my ear. It was true that while a part of me was scared of all the changes in my life, another part of me craved the

Rhett | 285

change. Another part of me was ready to see what else life had to offer.

We pulled up to a small-dilapidated house and I turned to Clementine with a frown.

"You sure this is the right address?"

"I'm sure." She nodded.

"Hmm." I sat in the car for a few more seconds and then got out of the door slowly and looked around. The roof was missing shingles and looked like it was in serious need of being replaced. The front of the house had peeling white paint and the yard as overgrown. This wasn't where I expected my mother to be living. I wasn't sure why she would have left my father and his mansion in Charleston to come and live in a dump in Beaufort, alcohol or not. My father had led me to believe that she'd cared more about alcohol and his spousal payments than me. My dad was rich, really rich and I couldn't imagine that she could have spent all the money he gave her on alcohol? It didn't make sense.

"Are you ready?" Clementine walked up to me and gave me a hopeful smile. "It's going to be fine."

"We'll see." I sighed, all of a sudden feeling apprehensive. "I don't know about this Clemmie." I was about to walk back to the truck, when we heard the front door open and a big black Labrador came running out and over to us.

"Jimbo." A voice called out and I froze. I recognized her voice right away. It hadn't changed one iota. It was my mom.

"Hey boy." I stroked the dog's face as he licked my hand eagerly. I didn't want to look up and see my mother. I didn't want to acknowledge that she was here.

"Clementine?" My mom spoke again. "Rhett, Rhett honey, is that you?" Her voice rose as she came closer and I kept my face down.

"Hi, Mrs. Madison." Clementine's voice was sweet and I wanted to tell her to stop being so nice.

"Rhett." My mom spoke again and finally I looked up. I turned to my mother and I felt the whole world go still around me. Everything seemed to freeze as I stared at her. I felt as if I had been transported to another planet and the only two people that existed were me and her. She still looked the same. Her face beautiful, and her eyes bright and blue. She had a small smile on her face and I stared at her wondering how she could smile at me as if everything were okay. As if, she hadn't been out of my life for more years than she had been in it.

"Rhett," She said again and her eyes widened in joy, the smile on her face more beautiful than a few minutes ago. "You're so handsome."

Still, I stayed silent. The colors in the world still more vivid than before. The sounds still more distant. I couldn't stop myself from looking at her. She walked towards me and my heart stopped as she reached up and ran her hand down my face. "My beautiful son."

I wanted to ask her how she knew it was me. I wanted to ask her why she left me. I wanted to ask her if she loved me, but I couldn't speak. Seeing her close up also showed me more of her imperfections. Her eyes weren't as blue, they were bloodshot and fuzzy. Her face was marred by lines. I wasn't sure if they were caused by stress or hard living. Her lips were cracked and shivering. Her hair, once so blonde and beautiful was graying and thinning. My beautiful mother was no longer as beautiful as she had been, yet, she seemed more real.

"I've been hoping for this day." She said, her eyes searching mine for a response.

"Really?" My words sounded bitter and full of disbelief.

"You sound like a man." She smiled again, this time her confidence was noticeably wavering.

"As opposed to the little boy you left behind?" I stared back at her with a straight face.

"It wasn't easy." I looked down and noticed her hands were trembling.

"Sure." I looked away then, somehow able to break her gaze. My eyes caught those of Clementine's. She was staring at me with an expression full of love and hope. She wanted this to go well. She wanted me to get my happy ever after with my mother. I could read it in her eyes. I could hear it in her brain. It was all she'd ever wanted for me. I wanted to walk away and never look back again, but I knew that Clementine wanted me to give my mother a chance. "So, where have you been?" I turned back to my mother and asked her a question. Even though I was no longer looking at Clemmie, I knew that she was smiling; happy I was making an effort.

"I kinda lost it when your dad cheated." My mom's face looked like a little kid. "I went to a house…" Her voice trailed off.

"To drink?"

"Among other things." She nodded, her eyes wide. "But I got sober."

"You're sober?"

"I went to AA. And a man friend of mine, he paid for rehab." She touched her lips and then licked them furtively. "He wanted me clean."

"A boyfriend?"

"No, he wasn't a boyfriend." She shook her head and her eyes widened again. "So I went to rehab. They got me off the coke." She nodded and smiled at me again, as if waiting for praise.

"That's good." I bit my lower lip and tried to remain calm, but I was starting to feel sick inside.

"I haven't taken any drugs in a long time."

"That's really good, Mrs. Madison." Clementine walked over to us and gave me a smile. "That shows you've really been trying."

"I wanted to see you." My mom looked at me and I could see a glimmer of some unknown emotion in her expression. "You were always my little boy. You loved me so much."

"Most sons love their moms."

"My blue eyed boy." She gazed at me and patted my hair. "I thought once I had my blue eyed boy, my life would be perfect." She paused and sighed. "It didn't stop your dad from straying though."

"You should have left him."

"I just wanted him to love me." She looked at Clementine then. "You know how it is. You just want them to love you. To see how perfect you are. To know that there is no one for them but you. But they just don't see it. They'll never see it. Don't waste your time like I did. Don't be a fool."

"What are you talking about?" My voice was high and angry as I spoke to my mom. "Don't try and project your life onto Clementine's. Clementine is not a drunk."

"It's okay, Rhett." Clementine touched my arm and shook her head.

"It's not okay." I said angrily, a volcano bubbling in my stomach as I looked back at my mom.

"You're mad at me." My mom's eyes narrowed and I saw her lips trembling. "Don't be mad at me, Rhett. I didn't mean to…" She paused and took a big gulp. "I always loved my blue eyed boy."

"Really? From what I can see you only loved dad."

"Does he ever talk about me?" She asked hopefully.

"No." I said it emphatically. "No." I said it again, wanting the rejection to sting her as her leaving me had stung me.

"At least I have you." She reached out and touched my arm. "You came to see your old momma."

"What happened to you?" This time my words were as sincere as the pain in my heart.

"Do you really want to know?" Her eyes focused then and she looked lucid. "It's not a nice story."

"I want to know." I nodded.

"Do you have any money?" She asked softly and then looked at Clementine. "It's just I ran out and I really need a bottle of…" She stopped and played with her fingers. "It will help me tell the story." I felt Clementine tense up next to me. I knew, just as she knew, that my mother wasn't clean, not at all. I didn't even respond then. I walked straight to my car and got into the driver's side and started the engine. I put the car into reverse and was ready to leave, with or without Clementine. I heard her tapping on the window as I stopped and I waited for her to get into the car and then pulled off again. We drove in silence for about five minutes and then she spoke.

"I'm sorry." She whispered. "I didn't know."

"You weren't to know." I didn't look at her. I didn't care. I didn't care. I didn't care. The pounding of my heart felt like the constant downpour of rain against a bedroom window. Pitter, patter, pitter, patter, pitter,

Rhett | 293

patter. It was continuous and non-stopping and I didn't mind because it stopped me from thinking too hard.

"I thought it would help you." She sighed and I heard her voice catch. "I wanted you to get answers. I wanted you to understand why…" She stopped. "Love isn't always a bad thing."

"It's isn't always a good thing, either." I grimaced. "Love means seeing what you can get from someone. It's never about doing what you can for the other person just because, it's always about doing something for the other person and hope you repay them for whatever you did."

"It's not always…" She began and I cut her off.

"It's about loving someone so much that you hope they repay you with gifts or money, or even more love back. When people say love is selfless, it's a crock of shit. People love because it makes them feel good because they get something from it. People who don't believe in love are more honest. They are letting you know straight up. I want this or I want that. No bullshitting. No, I love you, so please give me your virginity. Or I love you, lend me $10,000. Or, better yet,

I love you so take care of me now that I'm sick. Take care of me now I'm an alcoholic or a cheater or a fucking bitch." My voice rose as I shouted. "I don't say I love you because I don't mean it. When I tell someone, I want something, it's true and it's valid and it's not because I want anything other than what I want."

"Love doesn't have to be like that." Her voice was small. "It can be selfless. People can love and keep it inside without ever wanting anything other than seeing the other person happy."

"Stupid." I laughed. "Those people are stupid. What's the point? Maybe because they feel like martyrs? What's the point of loving someone who can't give two shits about you? Waste of time if you ask me."

"Your mom does love you, you know." Clementine touched my shoulder. "She didn't leave you because she didn't love you."

"Yeah, she left because she loved me so much. That's why she never even called as well." My voice was sarcastic. "So much love for her blue-eyed boy."

"I think she'd been drinking." She sighed.

"Never." I rolled my eyes.

"I'm sorry." Her voice broke. "This wasn't what I wanted."

"I know." I gave her a quick look. "But maybe this is a lesson Clementine. We very rarely get what we want in life, so maybe it's best not to go chasing rainbows and butterflies. Maybe it's best to live the life we're dealt and just deal with it."

"Do you remember when we first met?" Clementine changed the subject.

"Vaguely?" I shrugged. "Why?"

"You wanted to get those candies so badly." She smiled. "Every day the teacher would do a little quiz and every day, you tried so hard because you wanted them so badly."

"I didn't get them though." I laughed. "There was someone who was just a little brighter than me."

"You did get them though." She laughed. "You befriended me and so you got them through me."

"That's true." I nodded. "I guess I got them in a roundabout way. Poor you. All those smarts and yet you still got your candy taken."

"But that's the thing." I could hear the smile in her voice. "All I wanted was to be friends with you. We sat next to each other in every class, but you never spoke to me. You only played with the boys. And I very much wanted to be friends with the cute boy with the bright blond hair and blue eyes, even though he was a mean little boy."

"You wanted to be friends with me?" I looked at her again. "Why?"

"I know seven year old boys don't notice girls yet, but seven year old girls sure do notice cute little boys."

"Are you saying you had a crush on me?" My jaw dropped open in shock.

"I did." She giggled. "I used to go home every night and make my mom test me on my spelling and math, just so I could do well in the quizzes every day."

"What?"

"Yup. I saw the way you used to eye up my candy every day. I knew that the easiest way to get you to become my friend was to win the candy every day, and look it worked. We became best friends."

Rhett | 297

"You tricky little…" My voice trailed off and I laughed, trying to remember a seven year old Clementine. "But you were so quiet and sweet. Everyone thought our friendship was a mistake, that I'd turn you into some sort of hellion tomboy."

"I don't think anyone expected our friendship to last." She said. "I guess it's unusual for people to remain friends for so long and not have anything happen."

"Well we had something happen." My heart jumped and I took a deep breath. "I hope it doesn't ruin our friendship."

"It won't." She grabbed my arm. "I won't let it."

"Good." I made my way to the highway. "I won't either."

"In fact, I'm pretty sure I want you to take me to the hotel now." She whispered and I froze.

"The hotel?"

"Yeah." She nodded. "If you're not too sad."

"Do you know what you're saying, Clementine." I spoke slowly.

"Yes." Her voice was sure. "I know exactly what I'm saying."

There are certain moments in your life that define you. They don't have to be monumental or life-changing, but they are moments that you can look back on and say that defines your character. I've never been one to think much about character. I've always lived my life, done what I wanted, and gone about my business. Even when it came to Clementine, I'd never really put her first. It was always about me and how I was feeling. I've never really thought about if anything was convenient to her or stressful. I was a selfish friend. Granted, I'd never fully realized that before, but as we walked into the luxurious hotel suite I knew that this wasn't right. This wasn't how Clementine's first time should be. There was absolutely nothing special about losing her virginity in a hotel in Charleston. No matter how badly I wanted it and her. I wasn't sure how to tell her. She was so excited. I was so excited. I knew that it was the perfect informal place to have sex. If we had sex at my house or in her apartment, the memories would always remain and I didn't want the memories to be linked to any of the spots we spent frequent time in. I wanted it to be as forgettable as possible, so that when things went back to the way they used to be, there would be no awkwardness. It pained me to think of a time without intimacy with Clementine. Now that I'd had a taste of her, I wasn't sure that anything would ever be the same, but I also knew I couldn't give her what she needed. Seeing my mother had only reinforced to me how little love meant. It was an emotion created by humans to deal with the fact that sometimes life got shitty. At the end of the day, love caused more problems than solutions. At the end of the day, it was better to deal with lust, lust was a real emotion. Lust was true. No one ever complained about being in lust.

"The room is gorgeous." Clementine stepped in slowly and looked around. "Really Presidential looking."

She turned to give me a small smile and my heart stopped beating as I stared into her eyes. She trusted me infinitely. I knew that without a doubt.

"Maybe we shouldn't do this." I started talking and watched as her face fell. "I don't know that this is the right place or time."

"I want to." She said softly and walked towards me. "I want to."

"Not here." I shook my head. "Not like this."

"What's wrong with here?" She looked around and studied the room. "Have you done it here before?"

"No." I laughed and shook my head. "This is one of the few places I haven't done it."

"You're such a pig, Rhett." She rolled her eyes and I wasn't sure if she was joking it not.

"Not here, okay?" I touched her shoulder softly and she glared at me.

"What is going on Rhett? Why are you treating me like a little princess?" She glared at me and stuck her face up in mine.

"What?" I stared at her in shock. "What are you talking about?"

"I'm talking about the fact that ever since we made out you've been treating me like some fragile doll that might break if you do something wrong."

"Clementine." I frowned. "I'm not sure what you're saying."

"Do you know why our friendship has worked all these years, Rhett?" She poked me in the chest and I shook my head, choosing to remain silent. "Because we're honest with each other, because we don't judge each other. Because..." She paused and grabbed my shoulders. "We're both strong and know our own minds. I know you think you're this big man on campus. I know you're hot, handsome Rhett and you have all these girls and I'm little old Clementine, your best friend: I've never really dated and I've got no experience, but let me tell you something Rhett. I know exactly what I'm doing and this isn't going to work if you start acting like a pussy around me."

"Did you just call me a pussy?" My lips twitched. "You know what I mean." Her eyes sparkled into mine. "Stop messing around."

"I'm not messing around. I'm trying to be good. I'm trying to be careful. I'm doing this for you."

"Don't treat me like any other girl." She sighed.

"That's kinda hard." I frowned. "I like you."

"I mean don't just disappear, but don't be someone you're not." She paused. "Throw me on the bed, have your wicked way with me, use your famous lines, try and pawn me off on a friend. Wait." She laughed. "Don't do that last one."

"There's no way I'd hook you up with any of my friends." I gave her a look. "No way in hell."

"Not even Tomas?" She smiled sweetly at me.

"No, not even Tomas." I grabbed her and pulled her towards me. "Why did you mention Tomas? Are you into him?"

"No." She grinned and me, and I could see her blushing.

"Clementine," I said slowly. I could feel my stomach churning. "Do you have a crush on Tomas?"

"No." She shook her head. "He's cute, but he's not my type."

"Oh?"

"He's a player." She laughed. "Maybe a bigger player than you. Penelope told me that he made a move on her recently."

"Oh?" I felt my breathing coming out faster.

"Yes, he wanted to have some fun." She groaned. "I'd never wanna hook up with a guy that hooked up with Penelope."

"Oh really?" I looked away from her.

"Just seems icky," she made a face. "Two friends hooking up with one guy."

"Yeah, I guess." I sighed. "So are you ready for us to leave?"

"I don't want to leave." She mouthed slowly and grabbed my shirt and pulled me towards her. "Did you not hear what I was just saying?"

"I heard you, but I still don't think this is the right..."

"Rhett. If I was one of your bimbos would you be brushing me off right now?"

"You're not one of my bimbos." I sighed. "You're my..."

"I swear Rhett if you tell me I'm your best friend one more time I will scream. Right now I don't want you to treat me as your best friend. Right now I want you to treat me as your bimbo." She giggled. "I never thought I would say that." She leaned forward and kissed me. "I never thought I'd do that either." She pulled back slightly and then kissed me again softly. I was taken aback by her actions. This wasn't the Clementine I knew. This was a totally different creature. Clementine was acting like a vixen. It delighted and scared me. Where had this girl, no, where had this woman come from? I didn't have much time to think as she pressed her lips against mine harder. I could feel her lips trembling against mind as she pushed her tongue into my mouth hesitantly. I couldn't stop myself from responding then. I grabbed the back of her head and pulled her body against mine. I sucked on her tongue eagerly and I felt her hands reach up into my hair.

"See Rhett." She whispered as she grabbed me. "This is what you do with other girls. I want you to want me as much as you want them."

I frowned slightly at her words. Didn't she realize that there were no other girls that could compare to her? She was the only one that had turned me on in months. I'd had to fantasize about her when I was with other girls. I pulled away from her slightly as I realized I needed to tell her about Penelope.

"I need to tell you something." I ran my hands through her hair and took a deep brief. She looked back at me with bright expectant eyes. I could see the want in her expression. I knew if I told her now I would ruin the moment. I knew that everything would be ruined if I told her what had happened in the back of the truck.

"Yes Rhett?" She prompted me after a few seconds. I felt her hands around my waist and I knew that this was a defining moment for both of us.

"I want you so badly." I leaned forward and whispered in her ear. It wasn't a line, but the absolute truth. "I want you so badly that I'm scared that this moment won't be everything you want it to be and I want it to be perfect, Clemmie. I want every second to be perfect."

"It will be" she whispered.

"I don't want it to be in here. I want it to be in my bed, in my house."

"But..." Her voice trailed off.

"I've never taken anyone back there Clem. You're the only one that's slept in that bed."

"Sleep being the operative word?" She raised an eyebrow at me.

"No one has been in that bed with me." I shook my head. "So it will be both of our first times."

"Funny." She smiled at me and ran her hands down her back. "I still want to stay here tonight though."

"But, we're not going to..." I started and then stopped. "But we don't need to rush into that. Just being together will be good."

"Are you sure you're okay with that!" Her eyes searched mine, "I know it's not different to our usual routine. But it kinda is."

"Hey, let's watch a movie and order some pizza and just chill." I smiled. "I'm always down for spending time with you."

"They have a hot tub here as well." She smiled. "I was thinking we could go in there tonight."

"Really now?" I grinned. "Do you have a bathing suit with you?"

"No." She winked at me. "But I'll make something work."

"That sounds interesting."

"Interesting?" She raised an eyebrow at me and I threw my hands up in the air.

"Hey, hey, hey. I might be a player, but I'm not a pimp. I don't have sexy lines ready for every occasion."

"Why not?" She grinned and she ran over to the bed and jumped onto it.

"Wow, it's super soft."

"Are you trying to tease me?" I walked over to the bed quickly and flopped down next to her and took her in my arms. She curled up next to me and I ran my hands down the sides of her waist.

"Maybe."

"I told you, not here." I grinned at her and ran my fingers to her butt and squeezed her butt cheeks.

"You're such a tease." She pouted at me and her brown eyes laughed at me.

"Oh?" I smirked and pushed my fingers between her legs and rubbed gently.

"Rhett." She groaned and bit her lower lip, her eyes widening as I teased her slowly.

"Yes, dear?" I grinned and moved my hand back to her ass.

"Are you trying to drive me crazy?"

"Nah." I laughed. "I don't think so."

"Are you okay?" Her expression changed and she looked at me seriously.

"Yes, why?" I frowned.

"I meant about earlier." She nibbled her lower lip. "I just realized we never finished talking about your mom."

"Clementine, now is not the time to talk about my mom." I sighed. "To be honest, I never need to talk about her again."

"I just wanted to…" She started and I leaned forward and kissed her to shut her up. Her eyes widened as I bit down on her lower lip, hard, and kissed her more forcefully. My hands moved her closer to me and I rolled her onto her back and positioned myself on top of her body. I wasn't going to fuck her, but I was going to have her begging me to. I smiled to myself as I thought about what I was going to do to her. She wasn't going to know where her body ended and mine started when I was finished with her. And yet, she still wouldn't have her release. At least not here. Not tonight. I pulled away from her and yanked her top off of her body. Her breasts were almost spilling out of her bra.

"Is that the right size?" I looked down at her and smiled.

"What?" She looked up at me in a daze.

"Your bra seems a bit, uh, small." I laughed and ran my fingers over the tops of her breasts. "I'm not sure they're meant to spill over like this."

"You're such a jerk." She shook her head and laughed.

"So??" I waited. "Too small huh?"

"Yes, it's a bit small." She smiled up at me. "I thought if I bought a smaller size, it would make them look perkier."

"They don't need to look any perkier." I lifted her up and undid her bra. "Not at all." I stared at her naked breasts and grinned. Then I reached my hands down and squeezed her nipples. I watched as they hardened and smiled before running my fingers over them lightly. "You have beautiful real breasts."

"Huh?" She moaned slightly and looked up at me puzzled.

"Nothing." I laughed. "Tomas and I just saw this chick with fake breasts."

"I see." She gave me a look. "How did you know they were fake?"

"Well," I paused. Normally, I would tell her the truth. To be honest, I couldn't remember if I had already told her the truth about what had happened that night.

However, as I sat there with her on the bed, I didn't want to tell her how I knew. It felt cheap. And I felt like it would make this moment cheap. I didn't want her to think I was in the habit of playing with girl's breasts. I didn't want her to think that this wasn't special to me. Because in all seriousness, it meant everything to me. I didn't take this moment light-heartedly. Yes, I've squeezed a lot of breasts and played with a lot of nipples. I've titty fucked and sucked with the best of them. Yet, none of them had been as beautiful to me. In this moment, I felt as if this were the first time I'd ever truly appreciated just how wonderful breasts were. "Tomas told me." I shrugged and lied. "He felt them up at a bar."

"Did you feel them up to?" I could see the hesitation in her eyes as she asked me the question. She didn't want to know the truth. I was almost sure of it.

"Of course not." I shook my head. "Do you think I'm sort of pig?"

"Of course I do." She laughed, but I could tell she looked pleased at my answer. "What sort of guy asks a girl if she bought the wrong sized bra?"

"A guy with knowledge of breasts and bras." I winked at her and she groaned.

"Uh-huh." She rolled her eyes. "You're a breast man, huh?"

"I can't lie. I love breasts and butts equally." I licked my lips. "I love to fuck a girl from behind and grab her titties and then…" I stopped. "Okay, maybe that's too much info."

"It's fine." She reached up and stroked my face. "You don't have to speak to me differently, now that you know me more intimately."

"I guess." I paused and then bent down and took her right nipple in my mouth and sucked on it gently. She writhed on the bed beneath me and I started nibbling on it as well. She moaned loudly and I could feel myself growing hard as she moved below me. I moved my mouth over to her other nipple and sucked on it with more pressure. It was hard as a rock and I knew that Clementine was just as horny as me. My fingers made their way down her stomach quickly and to her pants. I undid her button quickly and slipped my fingers down into my panties. I groaned as I touched her wetness. She was soaking and I couldn't stop myself from rubbing her clit roughly, wanting to get her even wetter.

"Rhett," she groaned underneath me.

"Yes, Clementine." I muttered against her nipple as I licked it with my tongue.

"You put your fingers in my panties so quickly now." She laughed. "There's no hesitation whatsoever."

"Well you know." I grinned. "I figured I don't need to ask. We've been friends for years."

"All I want to know." She gasped. "Is why you haven't done it before now?"

I looked up into her face, her eyes were filled with desire and she had a cute little smile on her face as she gazed at me.

"I want to know the same thing." I muttered before leaning down to kiss her. "I think of all those nights we wasted."

"I don't know that my parents would have been so cool with you staying over if they'd seen your fingers in my panties." She grinned at me.

"Or your lips on my cock." I winked at her.

"You haven't felt my lips on your cock yet."

"I'm hoping that tonight…" I winked at her again and she blushed.

"We'll see." She licked her lips and I groaned and kissed her hard again. She kissed me back passionately and I felt her arms on my back trying to pull my shirt up.

"You trying to get me naked or something?"

"Or something." She moaned and I sat up straight and pulled my shirt off and threw it on the floor. "Take your pants off as well." She muttered and I looked down at her in surprise and then laughed.

"Bossy boots." I said as I jumped up and pulled my jeans off. "Shall I take these off as well?" I pointed to my boxers and she nodded softly, watching me carefully. I pulled my boxers off slowly and she gasped as she stared at my hard cock. It was pointing out and she reached out to touch it gingerly. "Oh shit, Clementine." I groaned as she ran her fingers up the shaft and then squeezed the tip.

"You're hard." She ran her fingers back and forth and then reached under and grabbed my balls gently.

"And getting even harder." I bent down and pulled her jeans off and then looked at her. "Can I take your panties off?"

"Yes." She nodded and then paused. "Do you think it's a good idea though?"

"What do you mean?" I stopped yanking them down and looked at her partially exposed pussy.

"I mean, if we're both naked and we're not going to have sex." She nibbled her lower lip. "Do you think it will be easy to stop?"

"I'll stop." I nodded, feeling confident of my abilities to control the situation.

"Okay." She grinned. "I don't mind if you don't, by the way." Her fingers ran to her breasts and she touched them casually and licked her lips.

"What are you doing?" My eyes narrowed as I stared at her. I could feel myself growing even harder.

"I wanted to see what my breasts felt like, seeing as you were so enamored with them."

"You've never touched your breasts?"

"Only to wash them, never in a sexual way."

"Have you ever masturbated?" I continued pulling her panties down and then looked back up at her.

"Not really." She shook her head.

"What do you mean, not really?" My eyes narrowed and I lay down next to her.

"I've tried to touch myself, but it didn't really feel like anything."

"I see." I grinned then and ran my fingers to her pussy. "We'll change that."

"How?" She frowned and ran her hands down my chest.

"I'll teach you what to do and we can get some toys."

"Oh." She nibbled her lower lip. "Okay."

"I'll keep them though." My fingers found her clit again and rubbed. "I don't want you using them without me."

"Why not?" She gasped as I slipped two fingers inside of her.

"I don't want you coming when I'm not there." I groaned as she spread her legs and started moaning. "Maybe if I'm on the phone, but not by yourself."

"I wouldn't want to do it without you." She gasped out and I laughed.

"Trust me, you will want to and you might even try, but I promise you that it will never be as good as it is with me."

"Oh, Rhett." She groaned as I moved my fingers faster. "I feel like I'm going to burst."

"Just relax and let go." I whispered in her ear and then bit her earlobe. She closed her eyes and I could feel her losing herself in the moment. I removed my fingers just as I felt her body tensing.

"What are you doing?" She opened her eyes and groaned.

"Let's try something." I grinned at her.

"What?" She looked at me with desire filled eyes.

"I want you to move your legs up to my face."

"Uh, okay." She frowned. "And?"

"And move your head down to my cock."

"Oh." Her eyes lit up. "You want to '69'?"

"Are you down for trying it?"

"Yes." She nodded eagerly and got on her knees and turned around. She got on top of me and straddled me, her face right in front of my cock. She bent down and took me in her mouth quickly and I pulled her back quickly. Her cool breath felt delicious on my cock and I knew that if she sucked me too hard and fast I wouldn't last very long.

"Wait." I grunted. "Go slow." I then pulled her legs up slightly and spread them a little wider. "Sit back a little." I instructed her and she gingerly moved back so that her pussy was directly above my face. "I need you to relax." I whispered as I grabbed her ass and placed it directly on my face. I could feel her body trembling as I licked her pussy, but soon my mind was no longer on just her trembling as she took me in her mouth again, this time even deeper than before. I licked her clit quickly and sucked on it hard, before sticking my tongue inside of her. She tasted so good and I couldn't get enough of her. It seemed as if she felt the same way because she sucked on my cock as if it were her favorite food. I knew as soon as she was going to come because her pussy lips started trembling against my tongue. She orgasmed hard and fast on my face and I licked her up eagerly. It was while I was sucking on her clit that I came. I tried to pull her up but she kept sucking my cock as I came in her mouth. She moved her lips up and down even faster as she sucked on the tip of my cock and swallowed every last drop of come. I felt completely exhausted as we both finished coming and we both collapsed. I pulled her back up to me and we kissed gently.

"Did you enjoy it?" I asked her softly, running my hands through her hair.

"That was amazing." She grinned and ran her hands to my penis. "It was absolutely amazing."

"Yes, it was." I held her in my arms and played with her breasts and kissed the top of her head. She placed her head in my chest and we just lay there silently. I knew the minute she fell asleep because her breathing changed. I held her in my arms and tried not to think of why this was wrong. I tried not to think about everything that was going to be different now. What we'd just done had crossed the boundaries of our friendship completely. I knew that as sure as I knew the sky was blue. It was even more than what had happened the previous night. My making her come had been huge, but this, this was completely different. She'd sucked my cock and she'd swallowed my come. She had taken all of me and given herself to me freely. We hadn't had sex yet, but this was just as intimate. I wasn't sure how she was going to act in the morning. What if she felt different about me and our friendship? What if she resented me? I knew that Clementine wasn't the sort of girl to just suck a guy's cock. I was scared that she would think that something had changed between us. I was scared that she would demand more. I wasn't ready to give her more. I couldn't give her more. I wasn't that guy. I'd never be that guy. I didn't do love. Or relationships. I didn't want to. I didn't want to be hurt. I thought back to my mother. Seeing her had been so surreal. At one point, I had actually thought, maybe, just maybe, things would be okay. Maybe she'd have a really good excuse or reason for leaving me behind. Maybe she'd be sober now. Maybe she wanted to make it all up to me. But I'd

Rhett | 321

been wrong. My dreams and hopes were for nothing. All she cared about was money and alcohol. I was nothing to her. Absolutely nothing. I knew that if my own mother couldn't love me, her flesh and blood, her son, then love didn't exist. I wasn't going to make that mistake. I just hoped that Clementine wasn't hoping for a miracle to happen. Because I wasn't about to make it come true.

I woke up early the next morning with my hand on Clementine's breast. This wasn't the first time we'd slept in the same bed and my hand had made it to her breast. However, this was the first time her breast had been naked and I kept it there. I moved closer to her and she settled back into me. My cock was nestled next to her butt and I could feel my morning hardness pushing against her. I kissed her neck softly and ran my fingers down her breasts to her stomach and then her pussy, slowly letting my fingers touch her. I groaned as I realized she was wet. Even in her sleep, Clementine wanted me. I groaned again and lifted her leg up. I didn't know what I was doing, but I knew I needed to feel her. I pushed my cock between her legs and rubbed it up and down her pussy. It felt like heaven and torture at the same time. I was so close to fucking her, yet I knew I couldn't. If we'd already been lovers, I would have entered her already. I would have woken her up with an orgasm. However, there was no way in hell, I was going to let her first time, be her waking up to me inside of her. That wasn't cool. I'd have to make sure she was cool with morning sex before I ever did it.

I grabbed my cock and rubbed it directly against her clit. I could feel her body moving slowly against mine as she slowly awakened.

"Morning." She whispered.

"Morning." I kissed her neck and continued rubbing her.

"What a great way to wake up." She moaned and squeezed her legs together. "I've never woken up feeling like I'm about to come before."

"I'm glad to hear that." I laughed, and then groaned as she reached down and moved my cock closer to her pussy opening. "What are you doing?"

"I want to feel you inside of me." She moaned. "I need to feel you."

"No, Clementine." I groaned as the tip of my cock sat in her pussy entrance. With one smooth stroke I'd be inside of her.

"Please," she groaned and shifted slightly. The tip of my cock moved inside of her and we both groaned.

"Clementine." I muttered, but didn't move. "I don't want to do this here."

"Why not?" She moaned and shifted again. She grabbed my hand and brought it to the front of her pussy. "Feel how wet I am for you."

"I know." I rubbed her clit and groaned as my fingers became soaked.

"Rhett, please." She sighed and pushed back against me. "Ooh." She cried out as my cock went further inside of her. I groaned and pulled her back towards me and slowly pushed my cock further inside of her. Her pussy felt wet and tight against my throbbing cock and I could feel her hymen. I paused for one second and then pulled my cock out of her quickly. "No." She cried out and turned towards me. "Why?"

Her eyes were full of desire and she was breathing heavily.

"I didn't have a condom on." I kissed her. "And I told you, not at the hotel. I don't care what you say."

She pouted at me and I growled and pulled her out of bed. "Get your clothes on now and we're going."

"What?" She looked dazed as she stood there watching me get dressed. "What's going on?"

"We're going to my place." I grinned.

"Oh?" A smile hit her face and she pulled her clothes on quickly.

"Yes, and I'm going to make love to you all morning." I winked at her. We both got dressed in record time and ran to my car. I drove quickly and all I could think about was how fantastic her pussy had felt when my cock had been inside of her. I knew that technically there was no way she was still a virgin, well, maybe she was. I hadn't popped her cherry as yet, but the fact that my cock had been inside of her kinda negated that fact, I felt. However, I knew that I wanted her official first time to be in my bed at my house. I wanted that for her and for me. We reached my house in record time and I started pulling my clothes off as soon as we hit the front door. I grabbed her around the waist and I carried her to the bedroom, both of us giggling.

"Are you sure you want to do this?" I asked her while pulling her shirt off.

"Yes." She nodded eagerly and I grinned at her before pushing her down onto the bed. My fingers were pleased to find that she was still wet and I quickly grabbed my wallet and pulled out some condoms.

"I'm going to try and make it so it doesn't hurt, okay." I pulled the condom on my hard cock and got on top of her.

"I don't mind." Her eyes glittered and she reached up and pulled me down. "I just want to feel you inside of me."

"Aww, fuck, Clementine." I groaned at her words. "You're going to make me come before I even enter you."

"Then what are you waiting for?" She whispered against my lips and I kissed her hard, while slowly lowering myself on top of her. I reached down and spread her legs and entered her slowly. It felt different being inside of her with the condom on, not as sensitive and not as primal. I knew that I was going to have to get her onto the pill as soon as possible. I wanted to fuck her with no rubber on. I wanted to feel every drip of cum on my skin. I watched her eyes widening as I entered her slowly. When I reached the hymen, I pushed through quickly. She gasped out loud and I paused and she shook her head.

"Don't stop." She moaned and I started moving my cock again slowly. I didn't want to hurt her, but I did want her to enjoy it. I knew that many women didn't come from missionary and I didn't want her first experience to lack an orgasm, so I fucked her for a few minutes in missionary and then I pulled her up and turned her around quickly. I entered her from behind with more force and then reached around and rubbed her clit as I moved against her. She cried out as I increased the pace of my cock entering her and I grinned as I felt her pussy lips tightening on my cock and her body trembling in an orgasm. I closed my eyes and

Rhett

grabbed her hips and pounded her quickly for a few seconds and then felt myself coming hard and fast into the condom. I pulled out of her and placed the condom on my night table before pulling her into my arms and kissing her. I stared into her eyes and she looked dazed and in bliss.

"That was wonderful." She gasped. "I never wanted it to stop."

"It was amazing." I kissed her and nodded in agreement. I'd never had sex where I'd cared so much about making sure the other person orgasmed. In fact, I'd never had sex where my body had felt like that before. "I want you to go on the pill." I whispered as I cuddled her. "I want to make love to you without a condom."

She looked at me with wide eyes and I could see that she had a question.

"Only if that's okay with you." I whispered into her ear, but I could see that something was still on her mind. "What is it, Clementine?"

"Is that something you do with a lot of girls?" She bit her lower lip and looked away.

"Never." I shook my head. "I've never entered another girl without a condom on, not even if they told me they were on the pill." I told her honestly. "I've never even considered it."

"Oh." She blushed and I saw a small smile on her face.

"This is because of you. This is special." I kissed her shoulder, my heart thumping and my stomach curdling. I was starting to feel uneasy about my emotions. I felt like I was coming under some sort of spell and I didn't like it.

"I want to feel you inside of me again." She whispered and I smiled.

"Soon, it'll take me some time to recover." I grinned at her. "I'm not superman."

"I want to feel it without the condom." She whispered at me and I froze.

"What do you mean?"

"I just want you to enter me, just so I know how it feels without the condom."

"I don't know." I sighed hesitantly. There was nothing I wanted more.

"Please, Rhett."

"Fine." I groaned and ran my hands to my cock and rubbed it until it got semi-hard. "I'm not going to fuck you."

"I know." She smiled at me and I kissed her again. When my cock was a bit harder, I entered her slowly. She wasn't as wet this time, so I ran my fingers over her nipples and along her clit again. She was wet again within seconds and I groaned as I felt her juices covering my cock. "Oh, it feels so good." She moaned and started moving her body.

"Clementine." I closed my eyes and moved my cock in and out of her slowly. I knew I was playing with fire, but I couldn't resist.

"Ssh." She grinded her hips back against me and I held on to them and started moving back and forth with more urgency. By this time, I was extremely hard and both of us knew that this wasn't a simple, let me feel it inside of me maneuver. I was fucking her and she was loving it. My hands reached up and squeezed her breasts and then I pushed her down flat on her stomach and lay on her back and fucked her slowly. She moaned and moved underneath me and then I pulled out and stopped.

"Oh," She moaned and rolled over.

"I can't fuck you without a condom, Clementine. I don't want to get you pregnant."

Her eyes widened at my words and she nodded. I sighed and pulled her towards me. I knew how easy it was to forget about protection when in the heat of the moment. I felt guilty for getting carried away so quickly. I grabbed another condom and pulled it on and then entered her again. This time, there was nothing slow and soft about my movements. I fucked her hard and fast so that she was screaming out my name. We both came at the same time this time, and I grinned as her eyes rolled in her head as she scratched my back and started breathing heavily. Sex with Clementine was wonderful. Better than I could have ever imagined. A part of me was glad that we'd gone to this step in our relationship. I was fine with being best friends and having sex. As long as we stopped here, everything would be absolutely perfect.

Chapter Eleven

"So how are we going to do this?" I asked her awkwardly as I drove to Nanna's house.

"Do what?" She grinned at me. "I'm not sure I'm ready for car sex."

"Very funny." I rolled my eyes though the thought of car sex was very appealing. "I mean what are we going to tell your parents?"

"What are you talking about?" She looked confused.

"About us..." I gave her a quick look as my stomach dropped. I could feel sweat building up on my forehead.

"There's nothing to tell." She shrugged. "Unless you want me to tell them you deflowered me."

"Very funny." I frowned. "I mean are you sure we shouldn't tell them something?"

"Rhett, what would we tell them? That we've moved our friendship up to the next level and that we don't mean a relationship, we mean friends with benefits." She laughed. "I think not."

"You're fine with that?" I looked at her suspiciously.

"I already told you that suits me fine,"

"I see." I kept my eyes forward, not sure why I wasn't happier. Clementine was being so grown up about everything. If I'd known that she'd be down for friends with benefits, I would have asked her earlier. Though I couldn't say that I felt ecstatic about the situation.

"So Jake is super excited about moving in with you."

"Your parents are going to let him?"

"Yeah." She grinned. "He talked them into it."

"Awesome."

"Yeah it will be. We won't be able to hook up at your place then."

"What are you talking about?" I pulled over to the side of the road and stopped, my heart beating fast.

"We can't hook up in your room when Jake is there, what if he sees us?"

"I don't care if he sees us." I gave her a direct look. "I don't care if he sees me running around like a monkey."

"Rhett, he can't see us. It will make things complicated."

"So?" I shrugged. "I don't care."

"I don't want my parents to know." She nibbled her lower lip.

"Why not?" I knew my voice was starting to sound pissed, but I was getting angry. Was Clementine ashamed to be with me?

"Because this isn't serious, they would be disappointed."

"Are you disappointed?" I asked softly and looked into her eyes to try and figure out what her emotions were inside.

"I'm fine." She grabbed my hands. "I knew when I went into this what your story was."

"What my story was?" I repeated and frowned. "What does that mean?"

"I know you don't do relationships."

"I see." My stomach churned at her words. Was she trying to use me as an excuse to not want a relationship with me?

"Let's not worry about this now." She sat back in the seat. "Let's go, my parents will be wondering where we are."

"Fine." I started the engine again, feeling put off. I wanted to talk about what was going on, but I didn't really understand myself.

"Last night was fantastic by the way." She touched my arm. "Better than I ever thought it could be."

"Thanks." I smiled and winked at her. "I wish I'd had time to show you how great morning sex is as well."

"Maybe you can show me later." She giggled.

"What do you mean?" My breath caught and I gave her a quick glance.

"Just because my parents aren't going to know what's going on, it doesn't mean we can't have some fun."

"At Nanna's house?" I said and smiled.

"Or in the yard."

"You wouldn't." My jaw dropped.

"I would."

"Holy shit, Clementine, are you for real?"

She burst out laughing then and I wondered if she would really go through with it. Shit, I wondered if I'd be able to go through with it.

"We'll see." She winked at me. "Maybe if you watch Devious Maids with me tonight."

"I'll watch it if you dress up like a maid." I grinned.

"Shit, you figured out my plan."

"You always were easy to read Rhett."

"What you trying to say?" I grinned as I pulled up to Nanna's house.

"Nothing." She grinned back at me. "Hey, I think you just got a text."

"Okay, Sherlock." I pulled my phone out and saw a text from Tomas. **What up, bro? Wanna go to the Q bar tonight? Met these two hot chicks from England and they are dtf.**

I read the text and smiled. Only Tomas could find two hot British girls who were down to fuck. I put the phone in my pocket without responding. I didn't want Clementine to read the text and ask any questions.

"That was just a friend." I looked at Clementine and she shrugged.

"I don't care." She smiled. "You don't have to explain to me."

"I was just saying." I was irritated by her nonchalance. She wasn't acting how I'd expected at all.

"Let's go inside. I'm hungry." She grabbed my hand and we walked to the door.

"There you are." Jake opened the door and looked at us. "Why are you guys holding hands?" He frowned and Clementine dropped my hand quickly.

"I was just pulling him along, little brother." She rolled her eyes and ran into the house. I followed behind her still feeling put off.

"I'm here." Clementine called out and her parents came towards the door.

"There you are." Her mom exclaimed and then smiled as she saw me. "And you brought Rhett."

"Yeah, we hung out last night so..," Clementine shrugged.

"Where's Elliott?" Her father asked casually.

"No idea. We broke up." Clementine shrugged and her mother cried out.

"What already?" She sighed and looked at her husband. "He seemed so nice."

"It didn't work out, mom." Clementine rolled her eyes.

"Maybe Rhett scared him off." Her dad joked, but we all knew he was serious.

"It's not that we don't love you Rhett." Her mom continued. "It's just that we want Clementine to find a boyfriend, and well, her being best friends with a handsome boy like you is a put off to most guys."

"Mom." Clementine moaned.

"I'm just saying." Her mom continued. "You guys hang out too much, people are going to think it's not as innocent as it is."

"Mom," Clementine frowned. "Stop."

"I'm just saying, maybe you guys shouldn't hang out so much." Her mom sighed. "Just until you get a boyfriend."

"Mom." Clementine's voice was angry and her face was red. "Come Rhett." She grabbed my arm and pulled me up the stairs with her and into the bathroom. She closed the door, locked it and looked at me.

"Fuck me." She said directly and I frowned.

"What?" I stared at her as she pulled her pants down and her panties off.

"I said fuck me," she half smiled. "Now."

"Clementine we can't." I shook my head and she smiled wickedly.

"Oh, but we can." She grabbed my shirt and pulled me towards her. Her hands fell to my jeans and she pulled the zipper down quickly and pulled my cock out before dropping to her knees and taking me in her mouth. She stopped sucking as soon as I got hard and then sat on the counter and spread her legs.

"I don't have a condom," I shook my head, as I moved closer to her.

"I'll risk it," she grabbed my head and kissed me. "Pull out when you're about to come."

"That's risky." I shook my head.

"Please Rhett," she whispered against my lips.

"Clementine," I groaned and ran my fingers to her pussy. She was already wet. I pulled her to the edge of the counter and rubbed my cock against her clit. "You're such a bad girl, you know that right?"

She grinned and kissed me again and I entered her hard and fast. Her legs wrapped around my waist and I groaned as my cock slid in and out of her wetness. She tilted her head back and I moved faster and faster inside of her, feeling incredibly turned on by the danger of the situation. I tried to pay attention to my body. I knew I couldn't afford to cum inside of her. It was too big of a risk. Already just fucking her with no condom went against my own practices, but I was loathe to deny her. I knew as soon as Clementine closed her eyes that she was about to come. I also knew that I wasn't quite there yet. I fucked her hard and fast for a minute and then pulled out quickly. I pulled her down off of the counter and pushed her to her knees. She grinned up at me and took me in her mouth, before I knew what was happening I was coming hard and fast and she was swallowing it quickly. About a minute later, she stood up and licked her lips. "I don't know if I need breakfast anymore." She grinned and I shook my head.

"That was risky, Clemmie. I nearly came inside of you."

"So?" She laughed and kissed me. "I knew you wouldn't."

"How did you know?" I frowned and shook my head.

"I just did." She licked her lips. "I like the feel of you with no condom."

"Then get on the pill." I kissed her firmly. "Then I can come inside of you as well and you can see what that feels like."

"I can't believe we're talking about you coming inside of me." Her eyes were wide and she was laughing. "We've so crossed over a line."

"It's just an extension of our friendship." I smiled at her, but I knew that wasn't true. This was getting bigger than our friendship. We had been lying to ourselves that we could be best friends and lovers. Especially now that we were fucking without protection. Shit was getting real. I closed my eyes for a second as I realized that I didn't know how I felt. I didn't know what to do. I thought back to what I'd just said. I'd told her I wanted to come inside of her. I wasn't even sure why.

The doorbell rang then and Clementine froze. "Shit, I think Penelope is here."

"Penelope?" I froze as well. All of a sudden all I could think of was my cock between her breasts.

"Yeah I forgot I invited her over last week. You're cool with that right?"

"Yeah, of course." I offered her a weak smile.

"I know you guys don't get along, but I'd like you to be friends."

"Yeah." I nodded and she gave me a quick kiss.

"We haven't made a mistake, have we Rhett?" She nibbled her lower lip and gazed at me.

"Never." I shook my head and picked up her panties and skirt and handed them to her.

"I hope not." She sighed. "I don't want to lose my best friend."

"You won't." I shook my head. "Of course you won't."

"You're sure?"

"As long as you don't expect more, we'll be fine." I stared at her, not blinking.

"Yeah." She nodded, her eyes fading a little bit. "Of course I don't expect more."

"Well okay then." I zipped myself up and frowned.

"Clementine, where are you? Penelope is here!"
Jake ran up the stairs and called out. I froze at the sound
of his voice and watched in surprise as she opened the
bathroom door. "Oh, hey," Jake looked at her and then
at me with a puzzled look. "You guys have a weird
friendship."

"You have a weird face." Clementine muttered
back to Jake and I heard her running down the stairs.

"I don't know how you've been friends with her
for so long." Jake shook his head and made a face and
for some inexplicable reason I wanted to tell him we
were more than friends.

"Oh Jake." I laughed and put my hands in his
shoulders. "She's a good girl."

"Uh-huh." He groaned. "She can't even keep a
boyfriend." He laughed.

"My parents are starting to get worried. They
really hoped Elliott and her would get serious."

"Why?" I frowned.

"So she'd have someone to look out for her at
Harvard."

"What?" My heart stopped. "What are you talking about?"

"She got in." His eyes looked worried. "She didn't tell you?"

"No."

"Maybe she was waiting to hear if she got a scholarship for transferring."

"I see." Though I didn't. I was angrier and more pissed than I had been in a long time.

"It's cool that she got in." Jakes voice sounded stiff and his voice trailed off. "She's always dreamed of going there."

"I guess." I frowned and looked at the wall. I thought back to high school when Clementine and I had discussed colleges. I thought we'd both been excited to go to State together. I thought that we'd both graduate together. I sighed as I realized that those were my plans. I could vaguely remember Clementine talking about going to an Ivy League school, but I'd never paid much attention to her. Maybe state hadn't been both of our dreams. I'd just thought we'd go through it all together.

"And what happens after graduation?" A voice whispered in my head. *"What then?"* I could feel my heart pounding as I realized that I had no idea what would happen next. I knew in that moment that I didn't want to continue working for my dad. In fact, I wasn't even sure I wanted to stay in Charlestown or South Carolina. What would happen if I moved? Could I convince Clementine to move with me? I frowned again. How in the hell was I going to expect her to move with me? That wasn't a realistic expectation of a friend. I felt sick to my stomach as I realized that life itself was going to change our friendship and not the fact that we were now lovers. I knew it would be too much to expect her to move with me, especially as I had no idea where I wanted to move to.

"You okay, bro?" Jake looked concerned again and I faked a laugh. I didn't want him to start getting suspicious.

"Yeah, I'm fine." I nodded as we walked down the stairs. I cringed as I heard Penelope's voice. I did not want to have to deal with her right now. I looked up and gave her a quick smile. "Hi Penelope." I said and everyone's jaw dropped including my own when she rushed over and gave me a quick hug and a kiss on the cheek.

"Hi Rhett." She smiled as she remained next to my side. Fuck is all I could think to myself. Fuck, fuck, fuck. I'd been worried that she might act obvious, but I'd never expected clingy.

"How are you?" I asked politely.

"Been thinking of you." She batted her eyelashes and ran her hands through her hair. I saw Clementine's parents looking at us curiously and even Jake looked confused.

"Where's Nanna?" I asked them all quickly. "I haven't seen her yet."

"She's in the kitchen with Clementine." Penelope placed her hand on my upper arm. "Let me take you to say hi."

"Uh okay." I nodded, thinking that now would also be a good time to have a quick conversation with her. We walked out of the living room and down the corridor and I pushed her quickly into the study.

"I missed you too big boy." She grinned and leaned forward to kiss me.

"No." I shook my head and cringed at the thought of her lips touching mine.

"It's okay." She smiled. "I can be quick."

"Quick?" I frowned and then stared at her through narrowed eyes as she started unbuttoning her blouse. "What are you doing?" My voice was annoyed and I was starting to get angry again.

"Rhett, darling, I want to..." She started and I froze. I couldn't deal with this shit right now. I took a deep breath and ran my hands through my hair.
"Look Penelope, I have to tell you something." I bit my lower lip. I wasn't sure if Clementine would appreciate the fact that I was about to tell her our secret, but I couldn't stand for her to not know.

"What?" Her eyes narrowed. "Are you ashamed that you fucked me? Am I one of your disposable girls?"

I stared at her in shock. "We didn't fuck. What are you talking about?"

"We almost did." Her eyes were bright and flashing and I realized my earlier assessments of her were correct. She was a crazy bitch.

"You sucked my cock for a few seconds and I couldn't get hard." I stared at her and watched her face go red.

"I sucked your cock, you got hard, you put your cock between my breasts and then you got soft cos you were drunk."

I stared at her for a few seconds and then looked away. I couldn't tell her I only got hard because I pretended she was Clementine. My stomach flipped as I realized that the shit was about to hit the fan and I had no way out.

"I don't understand why you're going so mean Rhett. I thought I was something special to you. I mean why fuck with your best friends other best friend?" She shook her head. "Only shit where you eat if you know it's all good." She reached out to touch me again. "Don't you like me, Rhett?" I stared at her aghast for a few seconds. This was my worst nightmare coming true.

"Rhett, Penelope, where are you guys." Clementine's voice drifted into the room before her. She gave us both a sweet smile and then spoke again.

"Nanna said to tell you lunch is ready." She paused and looked at us both again. "What's going on?"

"Nothing." I shook my head, all I could hear was the sound of waves crashing. I stared into Clementine's eyes and she looked taken aback and worried. My heart broke and I knew that she knew something was off. I looked over and watched as Penelope quickly did her shirt buttons up. Fuck it! I looked back to Clementine and she stared back at me with a hurt expression and a question in her eyes. I shook my head and she sighed.

"Are you ready to eat?" She asked brightly and walked out of the room. I stared at her retreating back and I knew that she was upset. Worse still, I felt like shit. My head was pounding and I felt like I was going to hyperventilate. I didn't know what to do. She was leaving me. She thought I was fooling around with her friend. Her family wanted her to be with Elliott. She didn't want to tell them that we were dating. I froze as I realized I was now considering her someone I dated. I stopped still and rushed back upstairs to the bathroom, closed the door and ran cold water over my face. I stared at myself in the mirror, not recognizing the face staring back at me. Yes, I had the same vibrant blue eyes, the same funky blond hair, same facial hair, same lips, same nose, yet there was something different about me. I was no longer composed and easy going. I was taunt and agitated. I was also freaking out because I wanted Clementine to be my girlfriend. I wanted everyone to know that we were together. I didn't want her family thinking about her with another guy. I didn't want her thinking about being with another guy. I wanted her to be all mine. It wasn't enough to just be friends with benefits. The benefits were great, but I wanted more. I splashed my face with water again. What had come over me? I didn't do girlfriends. This would complicate everything and I wasn't even sure if Clementine wanted that. Then I thought of Penelope. She would ruin everything. With one word from her big mouth, it would all be done. I was pissed at myself for fucking up, but a part of me was also calm about it. This was life. It never went the way it should. This was ultimately why I didn't believe in love. Someone or something inevitably came along to fuck it up. I sighed as I realized that Clementine and I were doomed before we even got together. There was no point in even trying to see what could happen. I pulled out my phone and texted Tomas back. **You know that I'm always dtf. That's my mo. See you tonight.** I hit send and put the phone back in my pocket. I walked down the stairs and right out the front door and drove away. I felt bad for leaving Clementine without an explanation, but I knew she could get a ride from someone else. My phone started ringing about two minutes later. It was Clementine. I turned the phone off and drove home. I collapsed on my bed and pulled her pillow towards me and sniffed. Her scent was the straw that broke the camels' back and for the first time in a long while, I found myself crying.

Chapter Twelve

I woke up the next morning feeling groggy and stiff. I was shocked that I'd slept pretty much all of the previous day and night away. I groaned as I stood up and stretched my stiff limbs. I walked into the bathroom and stared at myself for a few seconds and then laughed. I looked like shit. Certainly, no women would be fighting over me if they saw me right now.

"Oh shit." I groaned as I realized I'd stood Tomas up. Not that I cared that I'd missed out on the two girls, but I felt bad that I hadn't told him. My text message to him had been sent impetuously. I had no desire to be with another woman. No desire to even think about another woman. I was well and truly into Clementine. I

Rhett | 353

closed my eyes and groaned again, thinking about her. She must hate me by now. I was pretty sure that Penelope must have told her everything. I'd ruined everything. I walked back into my room and turned my phone on. I had five missed voicemails and twenty-five missed texts: ten texts from Clementine, five texts from Tomas, one text from Penelope and the rest were from random girls. I listened to the voicemails quickly. Only one was from Clementine and the rest were from Tomas. I smiled to myself as I listened to his messages. He was more concerned that I was okay, then about being stood up. I quickly called him back.

"Yo, bro, what happened? You alright?" He answered on the first ring.

"Yeah, my bad, my phone was off." I responded lightly, not wanting him to know why I'd backed out. "How was the night?"

"Epic." Tomas sounded proud of himself. "Threesome with two hot British chicks. Check."

"You didn't?"

"Yes, Sir, I did. I had to show them how we American boys roll." He laughed. "Let's just say they were impressed."

"Uh-huh." I laughed. "Dirty dog."

"You know it. We be the pimps of the dirty dog club." He laughed and I frowned into the phone. I didn't want to be a pimp of the dirty dog club.

"Yeah." I answered, less excitedly.

"Oh shit." Tomas exclaimed. "You been caught, ain't ya?"

"What?" I frowned into the phone. "What are you talking about?"

"It's your girl, Clementine isn't it? You boning her?"

"Tomas." I growled. "Don't use those words about her."

"Oh shit." He laughed. "I knew it."

"Knew what?"

"I knew you two were fucking."

"We weren't fucking. Well before." I paused. "We kinda are now."

"Shit." He paused. "That a good idea?"

"Why wouldn't it be?"

"I don't know." He spoke slower now. "She ain't like these other hoes. She's a good girl." He sounded more sincere. "She's one that can get hurt."

"I'm not planning on hurting her."

"So you going to wife her?"

"No." I was quick to respond. "I don't plan on getting married." My heart started racing at the thought.

"Exactly." Tomas sighed. "You gonna break her heart."

"No, I'm not." I sighed. "I think it's over already, anyway."

"What?"

"I messed with her friend that night." I sighed.

"That bitch, Penny?"

"Yeah, Penelope. I titty fucked her and now she thinks we're an item."

"Oh shit." Tomas's voice was awed. "A lot of shit gone down recently."

"Yeah." I groaned. "I fucked up."

"What you going to do?"

"Dunno." I sighed and then heard my doorbell ring. "Look, bro. I gotta go. Someone's at the door. I'll talk to you later." I hung up and walked quickly to the front and opened the door. "Hi."

"Hi." Clementine nodded and stared at me with a frown. "Can I come in?"

"Sure." I opened the door wider and she walked in.

"You look beautiful today." I smiled at her and took in her appearance.

"Cut the crap." She rolled her eyes. "What's going on?"

"What?" I frowned. "I can't tell you that you look beautiful?"

"Last week I was Big Bertha. This week I'm Cindy Crawford?"

"I never said you were Cindy Crawford." I shrugged and she laughed.

"Dude, I don't know what's going on." She sighed. "Why did you leave yesterday and then ignore all of my calls and texts?"

"My phone was off."

"Why?"

"I just needed to think?"

"Did I scare you?" She stepped towards me. "Is this too much for you?"

"Is what too much?" I stared at her in confusion. Was she worried about me or mad at me? Had Penelope not told her anything?

"I know you don't want a relationship, Rhett. That's fine. I don't want one either. We're friends with benefits. That's cool."

"That's what you want?" I frowned.

"This is what is right for us. You don't do relationships and, well, this works." She shrugged. "I don't need more from you."

"I see." I felt inexplicably hurt by her words.

"There's something you should know." She started and then paused for a second.

"What?" I took a step towards her and reached for her face, unable to stop myself from touching her.

"I got into Harvard." She bit her lower lip. "And I got a scholarship."

"Oh?" My heart stopped.

"So I can go." Her eyes lit up. "Are you excited for me?"

"You're leaving…" I took a deep breath. "I don't know what to say."

"Say you're happy for me."

"I'm not happy for you." I took a step away from her. "We said we were going to go through college together."

"There's only a year left." She took a deep breath. "It's not for long."

"Why are you going then?" I glared at her.

"Because I need to give myself the best start." She looked away. "I need a fresh start."

"Why do you need a fresh start?"

"It's just…" She sighed. "Let's not talk about this now."

"So you're definitely going."

"I have no reason to stay, Rhett." She sighed. "We'll still see each other. I mean, we're going to graduate and go our own ways soon."

"I wasn't planning on going anywhere." I frowned and walked to the couch. "But hey, blame this on me right. This is all my fault. Hey, Rhett doesn't do relationships, let me keep him a secret. Hey, Rhett doesn't want to get married, let me move away from him and go hook up in fucking Boston with my new jerk of a boyfriend." I jumped back up and stared at her, her jaw was open in shock and her eyes were shocked. "But why the hell not? I don't have feelings right? I'm just your sap of a best friend that goes along with whatever you want. Let's watch slutty maids, sure Clementine, let's watch a bunch of maids, let's kiss, sure Clementine, I'll kiss you. Take my virginity, sure Clementine. I'll make it the best night of your life." I stared at her. "But hey forget my feelings. What do I matter? I'm here just to make you feel better."

"Rhett." She walked towards me. "What are you talking about? I've never made you think that you were in my life, just to please me."

"Why didn't you tell Penelope about us?"

"Huh?" She frowned. "What?"

"Penelope had no idea about us. No one does."

"Rhett, what did you want me to tell them? Did you want me to text my entire family to let them know we became friends with benefits?"

"No." I sighed. "No, that's not what I wanted."

"So then what?" She glared, her eyes what. "What did you want? What do you want from me, Rhett? I'm doing this for you. I've gone along with your rules. I'm doing things as you like them. I'm accommodating you."

"I want you to want more than that from me. I want you to want more." I muttered and looked away from her.

"So you want me to be like every other girl?" She glared at me. "Look at me." She grabbed my arms. "You want me to beg you to be with me. You want me to tell you I want more? Just so you can freak out and then run.

You want me to lose my best friend cos you can't stand that I'm giving you what you want?"

"I want more." I shouted and we both froze in shock. "I don't want you to be my friend with benefits." I spoke softly and her eyes looked into mine with a glazed expression. "I want you to tell me that you're not putting up with my shit. I want you to tell me that you want to be more than friends."

"Why would I do that, Rhett?" She sighed. "I know that's not what you want."

"I want that." I grabbed her hand. "I want to be more than friends. I want you to be my girlfriend."

"You don't do girlfriends."

"I don't want to lose you." I shook my head. "I need you to…"

"Rhett, this is because I'm leaving." She sighed. "You're just saying this because you don't want me to leave South Carolina."

"Would you stay if you were my girlfriend?" I asked hopefully.

"No, Rhett." She sighed. "That's not a reason to ask me to be your girlfriend. You can't offer to be my boyfriend, just so you can trap me."

"What if I get you pregnant?" I half-joked. "We could go to my room right now. I'll fuck you without protection and we'll see what happens."

"Rhett." Her eyes glittered at me. "You do know how fucked up that sounds right?"

"I know." I sighed. "I don't even know what to think anymore."

"We'll always be friends." She sat down on the couch. "I promise."

"I feel like I'm losing you." I sat down next to her. "I can't lose you."

"You'll never lose me." She shook her head and turned towards me. "We're friends forever."

"I know." I looked away. I felt like I had been kicked in the gut. I didn't want to be friends forever. I wanted more than that. It hit me like a ton of bricks. For so many years, I'd been fooling myself. I was in love with Clementine O'Hara. I was in love with her and I wanted nothing more than to be with her. Forever. Just thinking the words scared me. Forever was a long time. Forever didn't really exist. Forever was a word for saps, but all of a sudden it didn't matter to me. I didn't care about what was going to happen. I didn't care that it could fail. I didn't care that there was a possibility that I could lose her. I needed her like I needed the air to breathe. "Dumbass." I mumbled to myself as I realized what a dumbass I'd been. I'd been so jealous of Elliott and every other guy that I couldn't even think straight. I hadn't know what to think or feel and I'd talked myself into believing it was just because I was being protective over her. I was being protective, but I also didn't want another man to touch her or kiss her. It made me angry just thinking about her with another guy.

"Rhett." She whispered and touched my arm softly. I closed my eyes and just sat there. All the happiest memories in my life were from times I'd had with Clementine. She'd been there through everything. She was my rock in ways I'd never even realized. She was the love of my life. She was my soul mate. She was everything to me. And she was moving away.

"So, I think I need to tell you something." I opened my eyes slowly and looked into her eyes. She was gazing at me with such devotion that I was scared to even breathe. I knew in every fiber of my being that she loved me too. I knew then that sometimes, God did make miracles.

"Yes?" She asked softly and leaned towards me.

"So, I've been thinking..." I took a deep breath and was about to tell her I loved her when her phone rang.

"Hold on." She groaned. "It might be Nanna, I told her I was going to check on you and call her to let her know you're okay."

"Okay." I frowned, annoyed that my declaration was going to have to wait.

"Hello," She answered with a smile on her face. Her eyes gazed into mine with a sweet expression. "Oh hi, Penelope." She spoke and my heart stopped. "What's up? Can I call you back? I'm here with Rhett." She frowned then. "It can't wait."

Dear, God, no. was all I could think. I continued staring at her, and watched as her expression changed.

"Say that again?" Her voice rose and her expression changed. She looked at me for a second and I saw the shock and dismay in her expression. Shit! "What happened exactly?" Her voice was cold and she moved away from me. "I see. I'm sorry, I had no idea. Yes, he doesn't care who he hurts." She bit her lower lip and I knew then, that there was going to be no happy ending. "I don't know why he does it, Penelope. I don't know if he's a sex addict. I've got to go." She hung up the phone and put it into her purse slowly.

"So, you know?" I sighed after a few minutes of silence.

"I always wondered you know." She turned towards me. "Not about you and Penelope of course, but if you could be faithful. I always wondered if we ever hooked up, if you could be faithful. I know we aren't dating. I know that we're not exclusive. I know that. But I thought I'd be enough."

"We hooked up before you and I…" My voice faded as she held her hand up.

"The day before, Rhett. The day before."

"It wasn't like that." I shook my head. "I don't even like her. I'm not even attracted to her."

"So that makes it better?" She laughed bitterly. "You don't even have to be attracted to a girl to hook up?"

"We didn't have sex." I reached for her hands and she pulled away from me.

"I know." She jumped up. "Does that make a difference?"

"I thought of you."

"Oh that fixes everything then." She glared at me. "You thought of me as she touched you. You thought of me when you attempted to…" Her voice cracked and tears streamed down her face. "How could you Rhett?"

"I didn't want to. I didn't want to hurt you." I jumped up and tried to touch her, but she flinched.

"I gave myself to you. I trusted you. I would have done anything for you, Rhett." She sobbed. "I can't deal with this."

"Please, can we talk?" My heart broke as she sobbed.

"I'm done talking. I'm done trying to make everything work for you." She shook her head. "I'm over it, Rhett. You're a selfish son-of-a-bitch. All you care about is yourself. I've tried. I've really tried. But you just never saw me as more than your friend. I'm the person that's there when your lady friends are busy or you have nothing else to do."

"That's not true." I shook my head. "You're my everything, Clementine."

"Oh shut the front door." She shouted. "We both know that's not true."

"Shut the front door?" I smiled and she rolled her eyes at me.

"Whatever. I'm leaving."

"Clementine." I grabbed a hold of her. "Please."

"Whatever, Rhett. Save it." She shook her head. "I'm over it."

"What does that mean?"

"It means I'm over it. I'm over you. This is just too much." She sobbed. "Just thinking about you with, Penelope. I can't believe it."

"Please don't think about it." I grabbed ahold of her and tried to pull her towards me. "Clementine, please."

"I've got to go, Rhett." She ran to the front door. "I've got to go."

"But, Clementine." I shouted after her. "I love you."

She didn't even stop. She didn't look back or hesitate as I shouted after her. It was as if my words meant nothing to her. It was as if, after all these years, she didn't even care. How could she not care? I'd thought that was all she needed to hear. I thought my declaration of love would be enough. I thought that would change everything, but it meant nothing. It was too late. I'd figured it all out, too late.

Chapter *Thirteen*

Six Weeks Later

There's a saying, you only know what you've got once you've lost it. I'm here to tell you that's true. The last six weeks of my life have been shit. I've got a full-grown beard. My hair is unkempt, my eyes are bloodshot. I've lost weight. I look and feel like shit. I guess some people call what I'm going through heartbreak. I'm here to say, it feels more like heart extraction. My heart has been slowly and painfully pulled from my body. And that was why today, I knew I had to go and see her. I needed to get my shit together. Clementine's rejection had made me realize just how many things I hadn't been dealing with in my life.

I pulled up to the driveway and took a deep breath as I stepped out of the car. This time I didn't hesitate. I didn't feel sorry for myself. I didn't think back to my childhood. I didn't even feel sad. I knew what real heartache was like now. I walked up to the front-door with my shoulders squared and knocked on the door. I heard the dog running to the door and then it opened slowly.

"Rhett," her eyes opened wide in surprise and she patted her hair down.

"Mom." I nodded. "Can I come in?"

"Oh, sure." She stepped back. "Sorry for the mess. I didn't know you were coming. I tidied up last time cos your friend said you were coming, but she didn't tell me this time."

"She didn't know." I walked in and looked around. It was surprisingly clean and homey. It looked nicer than I thought it would. "It looks nice in here."

"Thanks." She smiled. "I try to keep it nice, just in case anyone drops by."

"Yeah." I frowned as I saw all the photos of the wall. "Is this me?" I walked up to the photos and stared at them in shock. There were photos of me and me and Clementine from kids all the way through to a few weeks ago. "Where did you get these?"

"Your friend Clementine sent them to me." She smiled. "This is my favorite." She walked over to a photo on her mantelpiece and handed it to me. "You both look so happy." It was from high school graduation. We were both making faces at the camera. Our eyes were shining bright and our heads were pressed together as we stuck out tongues out. My arm was around her shoulder and she was grinning. We looked happy. Really happy. My heart hurt looking at the photo.

"I didn't know she sent them." I frowned.

"Her and her Nanna used to come visit me, once every couple of months." She shrugged. "Make sure I was okay and give me updates on you."

"I see." I frowned. "I never knew that."

"They used to say they wanted to update me on you, but I knew it was to make sure I was okay. They wanted me to contact you." She sat on a chair. "They said you missed me and needed me, but I never knew what to say."

"They asked you to contact me?" My breath caught. "I can't believe they did that."

"They love you." She gave me a weak smile. "They wanted to see you happy."

"I was always happy." I lied.

"You don't have to lie to me. I know I haven't been the best mother." She closed her eyes and covered her face. "I tried to stay sober, you know."

"Yeah." I nodded, unsure of what to say.

"They sent me flowers every Mother's Day as well." She sighed. "They tried to say it was from you, but I knew."

"Yeah." I looked away. How had I not known any of this?

"That Clementine loves you." She gazed at me. "I used to think she was stupid. Doing so much for you. You didn't even know. I used to feel bad for her. She was just setting herself up for heartache." She sighed. "But I guess, that's the beauty of love isn't it? Doing

Rhett

stuff to make people happy, without them ever knowing."

"I guess so."

"She's beautiful. She's really grown into a beautiful girl." She smiled at me. "I used to be beautiful too."

"You're still beautiful."

"You're just saying that." She sighed. "I didn't love as selflessly as she does. All her life she's loved you."

"Yeah." I looked down. How had I not seen it? "I don't get why she never told me?"

"I think she didn't want to get your hopes up, if I never came through. I have a habit of bailing on people."

"Why did you leave?"

"I loved alcohol more than myself." Tears sprang to her eyes as she stared at me. "Every day that I'm sober, I wonder what could have been."

"Dad still wouldn't have been with you."

"I meant if I'd stayed for you." She offered me a small smile. "If I'd raised you. If I'd been there for you. What would life have been like?"

"You choose a different path."

"I never stopped loving you." She started crying. "Every day, I think of you. I see your face as a little boy. I see you asking me for ice cream. I feel you hugging me. I see your big blue eyes. I screwed up Rhett. I love you so much. I can't even stand the pain I've caused you. The pain I've caused myself. Every night I go to bed and I pray that I'll see you again. Hold you again." The tears streamed out of her eyes as she sobbed. "Do you know what it's like to mess up and keep messing up? I just can't seem to get it right. I don't wanna be this person. I don't want to let you down. I don't want you to hate me."

"I don't hate you." I said softly and in this moment I knew it was true. I didn't hate her. I'd never hated her. I'd been heartbroken, scared, rejected, confused, but I'd never hated her. Pitied her, yes, felt bad for herself and for myself, yes, but hate. Never.

"You're a good boy." She nodded and touched the top of my head. "You've got a kind heart."

"Not sure how." I joked.

"Clementine." She ran her fingers to my beard. "Her soul is angelic. It's only natural that it touched you."

"She hates me now." I sighed. "She hates me."

"She'll never hate you, Rhett." Her eyes smiled at me. "That girl loves you more than life itself."

"I…" My voice cracked and I looked away. "I screwed up."

"That's the beauty about love." Her voice sounded wistful. "I was wrong before, when I told her she was like me. When I told her she was loving in vain. I was wrong. You love her don't you? You really love her. Your face is different when you talk about her. She's in your heart."

"Why…how…" I sighed.

"I don't know what happened with her, Rhett, but don't let her get away." She whispered. "You'll regret it for the rest of your life."

"I don't know what to do."

"Follow your heart, Rhett."

"I didn't know I had one until recently."

"It always takes men a little longer to figure it out."

"I'm sorry about dad, I know it must have hurt."

"It's not for you to be sorry. I'm the one that's sorry."

"I have to go now." I jumped up, my heart beating and my head full of Clementine. "I need to speak to Clementine."

"I know." She licked her lips. "And Rhett…" She paused and looked at me with hopeful eyes.

"Here," I opened my wallet. "I have $40 to give you." I pulled the notes out and handed them to her.

"No." She shook her head and refused the money. "I don't want it. I'm back in rehab." She half-smiled. "It's hard, but I'm trying. I'm really trying."

"Good for you mom." I dropped the money on the table. "What were you going to say?"

"Will you come and see me again?"

"Do you want me to?"

"I'd like nothing more." She stood up and walked towards me. "There's nothing I'd like more, except maybe a hug."

"Come here, mom." I pulled her into my arms and hugged her hard. She hugged me back, even harder and I could feel her crying against my chest. I rubbed her back and we stood there for ten minutes just hugging.

"I love you, Rhett." She sobbed against my chest. "I love you so much."

"I love you too, Mom." I whispered against her ear. "I promise I'll be back to see you soon. I promise."

I walked out of my mom's house feeling like a completely different man. I was ashamed of myself. Really ashamed of myself. Clementine had been right. My entire friendship with her had been selfish. Completely selfish. Only I'd chosen to ignore all the signs of my complete and utter jerk ways. Knowing that Clemmie and Nanna had come to see my mom all these years made me realize just how important I was to both of them. Both of them loved me more than I deserved. I thought back to a conversation, I'd had with Clementine many years ago. She'd told me that she would only give her virginity to a man she loved, but of course I'd chosen to forget that fact when I'd taken her. I'd been blind for so many years to her feelings and to my own. She'd been my de facto girlfriend. She'd done everything with me. Only I had not wanted to acknowledge the truth of my feelings towards her.

I got into my car, ready to call Clementine and beg her to meet me. I needed to talk to her. Yet, I knew a talk alone wasn't going to be enough. I needed to make a grander gesture. I pulled out my phone and called Nanna.

"Nanna, it's me Rhett."

"Rhett," her voice was cheerful. "I've been waiting on your call."

"You have?" I knew I sounded surprised.

"I've been waiting for you to come to your senses."

"What?" My jaw dropped.

"I presume that you've come to your senses?"

"I love her, Nanna." I whispered.

"Yes, so you've come to your senses." She sounded pleased. "I was worried that you were going to be stubborn."

"How long have you known?"

"Clementine has loved you since she was a child, Rhett." She laughed. "I knew you were in love with her when you were 13."

"What?" My jaw dropped. "What are you talking about?"

"A grandma knows these things, Rhett."

"She hates me now."

"She doesn't hate you." Her voice was firm. "Though I was ready to slap you when you started sleeping with her."

"I'm sorry, Nanna."

"It's fine." She sighed. "You young people do things so twisted these days."

"I didn't meant to take…"

"Rhett, let's not discuss this." She laughed. "I'm still an old-fashioned lady you know. I'm just glad you've come to your senses."

"What if she won't have me?" I sighed. "I kinda messed up."

"You mean the issue with that Penelope?"

"Yes." I sighed. Why did Nanna have to know everything?

"You didn't sleep with her, did you?"

"No." I was adamant and she laughed.

"Clementine's just being melodramatic. You broke her heart, Rhett. Here she's been loving you for years and just when she thinks you're within reach, you betray her with her best friend."

"I didn't betray her. We weren't even hooking up yet."

"It doesn't matter when it happened, Rhett." She sighed. "Jealousy and love have minds of their own."

"I haven't even thought of another girl since we've been together."

"Tell her that."

"She's not talking to me."

"Well, that's definitely a problem."

"Can I come over this Sunday? I want to tell her how I feel."

"In front of the family?" She sounded surprised.

"Yes."

"A grand gesture then?" She sounded pleased.

"Yes. I want the world to know."

"Good." She sounded happy. "Come over around noon."

"Great."

"Oh and Rhett."

"Yes, Nanna?"

"Sunday is her farewell lunch. She's moving to Cambridge next week."

"Oh." My heart dropped. "Isn't that fast?"

"Life goes quickly, my dear. That's why we must seize every opportunity and live life to the fullest."

"Yeah, thanks Nanna." I hung up the phone, feeling excited and depressed. Part of me wondered what the point was. If she was leaving anyway, what did it matter? But I knew in that moment that it would always matter. She would always matter. I had to let her know of that fact.

Sunday came quickly. I felt like my whole life was on the line. This was the most important day of my life and I was scared that I was going to fuck it up.

"You guys sure you know what to do?" I looked at Tomas, Brody and Jake in my back seat.

"Yes," They chorused and grinned.

"Don't mess it up for me." I glared at them, feeling agitated.

"We won't." Jake smiled. "I'm glad you're finally admitting you have the hot's for my sister. I wasn't sure how long I could take it."

"Very funny." I groaned and grinned back at him. "Okay, sshh. I'm calling Nanna. She's going to bring your parents and Clemmie outside." I pulled up and parked a few houses up. "Hey, Nanna. It's me. Bring them outside." I looked at the guys and wiped my forehead. I was sweating bullets of fear.

"You're going to be fine, Rhett." Tomas grinned at me.

"I feel sick to my stomach." I groaned and adjusted my bowtie. "Do I look like a fool?"

"Honestly?" He laughed and I glared at him. "You look fine bro."

"Argh." I looked at my reflection in the window. My hair was recently cut and it looked as perfect as it could. I looked like a bit of a nerd in my tuxedo, but it was all a part of the act. "Brody, Jake, Tomas, you all know what you have to do?" I asked again.

"Yes," they chorused again and I sighed.

"Just checking." I looked at Jake and grinned. "That costume suits you."

"I would never have dressed up like a white horse if you weren't wooing my sister." He made a face. "I look like an idiot."

"You look fine." I grinned. "Brody, you got the camera ready?"

"Yes." He nodded.

"You ready to fight?" I grinned at Tomas and he nodded and played with his sword.

"Yes, Prince Charming. Let's go."

"They're outside." Jake exclaimed and I froze. "Let's do this shit."

"Okay, guys. Let's go." I took a deep breath and grabbed the reins on Jake's costume. I tapped his shoulder and he pretended to gallop down the road. I pretended I was riding him and my heart was pounding as we came to Nanna's house. Nanna and Clementine's parents started laughing as they saw me, but Clemetine's expression remained stoic.

"Has anyone seen the fair maiden, Princess Clementine?" I shouted out as we made our way up the driveway.

"Did someone ask where my Clementine was?" Tomas came running up the driveway with his fake sword.

"She's not yours." I shouted out. "I will fight you for her hand."

"Who do you think you are, Prince Charming?" Tomas came charging at me and I pulled out my sword.

"My name is Rhett Charming." I shouted and I could see Clementine's lips twitching. That gave me the encouragement I needed and I got into character even more. "I'm here to win over Princess Clementine. I've come to show my love and to prove myself." I turned towards Clementine. "I've come to woo you, Princess Clementine. Let me prove myself to you."

"What is going on, Rhett?" She looked shocked.

"A long, long time ago, there was a girl called Clementine. She had a best friend called Rhett. He was a dumbass and for many, many years, he didn't realize how much he loved her, until it was too late. Then one day, Rhett woke up and he remembered what his love had said. She said she wanted romance. She said she wanted a prince charming. She said she wanted her soul mate. She said she wanted someone who loved her more than life itself. I'm here because I'm that person. I never wanted or dreamed that I could be that person because I never believed in it. Yet, you've been here by my side this whole time. I never believed in it, because I was dumb. I didn't realize that we had everything this whole time. Clementine O'Hara, you're the anchor to my ship, the fire in my sun, the water in my ocean. You're the love in my heart, the breath in my air, the voice in my dream. You're my everything and I didn't even know. I messed up and I almost walked away, but you never gave up on me and I'm not going to give up on you and your love." I took a deep breath then. I could see Nanna grinning at me and crying. There was silence in the yard, asides from the sound from my beating heart. I walked over to Clementine ad grabbed her hands and fell to my knees.

"I beg for your forgiveness. I was young and dumb, immature and childish." I bit my lower lip. "I love you Clementine, please say you can give me another chance."

"Oh, Rhett." Her eyes were full of love. "I can't believe you're doing this." She shook her head and she pulled me up to join her. "I just can't believe this is you, Rhett."

"You gave me wings, Clementine. You let me fly. I don't want to hold you back from anything in life. I'll always be here to support you. I don't want you to think

Rhett | 387

I'm just saying this because I don't want you to go to Harvard. I don't want to hold you back. I want you to go to Harvard. I want you do whatever you want. Even if that means dating other guys. I'll wait for you. I'll wait however long it takes. All I want is you. I don't want you to think I'm doing this for me. I don't want to stop you from doing anything. I'll wait for you, forever, Clementine. I need you to know that I'm here forever. I'll love you forever. Whenever you're ready for me, I'll be here. All I want is you."

"Oh, Rhett." She said again and pulled me towards her. "I love you."

"I can wait for eternity, Clementine. You're my home. I'm not going anywhere."

"I love you, Rhett." She kissed me softly and everyone around us clapped. I looked around in shock. I'd completely forgotten that we weren't alone. "I love you so much."

"You don't know how much that means to me." I held her tight to me, my heart overflowing with joy.

"I'm just so shocked. Why are you doing this?" Her eyes searched mine.

"Because you once told me that you wanted a man who would give you the stars." I paused. "But I want to do more than that. I want to give you the moon, the stars, the entire galaxy. I love you with every beat of my heart. I can't live without you."

"I love you too, Rhett. I've always loved you." She reached over and touched my face gingerly. "I don't want to be with anyone but you. I've never wanted to be with anyone, but you." She kissed me then and I grabbed the back of her head and ran my fingers through her hair as I kissed her tenderly. I could hear everyone around us still cheering and when Nanna said "Finally," we both drew apart and started laughing.

"This is forever." I whispered in her ear. "I hope you know that."

"I've always known." She smiled at me gently. "I've always known, Rhett."

"I guess that you Clementine O'Hara will soon have to tell everyone you have a boyfriend." I grinned at her.

"Are you sure?" She winked at me. "I wouldn't want anyone to think I was getting serious with someone."

"You sure as hell better let everyone know." I grabbed her around the waist and swung her around. "I want the whole world to know that Clementine O'Hara and Rhett Madison are together and no one is going to break that apart." I put her back on the ground and she held my face in her hands and kissed me softly.

"The world already knew." She whispered against my lips and we both stood there holding hands, grinning like idiots. I felt like the happiest man in the world. I wasn't sure what was going to come next, but I knew that whatever happened, Clementine and I would get through it. We could get through anything together. That's what love meant at the end of the day. It meant taking life's journey together and supporting each other, no matter what happened.

Epilogue

"Would you go on Big Brother?" Clementine nibbled on her pen as she sat in front of the TV making a list.

"Nope." I shook my head and looked at the pile of clothes in front of me. "Would you?"

"Maybe. If I thought it would be fun."

"Do you think it would be fun?"

"Maybe." She grinned. "How's it going?"

"Not great." I sighed. "I don't know what to pack."

"Do you want me to help you?" She stood up and walked over to the table and stared at my stack of clothes.

"If I let you help me, I'll never live it down." I laughed. "You'll always tell me you really are my maid."

"I do have the French Maid's outfit now." She grinned mischievously.

"Are you trying to make it so we don't leave tomorrow?" I raised an eyebrow at her. "Because I will take you in the bedroom right now and I won't be finished with you until tomorrow morning."

"We're leaving at 6am."

"Not if you put on that maids outfit."

"Rhett." She giggled and kissed me. "You're a goof."

"A goof who's in love with you."

"I can't believe we're doing this." Her eyes widened. "I can't believe you're coming to Massachusetts with me."

"Hey, I didn't get into Harvard, but Boston College is just as good." I smiled. "I'll tell everyone about my girlfriend that's smarter than me."

"I'm not smarter than you." She blushed and I grabbed her and pulled her towards me.

"Hmm, can I say sexier then?" I winked at her and she pressed her body against mine. "Definitely sexier."

"I think you're pretty sexy yourself." She laughed and ran her hands up to my hair. "All the girls are going to go crazy over you."

"I couldn't care less. I'm a one woman man."

"I'm glad to hear it." She kissed me softly. "Let's just hope all those Harvard geeks aren't after me."

"They won't make it past the front door." I grinned and kissed her hard. "So don't even think about bringing them home. I don't care if you call them a friend or a study partner."

"Oh, Rhett." She shook her head at me. "This is going to be crazy. I can't believe we're going to be living together."

"I know." I held her hands in mine. "It's a big step."

"I'm surprised my parents said yes." She made a face. "I thought Dad was going to have a heart attack when I told him."

"Yeah, thank God for Nanna." I grinned. "I'm not sure they would have been cool with it, if she hadn't said something."

"She's just so happy we finally got together." Clementine started sorting through my shirts. "I think she'd almost convinced herself it was never going to happen."

"I finally came to my senses though." I shook my head. "Though, I have to admit, your sexiness helped."

"I was wondering how many bras I had to take off to get your attention." She grinned and I stared at her in shock.

"You slept braless to turn me on?" I growled and ran my fingers to her breasts. "Do you know how many times I stared at your nipples and had to turn away because I felt like a scumbag?"

"No." She giggled and moaned as I squeezed her breasts in my palms.

"You little tease." I shook my head. "You totally knew."

"Well, it's not like you ever tried to move your morning wood from my ass." She reached down and grabbed the front of my pants. "I'd wake up to your hardness every morning I slept over."

"I didn't know you felt it." I made a face. "You never said anything."

"What was I going to say? Rhett your cock is nestled hard against my butt, can you move it or do something else with it?" She giggled.

"You could have reached out and touched it." I laughed. "I would have liked that."

"I bet you would have." She whispered against my lips and then sucked on my lower lip.

"Don't worry though. I'll have plenty of morning surprises for you once we get to Boston."

"Promise?" She grinned and I groaned as I felt myself growing hard.

"You're down for morning sex right?" I winked at her and she blushed. Just that morning I'd woken up to Clementine sucking my cock. As soon as I'd woken up, she'd gotten on top of me and I can't say I was fully awake until she started riding me hard.

"As long as you are."

"I'm down for it any second of the day. I don't care where we are." I stroked her hair. "I'm so excited that we're starting the next part of our life together, Clementine. I didn't think that life could get any better, but I think this new journey is going to just be the beginning of a wonderful new life together."

"Me too." She whispered, her eyes sparkling. "We're not crazy are we?"

"That's the only way to be." I held her in my arms. "We're crazy in love and that's all I could ask for."

"I love you, Rhett Madison. It took us a while to finally get here, but boy am I glad that we did. Thank you for coming with me to Boston. Thank you for loving me. Thank you for giving me an awesome life to look forward to."

"Thank you, Clementine O'Hara. I can't wait for this next step in our lives. I know it's going to be wonderful. I love you my beautiful wonderful, Big Bertha." I grinned and she started laughing.

"You're an asshole, Rhett."

"And you love me." I kissed her and held her close to my heart. Nothing had ever felt so wonderful or so new. I was excited to see where the journey took us. I was excited to reinvent myself. I was excited for our new beginning. I had no idea what the journey was going to be like, but I knew that whatever came our way, we'd be able to laugh about it.

Author's Note

Thank you for purchasing *Rhett*. If you enjoyed it, please leave a review on Amazon, Barnes & Noble, iTunes or Kobo and recommend the book to your friends. Please join my MAILING LIST to be notified of new releases and teasers: (http://jscooperauthor.com/mail-list/). I love to hear from readers so feel free to send me an email at jscooperauthor@gmail.com at any time and tell me what you think about the book and if you would like a sequel.

List of Available J.S. Copper Books

You can see a list of all my books on my website:
http://jscooperauthor.com/books/.

Finding My Prince Charming

The Love Trials

The Forever Love Boxed Set (Books 1-3)

Crazy Beautiful Love

The Ex Games

The Private Club

After The Ex Games

Everlasting Sin

Scarred

Healed

The Last Boyfriend

List of Books Available for Pre-Order

Illusion

The day started like every other day...

Bianca London finds herself kidnapped and locked up in a van with a strange man. Ten hours later, they're dumped on a deserted island. Bianca has no idea what's going on and her attraction to this stranger is the only thing keeping her fear at bay.

Jakob Bradley wants only to figure out why they've been left on the island and how they can get off. But as the days go by, he can't ignore his growing fascination with Bianca.

In order to survive, Bianca and Jakob must figure out how they're connected, but as they grow closer, secrets are revealed that may destroy everything they thought they knew about each other.

Taming My Prince Charming

When Lola met Xavier, Prince of Romerius, she was immediately attracted to his dark, handsome good looks and sparkling green eyes. She spent a whirlwind weekend with him and almost fell for his charm, until he humiliated her and she fled.

Lola wasn't prepared to find out that Xavier was her new professor and her new boss. She also wasn't prepared for the sparks that flew every time they were together. When Xavier takes her on a work trip, she is shocked when they are mobbed by the paparazzi and agrees to go to Romerius with Xavier to pretend she is his fiancé.

Only Lola had no idea that Xavier had a master plan from the moment he met her. He wanted a week to make her his, so that he could get her out of his system. Only Xavier had no idea that fate had another plan for him.

Guarding His Heart

Leonardo Maxwell was shocked when his best friend, Zane Beaumont fell in love and got married. While he is happy for his friend, he knows that he definitely doesn't want to go the love and marriage route. He knows that there is nothing that can come from either of the two.

When his father calls him and tells him that it's time for him to take over the family business, he does so reluctantly. He's never liked the attention he gets as a billionaire's son, but he knows it's his duty.

Leo is not prepared for the animosity that he gets from his new assistant, Hannah on his first day of work. He has no idea why she hates him, but he's glad for it. He doesn't have time to waste staring at her beautiful long legs or her pink luscious lips. As far as he's concerned they can have a strictly professional relationship. However, that all changes when they go on their first work trip together.

If Only Once (The Martelli Brothers)

It's the quiet ones that can surprise you

Vincent Martelli grew up as the quiet one in his family. While his brothers got into trouble, he tried to take the studious route, even though he always found himself caught up in their mess.

When Vincent is paired up with a no-nonsense girl in one of his classes, he is frustrated and annoyed. Katia is everything he doesn't want in a woman and yet, he can't seem to get her out of his mind.

Then Katia shows up at his house with his brother's girlfriend, Maddie and he finds himself offering her his bed, when her car breaks down. When Katia accepts he is shocked, but he vows to himself that he won't let down his walls. As far as he is concerned there is no way that he could date someone like her. Only life never does seem to go as planned, does it?

Redemption

One fight can change everything

Hudson Blake has two weeks to get his best friend Luke ready for the fight of his life. If Luke wins the championship he will receive one million dollars to help out the family of the woman he loved and lost.

Hudson's girlfriend, Riley doesn't want Hudson or Luke to fight and so she enlists the help of her best friend, Eden. However, Riley didn't count on Eden finding a battered and bruised Luke sexy and charismatic.

Luke has never felt as alive as he does practicing for the championship. He has vowed that he is not going to let anything get in his way. He knows that he is fighting for redemption and love. And he can't afford to lose.

The Only Way

Jared Martelli is the youngest Martelli brother, but he's also the most handsome and most confident. There is nothing that gets in the way of what he wants and he has no time for love.

Jared blows off college to start his own business and it's his goal to make a million dollars within five years. He's happy working hard and playing the field. That is until he meets Pippa one night at a bar. Pippa is headstrong, beautiful and has absolutely no interest in him. And that's one thing Jared can't accept.

He decides to pursue Pippa with plans of dropping her once she submits to his charms. Only his plans go awry when he realizes that Pippa has plans of her own and they don't include him.

To You, From Me

Sometimes the greatest gifts in life come when you least expect them

Zane Beaumont never expected to fall in love with Lucky Morgan. He never expected to have a household full of children. He never knew that his life could be so full of laughter and love.

To You, From Me chronicles Zane and Lucky's relationship from the good times to the bad. It shows why marriage can be the best and worst experience in your life. Experience the gamut of emotions that Zane goes through as he goes through the journey of being a husband and father.

Crazy Beautiful Christmas

Logan, Vincent and Jared Martelli decide to spend Christmas together with the women they love. Only none of their plans are going right. When they find a pregnancy test all three of them start to panic about becoming a father. Only they don't know which one of them is the daddy to be.

Join the Martelli Brothers on their quest for the perfect Christmas holiday. They may have a few more bumps in the road than they planned, but ultimately it will be the season of giving and loving.

About the Author

J. S. Cooper was born in London, England and moved to Florida her last year of high school. After completing law school at the University of Iowa (from the sunshine to cold) she moved to Los Angeles to work for a Literacy non profit as an Americorp Vista. She then moved to New York to study the History of Education at Columbia University and took a job at a workers rights non profit upon graduation.

She enjoys long walks on the beach (or short), hot musicians, dogs, reading (duh) and lots of drama filled TV Shows.

Made in the USA
San Bernardino, CA
10 October 2014